INNOCENCE

A DARK MAFIA ROMANCE

STASIA BLACK

LEE SAVINO

ISBN-13: 978-1-950097-25-8
ISBN-10: 1-950097-25-0

Cover Design by Jay Aheer

Two Freebies!

Get these two exclusive books not available anywhere else ABSOLUTELY FREE when you subscribe to Lee Savino and Stasia Black's newsletter.

Sign-up for Lee's newsletter to grab your free copy of *Royally F*cked.*

Please visit: www.leesavino.com

Sign-up for Stasia's newsletter to grab your free copy of *Indecent: a taboo proposal.*

Please visit: bit.ly/indecentstasiablack

I'm king of the criminal underworld.
I always get what I want.
And she's my obsession.
Cora is new to the city of sin.
Her innocent blue eyes beg for me to claim her.
But I'm not the billionaire she thinks I am.
There's a darkness within me.
And Cora is a shining light.
She's beautiful. A virgin.
I'm ruthless. A beast.
She found me for a reason.
She'll be my queen.
I'll give her everything that her heart desires.
Except for one thing.
Her freedom.
She's mine to keep, and I'm never letting her go.

PROLOGUE

Cora knew she was dreaming.

She stood on the rooftop of a high-rise, goosebumps rising on her skin at the glorious view. Beside her stood the man who gave her everything, his face shadowed.

"It's beautiful." The city lights glittered like jewels in a black velvet night. The whole world laid at her feet.

"It's mine," Marcus told her. "Everything you see belongs to me."

She wore a red dress and heels with slender straps winding up her legs. Her wrists bore silver cuffs. Her ring flashed red as she tucked a strand of hair behind her ear.

"Everything?" She leaned against the ledge, striking a pose. The old Cora, country girl Cora would never be so brazen. The old Cora was a sheltered virgin, sweet and naive.

The old Cora was dead.

Marcus's footsteps echoed as he stalked to her. "Everything." The lines beside his grey eyes crinkled.

He grasped her hips and lifted her onto the ledge. Giggles escaped as her chest tightened. Before her stood the man she loved. Behind her, a dark expanse. An endless chasm.

"Marcus." She clutched his broad shoulders. The wind ripped at her garments and tugged her golden hair.

He caught her wrists and forced her hands back.

"Do you trust me?"

"Yes," she whispered. Her fingers fluttered. The garnet in her engagement ring caught the light.

Marcus moved closer as if to kiss her. She angled her face towards his—

—and he shoved her off the ledge. Her hands reached for him, her dress streaming around her floating body as Marcus grew further and further away.

The night rose up, surrounded, swallowed her. The city lights swirled, a dizzying kaleidoscope. One by one, the lights went out and Cora tumbled into darkness.

Cora jerked awake. Marcus's dark head was on the pillow beside hers, the shadows under his eyes lighter with sleep. The sight of him anchored her, grounding her spinning senses, the weightless sensation. If she closed her eyes, she was still falling.

Smoothing her pillow, Cora settled in. In the dark confines of Marcus's bedroom, she was safe.

Safe from everyone but him.

ONE

3 months earlier…

CORA SAT COLORING with little Timmy when his parents started up in the other room. Again.

"You know I hate this shit, Diana. I don't see why I have to go."

"Maybe because I expect my *husband* to support me when my firm wins a big case!"

Cora grabbed her phone and turned on the playlist Timmy loved best. He was three years old and apart from the occasional tantrum, he was a sweetheart. It wasn't his fault his parents didn't know how to use their inside voices.

The opening strains of *I'm Walking on Sunshine* started pounding out of her phone's surprisingly good speakers, drowning out the parental dramatics in the other room.

"Rolly monster time!" Cora said, grabbing Timmy out of his chair and lifting him in the air. Whew, she was getting some serious ab and arm muscles out of this job.

Timmy giggled and she breathed out in relief. Distraction managed.

She put Timmy on the floor and he immediately assumed the position, laying down on his back in the center of the play room. Cora cleared out the toys around him so he had a clear space to move and wouldn't hurt himself by rolling over stray Legos and magnatiles.

"Cora rolly monster, too," he demanded, except he couldn't say his 'r's so it came out sounding like 'Cowa wowy monsta too.'

Cora pursed her lips like she was thinking about it, but she grinned and dropped to the ground, lying down next to him.

"You ready?" she asked.

"Yes!"

"All right. Staaaaaaaaaaaaaart rolling!"

They both started rolling across the floor. The giggles began immediately. The playroom was huge, especially considering the Donahues lived in the prime real estate of the Upper East End. They could afford a live-in nanny like Cora, so they obviously weren't hurting when it came to the bank account. Too bad the money didn't seem to be able to buy them happiness.

Timmy finally reached the wall and Cora kept on rolling until her body smashed into his. "Uh oh! Collision! You know what this means."

Timmy squealed when she started tickling him.

"You gotta escape and start rolling again. That's the only way out."

She shifted him so he could wriggle over the top of her and off the other side. He started to roll away.

"Chase me. Chase me, Co-wa!"

"Oh I'm coming." She gave him a fair head start before

rolling, her long blonde hair catching crazy static electricity the more she did it.

As she finished a roll and started to twist into another, she caught sight of a figure standing in the door and yelped.

"Daddy!" Timmy cried. "Daddy, come play wowy monsta with us!"

Cora yanked down the hem of her shirt that had ridden up and got to her feet.

Mr. Donahue was looking at her, not his son. He was in his mid-forties, an architect who was always well-dressed and put together, if a little overly fond of hair gel. He was holding a glass of scotch. "Looks like you can have the night off after all. I decided not to go out."

"Oh." Cora blinked. "Thanks." She had asked for the night off a couple of days ago. Some of her friends, fellow nannies she'd met at the park when she took Timmy every day, had invited her out. But Mrs. Donahue told her no because her firm was having some celebratory dinner tonight. Which apparently Mr. Donahue had just begged off from. Eeek. As desperately as she needed this job, the family dynamics could get seriously weird sometimes.

But who was *she* to judge family dynamics? Her and her mom qualified for the screwed-up family Olympics.

"Daddy. Daddy!" Timmy ran up and started tugging on Mr. Donahue's pants leg. "Come play."

Cora looked between Timmy and Mr. Donahue. He was always asking her to call him Paul but she preferred Mr. Donahue.

"Are you sure it'd be okay?" she asked, eyes flicking toward the door. Mr. Donahue noticed and glowered, taking a swig of his scotch.

"Go. Have a good time. You're young. You deserve a damned night off now and then." She flinched at his tone and he paused and ran a hand down his face. "Jesus, I'm sorry. Seriously. I'll put Timmy to bed." He offered a tired smile. "You're officially off duty."

Cora bobbed her head. "Thanks. I really appreciate it."

She hadn't done much else other than work, aka, spend time with Timmy, since she got to the city six weeks ago.

As much as she loved the little guy, she'd come to the city because she wanted to live bigger. To see the world. To have friends.

To live free.

She bent down and gave Timmy a kiss on the head. "See you tomorrow, monster."

He made a roaring noise and she made one back.

She snagged her phone and hurried out of the room and up the stairs to shower and get ready.

She texted Helena when she got to her room: I CAN COME TONIGHT AFTER ALL!

It was several minutes before Helena texted back. WE'RE MEETING AT THE STYX AT 10.

Ten? She was usually in bed by ten. Timmy was usually jumping on her face at five-thirty in the morning. Some days earlier.

Her thumbs moved clumsily over her phone screen. Unlike her peers, she hadn't grown up with a cell phone glued to her side. She was still getting used to all the marvels of technology. Back at the farm, they hadn't even had TV. Much less internet or cell phones. No, mom wouldn't dare have any of the outside world corrupt *her* daughter.

Cora shook her head angrily and hit send on the message. SOUNDS GREAT. SEE YOU THERE.

She pushed play on the music again, leaving it on the Timmy playlist. Smashmouth's *All Star* came on.

Let go of the past. She wasn't on the farm anymore. She was in the big city. Living on her own. She had a job, a cell phone, friends and now a night out on the town. This was what life was supposed to be.

Her head started bopping along to the music. Then her hips. Then she was dancing around the room and laughing, arms spread wide.

She was *free*.

And tonight she'd go dancing and maybe meet a cute boy. The whole world was in front of her and she was ready to meet it, arms wide open.

TWO

3 Hours Later

HOW HAD it all gone so wrong, so fast? Cora lifted a hand to her head as the lights of the club swirled and danced in a crazy pattern. She shook her head and staggered, sluggish and bleary in the rowdy pit.

Helena. She needed to find Helena. Or Europa.

She was supposed to ask them if she could sleep on their couch tonight.

Because she couldn't go home.

Ha. Home. What a crock.

It had never been her home. And now she couldn't go back there.

Not after *Paul* had waited up for her and accosted her at the bottom of the stairs when she tried to leave to meet her friends.

The house had been dark, Timmy asleep and Diana still out at her dinner.

Paul had been drunk, that much was clear. He'd leaned against the wall of the foyer, blocking the front door so she couldn't leave.

"You're so beautiful, Cora. I think it's time to stop with all the pretending."

Cora had tried to edge around him and get to the door.

"I need to go, Mr. Donahue. My friends are expecting me."

"Paul," he said, slamming his hand to the wall behind her head, boxing her in. "How many times do I have to tell you? Call me Paul."

His breath had been sour from the scotch. He'd reached up a hand to touch her face and she'd shoved it away.

"Stop it!" she'd hissed incredulously. "What are you doing? You have a wife! And a beautiful little boy."

But he crowded her in with his body. "I can't stop. I love you, Cora. You drive me crazy. Seeing this tight little body." He put a hand on her waist and squeezed. "Hearing the shower earlier and knowing you were up there, naked."

She tried to twist away from him but he grabbed her with both hands and shoved her against the wall.

He kissed her.

Or, well, she should say, he smashed his mouth against hers and tried to shove his fat tongue between her lips.

She'd kneed him in the balls and shoved him backwards. "I quit!" She'd fled with only her phone, the small bit of cash she had shoved in her bra, and the clothes on her back.

And she'd come here.

Only to find her so-called *friends* could barely give her the time of day. They were too busy flirting with guys at the bar. She tried to tell them what had happened. Helena made a few sympathetic noises, then said Cora should get drunk and forget all about it.

Cora had stared at Helena. What did she expect? She barely knew these girls. So they'd talked a few times at the park while their charges played on the playground. She'd built it up to be more in her head because well, she'd never had friends. It had felt monumental to have girls she talked to and hung out with regularly. But to these girls, she was no one. Barely a blip in their busy lives full of friends and lovers.

So, doubting herself, she'd wimped out of asking to crash at one of their places. She told herself she'd do it at the end of the night. Besides, maybe Helena was right. Maybe loosening up and having a good time tonight was the answer. Maybe everything wasn't as dire as it all felt.

So she'd let a guy buy her a drink just like they did in the books and on TV—she'd been doing a lot of catching up in the last six weeks—and tried dancing.

But he must have gotten her order wrong. She'd asked for cranberry juice but there must have been alcohol in it because she felt weird. Really weird.

She stumbled forward and only barely caught herself from head-butting a chick who was dancing seductively up and down on a guy like she was a stripper and he was the pole.

Cora fumbled in the side of her bra for her phone. Why couldn't she feel her fingers? Her hand was a clumsy stump.

Okay, this was starting to really freak her out. She was never drinking alcohol again.

She frowned as she finally got hold of her phone and pulled it out. Everything kept going in and out of focus. And the lights. Too bright. She winced and stumbled her way through the crowd.

She'd text Helena. Maybe they weren't best friends, but she was one of the only people Cora knew in the city.

And Cora needed to lay down. This day had officially been *too long*. It needed to be over. Now.

It took her three tries to swipe the right sequence of dots to unlock the phone. She squinted blearily at the little screen. It kept moving and dancing. It was hard to figure out which screen was the real one. She stabbed at it with her weird stubby hand but couldn't seem to do anything right.

She felt frantic and sleepy at the same time. She needed help.

She finally got to the text app, somehow. Thank the Fates.

Tears of relief flooded her eyes.

But when she started to type a message, she fumbled the phone and dropped it.

"Shit!"

The club floor was a dark abyss. Would she even be able to find it—

"Hey, I remember you. Did you drop your phone? I saw you from over there." A man dipped down in front of her and came up with her phone. She could have hugged him.

She tried to say, "Thank you," but her tongue was thick and it came out more like *tank ya*.

She squinted up at him as the strobe lights flashed their way and she winced. Still, she could see it was the nice guy from earlier and she relaxed. He hadn't laughed or looked at her funny when he asked to buy her a drink and she said she was only drinking cranberry juice.

"I think I—" she started, but the world dimmed.

The next thing she knew, the nice guy's arm snaked around her, supporting her weight as he led her around the edge of the crowd.

"Let's get you to the restroom so you can splash your face," he was saying. "I texted your friend to meet you there."

Cora nodded. Talking was too much work. *Walking* was too much work but she fought to stay up on her feet and to keep stumbling along beside the nice man. He was strong and solid beside her and she clung to him with the little bit of strength she had.

She lifted her head and was blinded by the lights again. It was too much. All too much. The music pounded in her head with the force of an icepick. She needed quiet. Dark. She'd even take Mama's cellar over this.

The thought made her feel hysterical.

Look how far I've come, Mama. The big city is as scary as you said after all.

No. Today was a bad day. She focused on lifting her feet. One and then the other. Holding on to the man to stay upright.

It felt like they'd been walking *forever*. Weren't they to the bathrooms yet?

She finally hazarded looking up again. And frowned when she saw they were in a hallway. She twisted and looked over her shoulder.

Wait, they'd passed the bathrooms. She tried to dig her feet in. She needed to let the man know he'd made a mistake.

"Bathr—" she tried to say but he cut her off.

"Shh, quiet, kid. Everything's gonna be fine. Just fine."

But his voice didn't sound right. More like he was talking to a child he was annoyed at.

"No." She shook her head. Not right. This wasn't right.

She tried to pull away from him but his fingers closed

around her arms like talons and instead of gently leading her, he was yanking her forwards.

Stop! Help! she screamed in her head. But only little whimpers came out.

He was shoving her out the back door of the club. The cool night air hit her like a thousand tiny needles and she finally managed a shriek.

But it was too late. The door closed behind them as quickly as it had opened.

"Shut up, bitch," the man said, pulling keys from his pocket. There was a black car parked in the alley not far away and the lights lit up as he pressed a button on the fob.

No! No no no.

Cora tried to fight. In her head she was fighting tooth and nail. Screaming and flailing and clawing.

But outwardly, she must not have been putting up much of a fight because the brute lifted her slender body with no problem at all. He shoved her in the back of his car, face first into a leather seat. The car door slammed.

He didn't even bother to restrain her. He didn't have to.

She was helpless as he hit the gas, tires screeching. She was tossed against the back of the seat and, when he stopped, she was dumped into the footwell.

Ow!

But no. Pain was good. She blinked and tried to focus on it.

She couldn't let herself pass out. He must have drugged her cranberry juice. Stupid. So freaking stupid! She hadn't let the drink out of her sight. At least she thought she hadn't. But he had taken it from the bartender to hand to her. If he was good at sleight of hand, he could have dosed the drink while passing it.

Tired. *So* tired. She blinked her heavy eyelids closed. Once. Twice.

The car accelerated fast and the jolt had her eyes shooting open again. Shit! Had she almost fallen asleep?

What the hell was she thinking? If she fell asleep, she was dead. She'd be raped and murdered and all the terrible things her mom had warned her about. It was all happening. First with Paul, and now being drugged and kidnapped, oh gods oh gods—

Stop it! Stop freaking panicking.

She forced her eyes open as wide as they could go and she tried to focus. She'd only sipped about a third of the glass of cranberry juice. She had to try to get out of this. The man was taking her somewhere but they weren't there yet. There was still time.

Rain spattered the windows as the car rolled down the dark streets. They were still in the city. Okay. She had to escape the car the next time it stopped. The man was obviously counting on her being passed out by this point or too incapacitated to try anything.

Probably because you weren't even able to walk on your own back at the club.

But she hadn't been terrified for her life then. Adrenaline surged through her veins, painting her options in stark black and white.

The car turned a corner and her body seemed to flip 360 degrees, everything went so topsy turvy... until she realized she was wedged so tightly in the footwell, she hadn't moved at all, frozen like a rabbit hiding from a wolf.

So maybe her head wasn't *perfectly* clear. Still, no way she was gonna lay here and accept whatever this guy had planned for her.

When the car next slowed, she exploded into action.

Meaning she sluggishly climbed back up onto the seat and reached for the door handle. Her limbs were concrete. It took her several precious seconds to figure out how to flip the lock, but she pulled the handle right as the car came to a stop.

The door opened and she hurled her body into the night.

"Hey!" she heard the guy shout as she hit the wet pavement. Raindrops smacked her face.

Up. Get up, now, she shouted at herself. Instead she lay there dazed. The city swirled around her, towering skyscrapers stretching into the endless night. She was small as a raindrop, a wet splat on the blacktop...

Feet hit the ground as the driver side door opened and her kidnapper got out.

She dragged herself off the ground, using her door for leverage. She spared only the quickest, frantic glance around. They were stopped at a red light. Rain beat down on the empty sidewalks. Everywhere she looked, shops were dark and silent.

But far ahead down the sidewalk off to her right, one door was illuminated. *Light*. Light meant people. People who could help her. Or if nothing else, it meant a place to hide.

She ran towards the light. The world narrowed to a dark tunnel, her hope shrinking to the size of the cone of rain-washed light. She ran, bare feet smacking cold puddles. Her heels had fallen off somewhere along the way, thank the Fates. She was much steadier without them. The rain biting at her cheeks sharpened her focus. She ran, adrenaline powering her forward, the man's shouts chasing, but not catching up. Yet.

She tumbled down the steps that cut below street level

and slammed into the door. The man's shouts were closer than ever. He was almost on top of her. She yanked at the door handle, managed to drag it open, and rushed inside.

Her refuge was a bar or club of some sort, probably private, judging from the subdued lighting and mahogany wood that filled the place with shadows. Dimly she could make out an empty bar and booths lit by small lamps.

Crap, why was she standing here taking in the décor? Her kidnapper would be on her any second. Trying to quiet her breathing, she slipped towards the wall on her left, hugging the shadows and dripping as she went. She passed a doorman's stool and a coat room. Where was the bouncer? If this was a private club, would they kick her out?

She looked down at herself. Her little black dress was smeared with mud from the street and she was sure her face didn't look much better.

But she was thinking more clearly. Finally. So there was that.

And there wasn't a bouncer that she could see. When she paused and listened hard, all she heard was the pounding of her heart, and a few subdued voices in the back. The place was closed for the night, or very, very exclusive. If she moved quietly enough she might be able to find a back door and leave unnoticed.

Her plan held for a few seconds, but the door behind her burst open, slamming into the wall with a loud *bang*. No! She bit back a scream, cringing in the shadows. The arrival of her pursuer caught more than her attention, though.

From the far left came a shout. The bouncer, finally making an appearance.

"Hey, man, you can't come in here."

Cora blindly felt along the wall until she nearly fell into a corridor. She waited a moment, listening.

"I was with my girl—I need to see if she came in here . . ."

Scared as she was, everything in Cora protested: *I'm not his girl; I'd never met him before tonight.* The bouncer was also arguing with him, telling him the place was private.

"If you remain here, Mr. Ubeli ain't gonna be happy with you." The man's voice was unnaturally deep, and Cora imagined he was a huge man, a brute in a suit. "You need to leave."

"No, I'm telling you, she ran this way . . ."

The seconds ticked by, and Cora realized that her pursuer wasn't going to leave.

Thumping footsteps, a shout— "Hey, you can't go in there!"

Cora backed deeper into the hallway. She turned and grabbed the closest door knob she could find. Locked. Frantic, she moved down to the next one. The voices were getting closer.

The door opened. Blindly, she rushed through and closed it, cutting off the shouts.

Inside the light was subdued, the room a long dim expanse filled with as many shadows as the club. Cora stood with her back to the door, and gasped as soon as her eyes adjusted to the light.

In front of her, beyond an expanse of rich red carpet, was a desk.

Behind the desk was a man.

She froze. Her sluggish mind turned to this new problem. The man wore a suit tailored to broad shoulders. His head was bent, his dark hair gleaming, as he worked by desk light in the long, dark room.

He looked important. Interrupting this man with his imposing office in a very private club would probably only lead to trouble. Still, anything was better than the situation she'd escaped. Right?

She stood, barely daring to breathe, water dripping from her hem onto the beautiful rug. For a second Cora thought that the man hadn't seen her, he was so absorbed in the papers in front of him. In a fluid movement, though, he raised his head and looked straight at her the next moment.

Cora moved back against the door. He was handsome but in a terrifying way, like he'd been cut from marble but the sculptor had forgotten to smooth out the edges to soften the features. She could only guess at his age. Early-thirties, maybe? Shadows rested on much of his face, especially under his eyes. These he moved over her, taking in her too short dress, her unshod feet, her wet hair.

Cora, heart racing painfully, stood like a statue.

Neither of them said anything.

Slowly the man rose, a question forming on his lips. Cora also stepped forward, mind racing with possible explanations.

But she met the man's eyes, dark gray, accented by the brooding light, and her mind went blank. She wasn't sure if it was the remnants of the drugs in her system or just being near this man. She swallowed hard.

Behind her, a knock sounded sharply against the door. Cora shot backwards, her arms wrapped around herself.

"Mr. Ubeli?" someone called.

"Yes?" the man answered without taking his eyes from her.

The door opened slightly and Cora shrank back. The speaker didn't enter the room, though, and she was completely hidden behind the door.

"We got a guy out here, says he's lost some lamb he's lookin' out for. You hear?"

"I hear, Sharo," said the man called Mr. Ubeli. "Get rid of him."

Cora felt her whole body relax. Her breath escaped silently, even as Sharo said, "You got it, boss. Do you want me to dump him?"

"No, turn him away." Mr. Ubeli glanced down at his desk, shifting some papers as he called out orders. "Smack him a bit if he means trouble."

"Yeah, Mr. Ubeli. Will do."

The door closed, leaving Cora exposed again, alone with Mr. Ubeli. For a moment, he studied her with narrowed eyes.

"Was that guy giving you trouble?" he asked, moving out from behind his desk.

"Yes," Cora whispered. "Thank you."

Hunching her shoulders, she shivered, and Mr. Ubeli came forward, carefully like she was a wild animal that might run.

She shrank away, but he walked past her, going to the coat rack beside the door and lifting a coat from it. Returning, he held it out, shaking the sleeve toward her arm.

For a second Cora didn't move. She stared up at the man, into the deep, shadowed eyes. Turning, she put her arm through the sleeve, and let him help her into the coat. Once it was on, she realized it was a suit jacket, gray and too big for her, hanging slightly over her hands.

But as she wrapped it around herself, it felt like a shield against all that had happened tonight. The wave of relief hit her so hard that she all but collapsed into the chair the man guided her to in front of his desk.

She was finally safe.

It was over.

She sank back into the chair. She hoped her wet dress wouldn't ruin the red leather but she couldn't give it more than a moment's thought. It was so warm in here. Warmth and safety felt like everything that mattered in the world.

Stupid, really. She was still out of a job. And since the job had been a live-in nannying gig, she was also out of a place to live. She drew the coat even tighter around herself.

"You were his girl?"

It took a second to register his meaning, but as soon as it did— "No," Cora said violently, shaking her head and shuddering, "No. I didn't know him before tonight. He put something in my drink. And he—he—"

"Hey," he said softly, his eyebrows furrowed. "I'll make sure he never shows his face around here again."

Who was this man, to make such a promise? But the way he stated it, with such authority, made her believe it. It should have disconcerted her maybe.

Instead all she felt was relief.

Relief and warmth.

She nuzzled her head into the plush leather of the wing-backed chair. She was *so* tired. More tired than she'd ever been in her whole life.

"What's your name?" he asked.

"Cora," she said automatically, and then pressed her lips together. Should she have told him her name? *Strangers are dangerous*, her mother's words rang through her head. *The outside world is treacherous. It's only safe here on the farm. I'm the only one you can trust.*

"Nice to meet you Cora. I'm Marcus. Marcus Ubeli."

She nodded sleepily.

"Nice...to meet you...too."

Her eyes kept falling shut. It was rude and she struggled to blink them open. She really did. Well maybe she'd rest them. But only for a moment.

Only...a...moment.

But the warmth folded her under and she fell asleep.

THREE

When Cora woke up, she remembered the drink—the red liquid, shining jewel-like in the glass. She startled awake, her heartbeat racing like a terrified rabbit's.

But she wasn't in the backseat of a car. She sat up and looked around, head swinging back and forth, her messy hair falling about her face.

She was in a hotel room. A really, really fancy hotel room, judging from what she could make out by the light of the single dim lamp.

Was she still dreaming? She scrubbed groggily at her eyes but slowly, she started to remember the night before. Paul, the club, her so-called friends, the man who'd bought her the drink. The backseat of the car. Wet pavement as she ran away, down the street until she found the basement stairs, and the door, and everything that lay behind it.

That part seemed like a dream, and she would deny it happened, except she was lying between the smooth sheets and the velvety soft pillow of a five-star hotel bed.

And she was still in her dress from last night.

She blew out a sigh of relief.

What had she gotten herself into?

Well you can't stay here in bed all day. Time to go face the mess that is your life.

"But I don't wanna," she groaned and coughed. Ugh, her throat was dry.

As she got up, she noticed a glass of water on the bedside table. She almost reached for it but stopped at the last moment. She was done accepting drinks from strangers, no matter that her throat felt drier than the Mojave Desert. She yawned and stuck her tongue out as she stretched.

Ugh, her muscles ached like she'd been run over by a truck. And her head hurt. A lot. She groaned as she stumbled out of bed. She headed towards the bathroom adjacent to the room, clawing back the tangled fall of her wheat-colored hair.

How long had she slept? She'd have to look for a clock when she went back to the bedroom. The cool marble of the bathroom stung her tender feet. Squinting over the two sinks—both made out of a striking black marble—she saw the color had returned to her cheeks. She must have slept for a long time.

She yanked hard on the knobs on the bathroom sink so the water blasted and cupped her hands underneath it, and then she drank swallow after swallow.

She washed her face afterwards. The cool water washed her clammy skin clean and by the time she was finished and toweled off her face, she felt marginally better.

Especially when she saw a new toothbrush and tube of toothpaste arranged beside the sink.

"Thank the Fates," she moaned and grabbed both. She brushed long and hard, not caring if she was taking off the top coat of enamel, she was so determined to wash last night off of her. Especially when she remembered Paul trying to kiss her. *Shudder*.

A shower was up next.

She felt slightly more human after she finished and stepped out. The headache was dissipating with the more water she drank.

As she toweled off her hair and walked back into the bedroom, she found that someone had left a shopping bag on a chair near the door of the hotel room. The skirt and top she found inside were her size. Along with some underthings. She paused, not sure how to feel about that. Was it considerate, or creepy? Probably considerate seeing as the only other clothing she had was the little black dress she'd gotten at a thrift store for ten dollars. And it wasn't like she wanted to put dirty underwear back on after her shower.

Was it the man from last night who'd bought her these things?

Duh, who else? But he'd probably had his secretary get them or something.

Would she ever see him again? Or had he taken pity on her, arranged for her to sleep it off in this nice hotel room, and gotten her clothes so she wouldn't have to do the walk of shame? And that was that, he'd done his good Samaritan act for the year?

She dressed quickly, feeling embarrassed for having taken so long to get out of the hotel. She was probably overstaying her welcome. What was check-out time? Jeez, she didn't want them to charge the guy extra because she'd washed her hair twice. The shampoo had smelled so *good*. And why wasn't there a dang clock in this room? She hadn't bothered pulling back the heavy drapes to see how high the sun was in the sky because she'd been naked and changing and now she was leaving so she didn't bother.

She quickly folded her old clothes before cracking open the bedroom door.

"Oh!" she squeaked in surprise. She'd been expecting the hallway of a hotel but instead, she was met with an even larger room.

She was in a hotel *suite*. A really, really expensive hotel suite by the looks of it. With as big as the room was… was this the *penthouse*? Holy crap.

The long wall of windows was dark—there weren't any city lights visible, so Cora assumed it was the kind of glass that could be turned dark on command—and there were no lights on in the living room. What time *was* it? She ventured forward, wondering if she should call out *hello* or go knock on some of the other doors in the suite.

"How did you sleep?" a voice snaked from the darkness.

"Oh!" Cora squeaked again, hand clutching her chest.

There, in an armchair in the sitting area down by the bar, was Marcus Ubeli.

"Fine," she said, smiling timidly. "I slept fine."

She moved down towards him, still looking around. The room stretched out in shadow. The penthouse must take up one whole side of the building, she realized. There was a kitchen and bar, sunken areas for lounging, TVs and, in one corner, a baby grand piano. Everything was in grey or black, with touches of cream.

"Do you like the place?" Marcus Ubeli stood with his hands in his pockets, the shadows grey on his face and under his eyes as he watched her.

Right. She was probably staring like a country bumpkin. "It's nice," she said and inwardly cringed. *Nice?* "I mean, it's really fancy." Cringe. *Fancy* was worse than nice. "Elegant, I mean. Really elegantly decorated."

Shoot her now.

To get into the lowered seating area, she passed a statue, a contorted figure in white marble.

"That one's mine," he commented, and she paused politely to stare at it. "The hotel lets me furnish this place to my tastes."

The statue was of a woman, a body and thin cloth all finely sculpted. It looked Greek, and well done, but the figure's face unsettled her—a sweet youth's features twisted as if in some horror or fear. She moved on, descending into the sunken area where her host stood.

"So you live here?" Cora asked.

Marcus Ubeli chuckled. "No, I keep it in case I want to get away."

Of course he did. Drawing in her breath, she nodded as if this was normal. But holy crap, what must a place like this cost? And he kept it as what, a place to crash when he was up late in this part of the city?

Or a place to bring women. Her cheeks heated at the thought.

"Would you like a drink?" He approached, and she shrank away from his tall, dark figure, suddenly imposing. But he only turned and went up the steps to the bar.

"No, thank you." She shook her head, still feeling a little sluggish. At the bar, glass clinked and then he was back. "How long did I sleep?"

Again, a small chuckle. It wasn't unkind, but it made her feel like she missed the joke. "I just watched the sunset."

"What?" She was horrified. "No way." She went to the window. "Can you turn these clear?"

"Of course." He reached for a remote control and with the tap of a button, the dark windows became transparent. Cora gasped as the view became bright with rows of light that outlined skyscrapers, artificial and multicolored against a black velvet sky. She really had slept for an entire day.

"Oh, no," she said, lifting a hand to her forehead and feeling completely disoriented. She turned back to her host, who was now standing, his figure cut half through with black, half in grey.

"Forgive me," he said, and she was startled again. He didn't look like a man who would apologize. "I let you sleep as long as you could."

Shadow shrouded his face; she couldn't make out any expression beyond what was in his voice. "I made sure you were okay. Someone stayed here, in case you woke. But when I returned you were still asleep." His voice dropped and became softer. "I figured you needed it."

"It's okay," Cora said, although she felt weak. "I mean, thank you." She'd slept a whole day! And someone had stayed with her—she wondered who, and hoped it wasn't the muscular bouncer she had seen in the club. She had so many questions—who *was* this man? Why was he being so nice?—but she bit them back, feeling his dark gaze on her.

"You hungry?"

She shook her head sharply, remembering the pitch of her stomach during the chase. The memory didn't seem a day old.

Too late, she thought of her manners. This obviously wealthy man had taken time out of his day to check in on her when she was sure he had a million more important things to be doing.

"I'm sorry. I'll get out of your hair. And I really should be getting home."

She didn't even cringe as she said it. Well, not too much. But whatever her problems were, she was done foisting them on this man.

He tilted his head sideways, examining her in a way that made her mouth go dry again. "Last night you said you didn't have a home."

Cora felt her eyes go wide. "Oh." Shoot her now. She knew she talked sometimes in her sleep. She tried to laugh it off. "Well I was working as a live-in nanny."

"And?"

Cora opened her mouth and a helpless little noise came out. How could she even begin to— And it wasn't like it was *his* problem—

But Marcus Ubeli arched a dark eyebrow in a way that demanded the truth.

"Well, I sort of quit."

"Sort of quit? Either you did or you didn't."

She let out a breath in a rush of air. "I did quit. But I still need to go back and get my last paycheck and all my stuff."

She couldn't help her frown thinking about what sort of scene that might be. But all the money she'd made in the last six weeks was there, and her backpack full of clothes and the few other things she'd brought from Kansas—

"I'll have your things picked up. You can stay here until you're back on your feet again."

"What?" Cora's back went stiff. "No!"

Dang it, she was being rude again when this man had only been kind to her. "No, I mean, thank you. That's very nice. But I'm fine. I'll be fine. I'll go by and pick up my things and go to my friend's house."

He didn't have to know she was speaking about a hypothetical friend. Especially since her phone was gone. That creep from last night had kept it after he'd picked it up and she hadn't memorized Europa or Helena's numbers.

But the Donahues paid well. She'd have almost fifteen

hundred dollars all together once they paid the half of this month's paycheck she was owed. Maybe she'd catch a bus and find somewhere cheaper to live. The big city was the best place to hide from her mother, but it was too expensive.

"Sounds like you've got it all worked out," he said. "I'll have my driver drop you wherever you want to go." He pulled his phone out of his pocket and touched a button. "Sharo. Yes. Bring the car around. You'll be escorting Miss..." Marcus's eyes came Cora's way.

"Vestian. Cora Vestian."

"...Miss Vestian wherever she'd like to go."

He hung up the phone and slid it back in his jacket pocket in one fluid gesture. "It's nine p.m. I'd be happy for you to stay here another night and let all your responsibilities rest until daylight. What can you really accomplish tonight?"

Cora clutched yesterday's dress to her stomach. "Oh, it's fine. I'm a night owl. So are my friends." Lies. All lies. She was usually in bed before the evening news.

If Marcus could tell she was lying, he didn't call her on it. He merely inclined his head and held a hand out toward the door. "Sharo will be waiting by the time you get to the front of the hotel. May I walk you?"

She blinked, then nodded. She'd never met anyone so... well, so courteous. Courtly, that was the perfect word for Marcus Ubeli. He was like some old timey knight with his chivalry, coming to her rescue when she was a damsel in distress.

Books had been the one entertainment her mother allowed and she might have swooned over a knight or two throughout her adolescence.

Marcus held out an arm. She shoved her dirty dress behind her back, more glad than ever that she'd balled up her dirty undies and bra inside it, and took his arm with her other hand. Electricity crackled through her body the moment they touched.

Not to mention that the strength that emanated off his body was... wow. Just *wow*. She'd never felt anything like it. Being so near him made her feel a little light-headed all over again.

He led her smoothly across the living room of the penthouse, out the door and to the elevator. Cora had never wanted an elevator to come faster and wished it would never show up at the same time.

"So," she said, hating the way her voice came out as little more than a squeak. She must seem like such a little girl to someone like Marcus. "What do you do? Like, I mean, as a job?"

She glanced up at his face.

Bad idea. *Really* bad idea.

She'd only seen him in dim lighting before. The hallway didn't have fluorescents or anything but it was enough to see that, holy crap, Marcus was gorgeous. Freaking stunning from the top of his elegant cheek bones to the strong set of his jaw.

And the way he smiled down at her, still all dark and broody but like she amused him at the same time—it took her breath away. Literally she was having a hard time remembering how to breathe.

His grin deepened until a dimple popped in his cheek and she jerked back like she'd been struck.

"I own many business and investment properties. You all right?" Marcus's brow wrinkled. His eyelashes were black and long, a hint of beauty on a hard, masculine face.

Of course his eyelashes were freakin' perfect.

"Cora?"

"Yeah. Yes. Yep." She bobbed her head like a fool and got hit with another smile. They say Cupid shot arrows, but this felt more like a punch, a battering ram, smashing her right in the gut, pushing her insides out and replacing them with a golden glow.

Was this because she'd been completely deprived of male company her whole life and so now she was boy crazy, the first time she got to be this near a man?

No, it couldn't be that. She hadn't felt anything but disgust when Paul tried hitting on her.

She was pretty sure this was all Marcus.

He didn't move back. He stared down at her, the smile slowly falling away, replaced by an intensity that pinned her in place like a butterfly to a board.

When the elevator pinged its arrival, she all but jumped out of her skin.

The corner of Marcus's mouth tipped up and he let go of her arm. "After you."

Feeling like an idiot, she stepped onto the elevator. She thought he'd leave her there but he stepped on with her. The space shrank and the air heated. Cora held her arms stiff beside her body. She was an awkward mannequin next to the tall, broad shouldered god filling the small box.

The hairs on her arms rose where his suit coat brushed against her. The rich fabric felt like the suit coat he'd draped over her last night. She'd never been so *aware* of anyone in her whole life.

She thought that surely it would pass but nope, the entire ride down, the electric awareness hummed under her skin. She about jumped off the elevator once they got to the lobby.

"Thank you again," she said. "You have no idea how much I appreciate what you did for me. I mean," she shook her head as a shudder worked down her spine, "I can't imagine what would have happened if it hadn't been for—"

She sucked in a deep breath and cut off her word barrage. She looked Marcus in the eyes, tried as hard as possible to ignore the way his intense gaze made her stomach go absolutely liquid, and said, "Just, thank you."

"All right, Cora," he murmured. A flush came over her —she was freakin' light headed at the sound of her name on his lips. "You ever need anything, you reach out to me, yeah? I'll take care of you."

He was so nice. She reached out and gave his hand a quick squeeze.

His nostrils flared at the touch and she immediately let go and spun on her heel, her own eyes wide. Oh gods, why had she touched him? What was she thinking?

Glancing around, she saw all eyes in the lobby were on her and Marcus. And here she was, making a fool of herself. She squeezed her eyes shut briefly, horrified at how silly and naïve Marcus probably found her.

But she shook it off. Oh well. It was done. For one shining night, okay, two shining nights, she'd been a brief blip on Marcus Ubeli's passing radar, and that had been enough.

She bit back the impulse to thank Marcus again and instead, kept her back to him and walked across the lobby. It felt like the longest walk of her life. She could feel every eye in the place on her. But was *he* still watching her?

Duh, no, stupid. He probably turned around and went right back up to the penthouse. She'd likely never see him again.

The huge bald-headed bouncer, Sharo, was waiting for her as she pushed through the revolving doors.

Cora stopped up short at seeing him. Wow. She

hadn't realized quite how... *large* he was. All his proportions were normal, he just came in extra, extra-large. He must be six foot five and could have had a career as a linebacker. He wore a suit that had to have been specifically tailored for his frame and he had a small earpiece in his ear.

He nodded at her and walked around to the back of the sleek, black expensive looking car. "Miss Vestian."

"Thank you."

She slid onto the cool leather bench seat and Sharo closed the door behind her. She clutched her old dress in her lap nervously.

"Seatbelt," Sharo said from the front seat.

"Oh, right." She finally relinquished her clothing to the seat beside her and pulled the seatbelt across her chest, clicking it into place.

"Address?"

She gave him the address and he plugged it into a screen on the dashboard. They pulled out of the hotel's drive and the lights of the city slid over the car. Cora stared out the window like she always did when she was in a car or on the bus.

Six weeks here and the city still awed her. She'd read books about cities and buildings so tall they scraped the sky but reading about them and seeing them for herself were two entirely different things.

Cora had grown up surrounded by corn and sorghum crops. Rows and rows as far as the eye could see. And that was all. The idea of a place so packed with people they had to build upwards and stack them on top of each other to fit was something Cora hadn't really even been able to comprehend before coming here.

The ride was silent. Sharo didn't say anything and Cora

was glad because she was too intimidated to talk to the big man. If he didn't talk, that meant she didn't have to, either.

And soon enough, she began to recognize the landmarks of the Donahue's neighborhood.

She sat up straighter and looked at the clock on the dashboard screen. Nine twenty. Okay, at least Timmy would be asleep. Her heart squeezed in her chest. She'd miss the little boy. He wouldn't understand why she'd suddenly disappeared. It wasn't fair to him. But there was no way she could stay. Not after what Paul had done.

She took a deep breath as the car came to a stop.

Okay. She'd go in, get her money and belongings, and move on from there. She could get a hotel for the night. She almost laughed thinking about the kind of hotel *she* could afford compared to where she'd stayed last night. She'd have to take the train to the outskirts of the city and look for the cheapest motel she could find, but at least it would get her through the night. Tomorrow she could look for another job and—

"Miss Vestian?" Sharo questioned. "If you're having second thoughts, I know Mr. Ubeli wouldn't mind—"

"No." Cora's attention snapped back to the present moment and she shoved her door open, hiking her feet to the pavement. She cringed, thinking of how the beautiful heels were probably already getting scratched. She'd wanted to return the clothing in perfect order to Mr. Ubeli along with her thanks.

Oh well, she sighed. It wasn't like he could return them to the store after she'd worn them.

"Thank you. And thank Mr. Ubeli again for me." She closed the car door before she could start babbling again.

Sharo had gotten out of the car as well and she looked upwards at his face, so far above hers. "Mr. Ubeli asked me to give you this." He held out a card. "If you ever have need of him for any reason, any reason at all, you give him a call. You understand?"

She nodded quickly and took the card. She gave a quick smile and turned to hurry down the sidewalk toward the Donahue's brownstone.

She waited until the black car pulled away and drove down the road before knocking on the door. She didn't ring the doorbell because she didn't want to wake Timmy.

It felt weird to knock on the front door rather than letting herself in with her key, but she hadn't even had time to grab those before Paul had accosted her last night.

She shook her head. Had that really only been last night? Because as much as she'd been shocked to find out that it was evening when she woke up today, the events of last night had already begun to feel very distant, like they'd happened to some other girl. A defense mechanism probably, but she didn't have another moment to think about it because the door swung open.

"Mrs. Donahue. Hi. I'm here to pick up my things. I don't know if Paul— If Mr. Donahue told you, but I quit yester—"

"Whore! How dare you show your face back here?"

"Wha—"

But before Cora could even get the word out, the middle-aged woman stepped out onto the front stoop and slapped Cora. *Hard.*

Cora jerked back and lifted a hand to her face.

Ow.

For such a small lady, Mrs. Donahue packed a mean hit.

"Wait," Cora held up her hands, "there's been some kind of misunderstanding here—"

"Did you or did you not try to fuck my husband?" Mrs. Donahue sneered.

"Of course not! I would never!"

But it was clear by the expression on Diana Donahue's face that she didn't believe a word coming out of Cora's mouth. And why would she? It was Cora's word against Paul's.

"You're way out of line," Cora said, fists clenched, "but you're never going to believe me and I get it. So just pay me the money you owe me and let me get my things and you never have to see me again."

Mrs. Donahue made a disbelieving noise. "You're not stepping one *foot* inside my house, you homewrecking whore. I had to miss *work* today to stay home with Timmy. The gods only know what sort of influence you've had on my baby." She shook her head and went to close the door.

Cora shoved her foot in the way and pushed on the door. It startled Mrs. Donahue into stumbling several feet back into the foyer. But that only seemed to anger her more.

"I'm calling the police," she shrieked.

"All I'm asking for is what you owe me," Cora said, barely able to believe what was happening. "You have to pay me. I did the job. And I need my things."

"I *burned* your things. The second Paul told me what you tried to do after you didn't come home last night. I threw them in the trash and set them on *fire*."

Cora felt her mouth drop open. She'd burned— But that was all Cora had— All she owned in the whole world—

"But—" Cora broke off, biting back tears. Paul stalked into the room behind Diana. "Paul, tell her," Cora appealed. "Tell her what happened. Please. I need the money for the work I did. I don't have anything else. I need that money."

But Paul was stone-faced and when he walked forward,

he put an arm around his wife. "You need to go or we will call the police."

"I'm already dialing," Diana said, touching her phone and holding it to her ear. "Yes, hello. There's a psycho intruder in our house. Our former nanny who's stalking my husband."

Cora stumbled backwards and pulled the front door shut behind her. It wasn't fair! They shouldn't be able to do that to her. She'd been depending on that money.

She heard sirens in the distance. They probably weren't coming for her. Sirens were a normal part of city life but still, it had her running.

She didn't have any ID or even a social security number thanks to her mom's obsession with living off the grid. It was one of the reasons working for the Donahues was so perfect. They didn't mind paying her under the table in cash.

But now there was no cash.

No job.

No nothing.

She didn't even have her phone thanks to that bastard from last night.

She only slowed down when she turned the corner and ran down the steps to the subway.

She had twenty bucks on her from the night before and that was all. She spent five on a subway ticket and got on the first train that showed up.

Sitting on the grimy subway car, she looked around and the full weight of her situation finally hit her.

She had nowhere to sleep tonight.

Her eyes fell on a dirty, obviously homeless man sleeping in the corner of the train.

Well that was one option.

Her head dropped backwards against the window

behind her and she closed her eyes. Was she seriously contemplating sleeping on the subway car like the homeless bum? Was that how far she'd fallen?

Why are you being so sanctimonious? You *are homeless.*

She scrubbed her hand down her face.

She thought she was so brave, escaping the farm. She'd done it on the spur of the moment. She'd seen a chance and taken it. Cora was a terrible liar and no one could read her better than her controlling mother.

Controlling. Ha. Her mother was pathological.

Demi Vestian watched every single thing her daughter did. She monitored how much food Cora ate, how much she slept, if she'd done all her chores, if she did her schooling and did it perfectly. Most of the time Cora felt more like a science experiment or a prize show dog than a daughter.

Not that her mother ever showed her off.

No, that was the other singular rule of their lives. They never saw anyone. *Ever.*

If they had to have a vet out to look at the horses, Cora was locked in the cellar for the duration.

Her mom took the truck into town twice a month for food and supplies but Cora was always left behind. Cora only got to read about other kids in books. She never met any.

Until she was a teenager and got fed up with it.

One time when she was fifteen, she stole the truck and drove down the long road that led away from the farm.

It was stupid and reckless and she only knew the rudiments of how to drive. But the road was flat and straight and it was a bright, sunny afternoon. Within an hour, she'd made it to town.

She pulled the truck to a stop on the side of the road

and parked it as soon as she came to a grouping of buildings. She got out and started walking.

She walked from one store to the next, delighted and amazed by everything she saw, but most of all by the people. They seemed as surprised to see her as she was to see them. *Who was she?* they wanted to know. She didn't know how to answer their questions. She felt like it would be betraying her mom to say she lived down the road. No one was supposed to know she existed. She never knew why, but she knew that much.

But someone recognized her. The owner of the general store, a man so old his skin was papery with wrinkles and folds.

"You related to Demi? You're the spittin' image. The spittin' image, as I live and breathe. You a cousin come to visit? Or her niece?"

Cora nodded, not daring to speak. She backed out of the general store. Right into a group of teenagers.

One of the boys said she was pretty and he invited her to a party they were all going to. *A party!* Like she'd read about in her Sweet Valley High books.

She got in the back of a truck with the two boys and three girls and they drove out to an empty field. Cora couldn't stop smiling and laughing even though she started feeling self-conscious after one of the other girls whispered loudly about her, making fun of her worn overalls with the patches on the knees.

But not even that was enough to dampen Cora's mood. She helped the guys build up the bonfire and she felt a warm glow that had nothing to do with the fire when the boy who'd first called her pretty touched her hair and said it was the color of moonlight.

Cora had never heard anything so pretty or poetic and

when the boy invited her to sit on the hay bale beside him, she giggled but accepted.

They'd started breaking out the beer, which Cora politely declined, when suddenly the field was lit up by headlights and the blaring noise of sirens.

"Shit, cops!" the boy sitting beside Cora shouted.

Cora had jumped up and covered her ears, confused.

The boy who'd called her pretty ran away, along with all his friends, disappearing into the nearby cornfield. They all left her standing there alone as two police cars surrounded her.

Almost the second they came to a stop, Demi was jumping out of the first police car and running towards Cora.

Cora was both relieved and horrified to see her mother. She felt like crying, especially when her mother yanked her by her arm back toward the police car without a word.

She didn't say a single word to her as the police drove them back to her mom's truck where she'd abandoned it outside town.

And her mom didn't say a word after she'd hauled Cora into the passenger seat of the truck and slammed the side door shut after she was in. Or for the entire forty-five-minute drive back to the farm.

As soon as the farm came back into sight, Cora finally ventured, "Mom, I'm sorry. I just wanted to see how—"

"Do you know what could have happened to you?" her mom yelled, slamming her foot on the breaks and jamming the truck into park. "How could you be so *selfish*?"

Cora hunched down in her seat.

"After all I do for you." Mom shook her head. "After the years I have sacrificed for you, slaved for you, out here in the middle of *nowhere*. You think I like it out here with no one but you for company? But I do it. For *you*. To protect *you*. And you go and throw it back in my face like this."

"Why?" Cora sat up, slamming her hands on the seat beside her. "*Why* do we have to live like this? Why can't we live in town? Or a city? Why can't I have friends or go to a normal school?"

But Mom shook her head like Cora was being ridiculous. "How many times do I have to tell you how dangerous it is out there?"

"It wasn't dangerous today," Cora disagreed. "Those kids were nice. We were having a nice time."

Mom scoffed. "You're so stupid you don't even know what you don't know. You think those boys were being *nice* to you because they liked you? They wanted what's between your legs. If I hadn't shown up you would have turned out to be a statistic in the morning paper."

Cora shoved open her door and got out of the truck. "You're wrong." And she'd slammed the door behind her.

All of which was the wrong thing to do.

Because her mother got out of the truck just as quickly and before Cora could blink, she was around the truck and had Cora's arm in her iron grip.

She dragged Cora into the house, ignoring her cries.

"No. No, Mom!" Cora screeched as soon as she realized where Mom was taking her. "Not the cellar. Please. I'm sorry, okay? I'm sorry!"

But once Mom had made her mind up about something, there was no changing it. And though Cora was fifteen, she'd always been small for her age and she was no match for her mom's wiry, compactly muscled body.

Mom had her down the stairs to the damp, chilly cellar before she could even get another plea out. She shoved Cora to the floor and jogged back up the steps.

"Mom," Cora called, getting up and jumping to her feet. "Mama!" She ran up the stairs right as her mother slammed the cellar door on her.

And no matter how much she banged on the door or begged and pleaded and swore she'd do better, her mom wouldn't open up.

She didn't open the doors for three days and three nights. Not that Cora knew that until later. At the time, all Cora knew was that she was in the cold and the dark and that it was never ending. There was a gallon of water and a bucket for her to use the bathroom, and Cora finally got hungry enough that she opened some of the jam they had stored down there and ate it straight.

And when her mother finally opened the door and Cora had squinted up at the rectangle of light, things were never the same between them again.

Cora opened her eyes and looked around the subway car.

She couldn't go home. She'd sworn once she finally escaped that farm, and her mother, that she'd never *ever* go back.

Which meant there was really only one option, no matter how mortifying it might be. Cora pulled the card Sharo had given her out of her skirt pocket.

The subway car was almost empty. A weary-looking woman in business attire sat in the front, the seat furthest away from the homeless man. Cora stood up, holding onto the poles as she made her way over to the woman.

"Hi, ma'am, I'm sorry to bother you, but could I borrow your phone?"

FOUR

"We have to stop meeting like this," Cora joked nervously as Marcus opened the door to his penthouse hotel suite and gestured for her to come in.

The edge of his mouth quirked up in a half smile. Was he laughing at her joke or at *her*? Not that it mattered either way. He was doing her a huge favor.

"I really appreciate this," she said. "It'll just be for the night." She cringed. "Or maybe a couple of nights? As soon as I get another nannying gig, I'll be out of your hair, I swear."

Marcus didn't say anything, he just watched her with that inscrutable look on his face. He tilted his head, indicating she should come in. Well, further in than the foyer where she was babbling like an idiot.

"Sharo mentioned you hadn't eaten yet."

"Oh," Cora said, surprised to see an elaborate table set up in a small dining area. The windows were still not darkened.

She took several more steps forward, awed by the glittering tableau. She'd seen it earlier, but been too distracted to take it in properly. Now, she swayed as she faced rows and rows of skyscrapers, the entire city laid at her feet.

"I've never been so high up," she whispered. She wanted to go right up to the window but kept back. Looking down on the skyscrapers made her dizzy. "I mean, I knew we must be up this high from how long the elevator ride took but..." she trailed off, shaking her head.

When she looked back at Marcus, his head was tilted, his eyes narrowed at her like she was a particularly peculiar species of zoo animal.

She felt her cheeks heat and lifted her hands to them. Why the hell couldn't she keep her mouth shut? And not let every single thing she was feeling and thinking show on her face?

She moved abruptly to go sit down at the table. "Thank you, I am famished."

Marcus moved as she did, getting there right before her and holding her chair for her as she sat down.

His scent enveloped her, his arm brushing hers, and like earlier when he'd escorted her downstairs, the merest touch sent a jolt of electricity through her entire body.

She gasped and sat down, grabbing the seat of the chair and scooting herself in. "Thank you." She ran a hand nervously through her hair as she smiled up at him.

Her plate was covered with a fancy silver plate topper. She lifted it off and steam wafted up. "Oh!" she said, surprised again. Marcus chuckled as he sat down across from her.

"I hope you don't mind but I took the liberty of ordering for us. Roasted lamb shank, corn and leek grits, ruby chard, roasted rutabaga, topped with goat cheese."

"Oh," Cora said, yet again, nodding and looking down at her plate, eyes wide. She didn't think she'd ever seen such a large piece of meat. At least not on a plate set in front of her.

"You aren't a vegetarian, are you?"

"No," she said quickly. She and Mom *did* mostly eat vegetarian, but it hadn't been due to any choice on Cora's part. That was the point of leaving, wasn't it? So that she could finally have *choices* in her life?

Cora smiled and reached for her fork...only to find there were several forks. She grabbed the one nearest the plate and smiled wider. "Cheers," she said, lifting the fork like it was a wine glass she was toasting with.

Marcus chuckled again and she averted her eyes to her plate, digging into the lamb shank. It was so well-cooked and tender, it melted off the big bone. Tentatively, she lifted it to her mouth.

And almost embarrassed herself even more by moaning out loud. She stopped herself at the last second but holy *crap*.

Her eyes flew to Marcus and as soon as she finished chewing and swallowing the bite, she couldn't help moaning, "That's the best thing I've ever eaten in my *entire* life."

He sat back in his chair, brow wrinkled like he'd never seen anything like her before. He hadn't touched his food yet.

"Aren't you going to have yours? It's delicious. Trust me."

"Oh I don't doubt it," he said. "I'll give your compliments to the chef."

She nodded as she eagerly forked another big bite. "Please do," she said before shoving the forkful into her mouth. Dear gods, *this* was what she'd been missing out on the last nineteen years of her life? Now she had even more to begrudge her mother. It was a crime to have never encountered food this good before.

Her mom was a fan of boiled vegetables. And rice. Plain white rice. Food was fuel, that's what her mom always said. Just fuel.

"Wait till we get to dessert," Marcus said, finally taking a bite of his food, his eyes never leaving her.

"What's dessert?"

"Chocolate mousse."

Cora fought against licking her lips. She adored chocolate.

"So tell me. What made you change your mind and come back?"

"Oh." Obviously her favorite word for the evening. "Well I went by my former employers to pick up my, um, paycheck and my belongings but there was, um..."

Cora looked towards the window. "...a little bit of an issue." She glanced back Marcus's way and then down at her plate. "Anyway, I wasn't able to get my paycheck or any of my things. They'd already thrown them out. And I lost my phone last night when that man... So I didn't have anyone's phone number because they were all in the phone and I didn't know where to go without any money..."

She shoved another bite of lamb shank into her mouth if only to cut herself off from saying anything else. She hazarded another glance at Marcus. He had his glass of wine in his hand but he set it abruptly down on the table, frowning. "They didn't give you the money they owed you?"

Cora swallowed the meat and reached for her cup of water. All the sudden she felt hot. She fanned herself with her other hand. Did he feel like it was hot in here?

Marcus was still staring at her, obviously expecting an

answer, so she shook her head, three quick shakes back and forth.

It was embarrassing enough experiencing it the first time around, but now having to tell Marcus seemed like adding insult to injury. She didn't know what was worse, him knowing all the details of her pathetic situation or thinking she was a mooch, eager to eat his fancy food and sleep in his fancy penthouse hotel suite.

"That's not acceptable."

The dark look that crossed his face on her behalf both pleased and scared her a little.

She quickly waved a hand. "It's one of those things that happens, I guess. I'll be more careful in the future."

"But surely you have some money in the bank?"

Could she die of embarrassment?

"I don't have a bank account. I kept it all in cash."

She could feel his eyes on her even without looking up. "And, well, I don't exactly have an ID either. Or a social security number. My mom's kind of...intense, I guess is one way to put it. I grew up way out in the middle of nowhere on a farm and my mom homeschooled me and everything. Mom wanted to be off the grid."

Cora fiddled with her fork in her grits. "Like, *really* off the grid. Apparently she even gave birth to me at home and never, you know, got a birth certificate or social security card or anything for me."

Cora braced herself and finally looked up at Marcus. But she couldn't read a single thing from his features. It wasn't that his face was blank—his eyes were lit with interest, but he didn't look as shocked or appalled as she'd expected. It gave her the courage to go on.

"So when I left home and came to the city, I didn't have any paperwork. I didn't even think about it. I didn't know you needed that kind of thing to get a job. But it turns out it's really important."

"But you still got the nannying job."

She shrugged. "They were fine with paying me cash."

"And they didn't require references?"

"They told me they'd have a nanny cam on me at all times and I got along really well with Timmy during our trial play date. Plus I wasn't asking for as much money as other nannies, I learned later."

And it had been Paul who'd interviewed her, not Diane. Cora shuddered. Was that the real reason he'd hired her? Because he found her attractive and had hoped to have an affair with her?

"Well first of all, we need to start the process for getting you a social security card. You'll be crippled for life without one."

Cora's mouth dropped open. First by the *we* and second by how confident he sounded that she could actually get a social security card. She'd looked into it on the internet a few times but almost everything that came up was only for how to get documents for babies born at home while they were still babies. Not when they were *nineteen*.

She'd thought about going to the social security office and asking but had gotten afraid. What if she got in trouble for not having the documents? She couldn't actually *prove* she was who she said she was. She couldn't even prove she was a citizen and with how crazy everything had been with immigration lately, what if they tried to deport her to a foreign country? Yes, she was good at thinking in terms of worst-possible-scenarios. After living with her paranoid mom all her life, it was usually her knee jerk reaction.

Besides, she'd gotten the nanny position so it didn't seem so important and definitely not worth the risk.

Feeling stupid even as she asked it, she couldn't help herself. "Doesn't that seem, I don't know...risky? How would they prove that I am who I say I am?"

"I'll have my lawyer look into it, but I imagine it will involve a series of affidavits by your mother and people who knew her while she was preg—"

"No," Cora said sharply.

Marcus's eyebrows went up.

Crap. How to explain this? "My mom and I didn't part on the best of terms is all."

Marcus nodded, looking thoughtful.

Cora took another bite of her food if only for something to busy her hands with when Marcus asked, "Have you ever done any modeling?"

Her eyes bulged and she choked, grabbing for her napkin and dabbing at the red sauce she was sure was all over her mouth.

She hurriedly chewed and laughed. "Ha ha," she said. "Funny joke."

He wasn't laughing, though. His features were set with their stone intensity again. "When I'm telling a joke, you'll know it, Cora."

She scoffed. "I don't look like a model."

How many times had her mother picked on her appearance? *Why won't you let me cut bangs again? Your forehead is obnoxiously huge. It needs to be covered. And what have you been eating? I'm surprised you can make it through the door with those hips.*

Marcus's eyes narrowed. "Don't be one of those girls who pretends she doesn't know she's beautiful."

Cora's cheeks flamed. Did he think she was fishing for compliments? She waved a hand at him but he persisted.

"I have a friend who's a fashion designer, Armand, and I know he'd love to get his hands on you."

Her mouth dropped open again, the second time in as many minutes. *Get his hands on—*

"Not like that." Marcus tilted his head, his grey eyes turning dark. "No one will ever lay hands on you again."

The way he said it had a quality of finality that probably should have disturbed her. And was it just her or did she read an implicit, *"Except me,"* in his eyes in the silence after his statement?

"But it would be work I think you'd enjoy," he went on. "You'd get to meet people your age." He smiled in a way that made her feel every one of the years between them. "And wear pretty clothes."

She rolled her eyes. "I'd feel more comfortable in overalls and flannel. Farm girl, remember?"

Although more than once, she *had* snuck into her mother's closet and tried on the heels hidden in a box at the very back. She'd about broken her ankle the first few times she tried walking in them but had eventually gotten the hang of it. She'd dreamed about the sort of life Marcus was describing, but in the same way she dreamed about knights and castles from her books. Not as anything that could ever be *real*.

"You own businesses, right?" she asked. "Why can't I work for you?"

"Out of the question," he snapped and Cora shrank back from the table.

Marcus swiped at his mouth with a napkin. His eyes were on her again. "I own bars. Hotels that aren't in the best parts of town. Not where an angel belongs."

Cora frowned a little. She wasn't sure she liked being thought of as an angel all that much. The more she got to know Marcus the more she thought she might like to be right down here on the earthly plane with him. For him to see her as a *woman*.

A chair scraped and Marcus's shadow fell over her. "Cora," he took her hand and it happened again, the electricity, but far more intensely this time. Warmth pulsed up her arm, her blood simmering, the flush spreading over her chest and rolling down. Cora gasped and Marcus's forehead crinkled. "Cora?"

She stared at him as her body throbbed, her lips tingling and breasts swelling. From his touch. One touch. She never even knew that was possible.

"You okay?"

"Yeah. Yes." Her mouth still worked even though her throat had gone suddenly dry. A miracle. "I'm good," she whispered.

Marcus narrowed his eyes a moment before his face softened. His thumb stroked over her pulse. Her limbs turned liquid.

"Angel," he said softly, and the way he said it sent thrills through her.

He didn't say anything more, and he didn't have to. Did he... Was he... feeling it too? He had to know how he affected her. And he didn't pull away.

His grey eyes gleamed. Oh gods, he was. He was interested. In *her*.

Very interested, if the way his nostrils flared were any indication.

This was nuts, totally nuts. But it was happening. It was, wasn't it? She wasn't just making things up in her head? She searched his eyes, feeling desperate from all the sensations he was stirring inside her.

"Why are you helping me?" she blurted the question

that had plagued her since she'd woken this morning. "I'm no one."

A final squeeze, and his tall, powerful frame moved gracefully back to his seat. She felt breathless, all the nerves in her body still firing from his touch.

He looked down at his plate, his expression shadowed. The silence stretched.

"It's just, you're doing all these things for me. And I'm so grateful, don't get me wrong. But if I could understand *why—*"

"You remind me of someone," he said, eyes still on his plate, and she didn't miss the way his jaw worked. "Let's say helping you is paying a debt I owe."

"Oh." Cora's stomach sank to the floor, all the lovely feelings dissipating. She was a debt to him? So much for him seeing her as a woman. She felt so foolish. Like a schoolgirl with a crush.

"And this city is a dangerous place. I know better than anyone. I had a sister who was a little younger than you when I lost her."

A sister? And he'd lost her? Cora immediately felt like a witch for being so self-absorbed. Schoolgirl indeed.

"I'm so sorry. Marcus." She reached across the table and laid her hand on his. "What happened? No, gods, I'm sorry. You don't have to tell me." She gave his hand a squeeze and he exhaled a huge breath, finally lifting his grey eyes to hers. She couldn't look away. In front of her was a man, not a boy. He was a man who'd lived through things and survived them, things she couldn't even comprehend. She suddenly wished she was more...well, just *more,* so she might be any sort of comfort to him.

"I want to tell you." His eyebrows were drawn together and she could see a deep grief in his eyes that time obviously hadn't healed. Cora felt his pain cut straight through her own chest down to her bones. "She was my sister and I loved her more than anything else on earth. When she and my parents were taken from me, brutally, *violently*," his hand shook under Cora's, "for a long while, I wished I'd died with them."

"Marcus," Cora whispered, barely able to get the word out, her throat was so thick. She reached her other hand out and clasped his, both of her small hands only barely surrounding one of his huge ones.

She didn't know why he'd chosen her to share this with, but from her limited interactions with him, she felt sure this wasn't common for him, that he was a man who rarely if ever wore his heart on his sleeve. He was too in control of himself, too measured in everything he did. Whatever his reasons, she could only feel honored to have this peek beneath the mask to glimpse the genuine man.

"But I *vowed* to do everything I could to take the city they loved under control so that the monsters who killed them would never have free reign again. So you understand why I can't let you go," he said, gaze more direct than ever. "This city is a beast. A beast in a cage. Violent. Brutal. Innocents fall and the criminals go unpunished if left unchecked."

He believed everything he said and he believed it passionately. Absolutely. It sent a shiver down Cora's spine.

"But what about the cops?"

"What about them?" he sneered. "The police do nothing. They're either corrupt, or have no power. There's no law and order, just violence. The strong crush the weak, and death walks the streets. There's a reason they call the part of the city where you were clubbing The Underworld. But it's not just the south side. The whole city balances on a knife's edge. And it's men like me who keep it from going over and falling into chaos."

It's not safe. The world out there isn't safe.

How many times had her mother told her that? She'd repeated it over and over. *Not safe. Not safe. Not safe.*

"I don't want to live my whole life in fear," Cora whispered.

Marcus shook his head. "You won't have to." He flipped his hand and this time it was him squeezing hers.

She felt the strength of his grasp all the way down to her toes.

He leaned in, the burning intensity of his eyes flipping her stomach again as he vowed, "You'll live among the angels where you can't be touched."

FIVE

"Babe, babe, come on, move!" Cora turned and was blinded by the lights. She'd stepped into the studio and was immediately overwhelmed by the frenetic energy of the place.

"Out of the way! Move it!"

Cora took a step to the side, disoriented, and then noticed the harried cameraman trying to pass her.

"I beg your pardon," she said, moving out of the way even further. He shook his head at her as he rushed past. She stood unsure, looking this way and that until a short but well-built man came up to her.

"Cora Vestian?"

"Yes."

The man grinned broadly. "Armand." He was fresh-faced, dark-haired and olive-skinned, with sharp cheekbones and flashing black eyes. She wouldn't have thought anyone outside of the seventies could pull off a mustache, but on him it was dashing. Along with his big framed black glasses, tight jeans and suspenders over a striped vintage Parisian shirt, he looked incredibly hip in addition to handsome.

Cora tugged on the hem of her white t-shirt and rubbed her hands on her plain black leggings. Marcus had asked her what wardrobe basics she might like and she'd asked for the bare minimum, insisting she would take care of it herself as soon as she had her first paycheck. But maybe she should have worn the blouse and skirt he'd given her the first day.

Armand held out a hand and when she took it to shake, he pulled it to his lips and kissed her knuckles. "Enchanté. Thanks for helping a chap out in his hour of need. Now let's get you into hair and makeup." He took her arm and led her to a chair on the far side of the room in front of a row of mirrors, each lined with light bulbs.

"Armand!" Another man came running up to Armand, a tablet in hand. "It's a disaster! The zipper ripped on the nymph's maxi dress. Her tits are hanging out. And its Zephoria so there's not enough tape in upper New Olympus to keep those things in without the dress securely zipped."

Armand lifted a heavy eyebrow and smiled Cora's way. "A designer's job is never done." Then he looked to a skinny man with a receding hairline who was hovering by Cora's chair. "Mr. Ubeli said to treat Miss Vestian with the utmost respect. You understand?"

Cora sensed rather than saw the other man immediately come to attention at Marcus's name. "Yes, sir."

To Cora, Armand said, "Relax and be yourself." He leaned down and gave her a kiss on the cheek. His cologne was manly and as sophisticated as the rest of him. "You'll do *fabulous* out there darling, I know it."

With that he was off and Cora was left feeling extremely overwhelmed and out of her element.

First came hair, an extensive process of rollers and gels

and sprays. While her hair was 'setting,' the makeup artist had his way with her.

He murmured about good bone structure and classic cheekbones but never spoke directly to her for the entire hour he was working on her. Two hours after she'd sat down in the chair, hair and makeup were finally finished.

Cora looked at herself in the mirror and was stunned. She was covered in violet-shaded white makeup, topped with a powder that gave an iridescent glow to her face, chest, and arms. Striking purple, silver, and black makeup surrounded her eyes, topped off with the longest fake lashes she'd ever seen. It felt funny every time she blinked, when the lashes flapped against her cheeks.

Her hair hung in dark cascading waves down her shoulders, little wisps pinned up here and there that created a wild, ethereal effect.

She looked absolutely nothing like herself.

"Perfect," the artist said, and spun her out of the chair. "Let's get you to costuming."

Costuming. Cora could only internally shake her head. This certainly felt like playing dress up. Had she really been wiping a toddler's runny nose only three days ago? Though actually, that felt far more real.

This was the dream world. A strange realm full of beautiful, elfin people who were too tall, too thin, and perpetually grouchy. Apart from Armand, she hadn't seen a single person smile all day.

The assistants who dressed her acted as impersonal as the hair and makeup guys. The dress itself was gorgeous, though. In silver, charcoal and purple tones, it was a draped dress with fabrics that were sheer as clouds and had the effect of falling like water. With a pleased sound she turned in them and watched the material float around her. Armand was a genius.

The assistant was less happy. With a string of curses, he stepped in to pin something, and instead he stuck Cora's flesh.

Yeouch! Cora jumped.

"Well fuck, stand still and I won't accidently fucking pin you. Fucking amateurs, I fucking swear," he hissed under his breath. "Where the fuck did they find this one?"

Cora froze and gritted her teeth.

It's a paycheck. Grin and take it for the paycheck.

She waited for him to come at her again, with either more pins or more abuse. But another one of the assistants turned from the rack of clothes and pulled the second man away. He spoke in an urgent whisper.

"Mr. Ubeli," were the only words Cora caught as she waited, trying to keep a brave face. The first assistant returned and finished his work, silent and stiff. The second disappeared, and reappeared with a bottle of water.

"The lights can be hot," he explained. Cora noticed none of the other models being given water, but she accepted it. She was directed off to the side to wait her turn.

"But don't sit down," was the assistant's last instruction. "Don't crease the fabric." She gave him a thumbs up but he was already off.

With her clothing draped like a Greek statue and water bottle in hand, she felt like the Statue of Liberty.

She didn't have to wait long, though.

"Babe, there you are—" a photographer waved at her, "You're next."

Cora nodded and hurried forward. Another model, being unpinned from her clothes, turned her head. "Wow," she remarked on Cora's get up, "you look really cool. Who are you supposed to be?"

"Uh . . . I don't know." Cora stood aside as two men pushing a huge mirror came through. The thing stood six feet tall, and was still higher on its wheeled mount and gilt frame. They stopped in front of her, cutting off the other model's conversation.

Into the reflected surface, Cora stared at the striking woman in robes. She'd only been able to see her face in the makeup mirror earlier, but now she was hit with the entire effect.

Kohl-darkened eyes stared back at her. Her hair was big and wild around her but it didn't detract from the luminous, violet sheen of her skin. The tones of the gown only served to highlight the glow of her pale skin even more.

She looked larger than life. *Powerful*. She blinked in surprise at the thought. It wasn't an adjective she'd ever used to describe herself before.

"Well, well, if it isn't the goddess."

Cora turned around and saw a familiar face, lips quirked up in a half smile.

Marcus.

The room around them, chaos only a second ago, cleared out. Stepping back to look beyond the mirror, she could see another model's bare back, the assistant helping her with the bottom half of her costume as they both hurried away. Cora looked back into the mirror as Marcus approached behind her. His smile had dropped and instead his eyes held the intensity of a hunter.

"Marcus," she breathed, her stomach feeling strange and swoopy.

He was looking her up and down. With his handsome face and sculpted cheekbones, he looked like a model himself. He wasn't pretty, but the strength and symmetry of his features were powerful. Timeless. Next to him, regular guys were eye-wateringly ugly—until you realized that they weren't, they were normal looking and Marcus was a god. Mere mortals couldn't compare.

Her stomach did a sad little spiral. Marcus fit in better here than she did.

A few steps and he had crossed the distance between them. She gazed at him in the mirror. When he was right behind her, the two of them looked like a snapshot out of any style magazine. He was wearing a gray button up. He often wore gray or other dark colors. He wasn't wearing a jacket, and the shirt's smoothness couldn't hide the outline of his muscles. He was so *strong*. He didn't have the physique you would expect of a businessman.

Marcus's cheek tugged up in one of his signature half smirks. Oh no, he'd noticed her checking him out.

She felt her cheeks heat, and she looked at her own face in the mirror in alarm, but for once her blush didn't show because of the makeup.

But as she looked in the mirror—oh crap! There was plenty that *was* showing. Her gown might be gorgeous but all that sheer fabric was practically *see-through.* Had Marcus noticed?

She hurriedly crossed her arms in front of her. "I didn't know you were going to be here."

"Do I make you nervous?" he whispered, and she could feel the warmth of his breath on her ear as he skewered her with his gaze in the mirror's reflection.

Even with her arms over her chest, the outline of her body was perfectly clear through the gauziness of the dress. Her hips. The line of her inner thighs.

Marcus leaned his face over her shoulder so that their faces were side by side, cheek to cheek.

Cora felt paralyzed by his gaze.

"You are a goddess," he breathed.

"You shouldn't call me that..."

Marcus turned her to him. "Look at me."

She couldn't bear to obey, so she stared at his shirt. He'd undone the top two buttons, giving her a peek of the chiseled line of his pectorals with a faint dusting of hair. It was so...*masculine.*

When he raised her chin to look at him, she was able to follow the sculpted line of his neck up to his jaw and finally, over the strong features of his face.

"Perfect body, perfect skin," he murmured. "How could you not be a goddess?"

"That's very sweet but you don't have to—" she started.

"No, angel. In a second, you're going to walk out there, and everyone will know how lovely you are."

Her eyes darted away.

"Look at me." He took her in his arms, keeping her still. After a long pause, "Beautiful," he pronounced.

She laughed nervously. Marcus smiled and tightened his hold around her, "I'm telling Armand he owes me big for letting him borrow you. Not one—three or four favors."

Cora was unsure what to think about that. *Borrow*. Like Marcus owned her. The thought should disturb her but all she could think was, *yes, please*. What would it be like to belong to a man like Marcus Ubeli?

Cora looked at herself and Marcus in the mirror again, a gorgeous couple out of a magazine. The woman in the mirror's lips were parted slightly, while the man let his eyes browse along her bare shoulders and neck. When he raised his head, his look was cool, but his eyes smoldered. They consumed her.

"Goddess," he whispered again.

"Queen of the Dead, we're ready for you—" a woman with a tablet came out, saw the two of them and took a step back. "Oh, Mr. Ubeli, I didn't mean to interrupt."

"No, no," Marcus called back, "she's ready."

Cora was still feeling paralyzed but somehow she forced her feet to move forward anyway. Away from him. How, she wasn't sure. But she even managed speech. "Queen of the Dead?" she asked the woman with the tablet. "Do you mean me?"

The woman nodded.

"Come find me at the after party," Marcus called. "After the show. I'll be waiting."

Without looking back, Cora crossed through the door, into the lights.

AFTERWARDS, her eyes remained dazzled by cameras. She couldn't even remember walking the catwalk. All she could focus on was not tripping in the heels they'd put her in. She'd gotten to the end and posed like an assistant had instructed her, and the explosion of camera flashes had about blinded her. But she'd turned on cue and managed to get backstage without tripping herself or any other models so, *win*.

And now the afterparty. One of the assistants had brought Cora a dress to change into. The assistant said it was from Armand, but from the silent looks Cora got from all the other models, she guessed it was really from Marcus.

What are you doing? she asked herself as she walked

with the group of models and Armand's entourage and show attendees one block over to where the afterparty was being held. *Do you really think he's not going to expect something in return for all these so-called 'gifts'?*

Men were pathologically incapable of being trustworthy, her mother always told her. *They always want one thing and one thing only. That's why I keep you here where it's safe.*

But...would it be so bad if Marcus wanted her like that? She didn't need gifts. It would be enough if he was interested in her. He didn't need to do anything else.

And oh, the way she felt when he even *looked* at her...

And besides, he hadn't tried anything. Nothing like the 'one thing' men supposedly only wanted. If Marcus were a bad man, he could have tried to force himself upon her a hundred times over when he had her alone in his penthouse.

But he hadn't. Because he was honorable. He was a good man. And kind, and generous, and handsome and—

They got to the afterparty and if she thought the show and preparations for it had been overwhelming, she quickly realized it was nothing compared to when New Olympians really got down to *party*.

The party was held on a gorgeous rooftop terrace. The evening was cool but there were space heaters all throughout the terrace keeping it warm and everyone around her seemed to be in a jubilant mood. The show was apparently an unmitigated success according to early reviews and social media.

All around her people laughed and chatted and Cora smiled but she never seemed to be in on the jokes about this or that model or actor.

And all they served was champagne and other alcohol. Cora was parched and dying for a glass of water.

She went in search of one when she heard her name called.

"Cora! Darling!"

Armand came over to her and clasped her hand. "Our famous Queen of the Dead, in the flesh. I wondered where you'd gotten off to. Come, come, I have so many people I want to introduce you to."

And for the next thirty minutes, Cora was whisked around in a whirlwind of introductions, names and faces Cora knew she'd never remember. She tried to object when Armand kept introducing her as Marcus's girl but to no avail.

Finally, Cora managed to excuse herself from Armand's side to go in look of the water she needed even more desperately now.

She'd asked for a cup from the bartender and taken her first amazing, refreshing, beautiful sip when a shadow loomed in front of her, making her almost choke on her last swallow.

"Hello, goddess."

Marcus.

She rolled her eyes and coughed into her elbow, some of the water going down the wrong pipe in her surprise at seeing him.

How did he always sneak up on her like that?

"Not a goddess anymore," she finally managed to say once she got her breathing under control. She snuck another sip of water. "Just regular old me." She lifted her hands, *ta da, here I am*, like a dork.

"I beg to differ."

She shook her head at him. She couldn't even look him

in the eye. It had only been hours since she'd last seen him, but she was overwhelmed all over again. Every time. How could she not be? He was the epitome of power and masculine beauty. Plato's form of the perfect man, made flesh.

"Cora," he called softly. "Look at me."

She obeyed. She couldn't tell him she couldn't look at him directly or his perfection would scorch her like the sun. She met his grey eyes and welcomed the inner flutters, a thousand butterflies throwing a party in her middle.

"How do you like the party?" he asked, eyes crinkling. Like he knew how he affected her and he liked it.

The glittering terrace stretched before them. A jewel-blue pool was illuminated in the center and everywhere beautiful people stood gathered, chatting beautifully.

"Everything's so lovely." Cora tilted her head to the side.

"But?"

Cora blinked. She hadn't meant to let any dissatisfaction show through. She knew this was all meant to be a treat. Getting to be a model. Coming here to this fancy after-party. It was a Cinderella moment and she didn't mean to be ungrateful—especially since she was getting paid on top of all of the rest of it.

"Don't go shy on me now," he said. This was yet another reason she couldn't look at him. His intense, demanding stare always brought out the truth.

She leaned in. "This isn't exactly my scene. I sort of feel like..." She looked out at everyone again. "I don't know, like I'm a scientist and this is a sociological experiment. And I'm in disguise, getting to observe the beautiful people in their natural habitat. I feel like I should be taking notes for a paper or something."

Marcus lifted a brow.

"Like her." Cora nodded her head toward an especially emaciated model who'd been fascinating her for the better part of an hour. "Species modelsapian domesticus, approximately 95 pounds. Never actually eats food but holds it between her forefinger and thumb and pretends to nibble at it for thirty-eight and a half minutes. Then she casually sets it down on a passing waiter's tray and starts the whole charade again with another item of food. And don't even get me started on the mating rituals."

Marcus barked out a laugh, and looked surprised at himself.

And then, to *Cora's* surprise, he hooked her around the waist and pulled her away from the bar where she'd been standing and over to the shadowed corner, hidden behind two tall planted palm trees.

There was just enough light to see the glint in his eyes.

"I like you." He pronounced it so solemnly, Cora couldn't tell if he was happy about it or not. Cora was definitely happy to hear it. Exhilarated in fact.

"Really?" she squeaked.

This brought out the half smile she was quickly becoming addicted to. "Really."

He leaned in, his weight shifting to press her back against the wall of the building.

Wait, was he really about to—?

His lips were gentle against hers, but only for a moment. Like everything else about him, his lips quickly turned demanding.

And Cora was helpless to do anything other than obey.

Her lips parted on a gasp and he took the opportunity to plunge his tongue into her mouth.

She'd never been kissed, really kissed, and— She lifted her arms and wrapped them around Marcus's broad shoulders if only to have something to hold onto and ground herself. Because she felt like she could float up, up, and away.

He was kissing her senseless. Her stomach somersaulted with every powerful swipe of his tongue. Cora couldn't help arching her breasts up and into his chest. Oh gods, had she really done that?

She tried to pull back but Marcus wrapped a hand around her waist between her and the wall, securing her even more tightly against his body.

Her eyes flew open. He was— She could feel his—his *hardness*. She gasped for breath in between kisses and when he finally pulled away and cupped her face in his strong hand, she rolled her cheek into his touch, blinking dazedly up at him.

He had a satisfied smile on his face.

Would he take her home now and—and make love to her? That was what happened next, right? Even though he'd put a little bit of space between them, she could still feel him.

She didn't know much about sex but she knew she wanted it. She wanted everything Marcus had to give.

She'd never felt this way before. His presence rolled over her, overwhelming, taking no prisoners. Was this attraction? Or something more? Every molecule in her quivered, standing at attention.

Marcus dominated her senses, made her giddy. Alarm bells rang in her head. *Let him in, and he will rule your world.* Marcus wasn't a man who did anything by half measures. His control over her would be absolute, but she wouldn't hate it. She'd revel in it.

It was too much. It was happening so fast. She closed her eyes, dizzy.

Now she knew why the poets sang of "falling in love." Because it felt like falling. A wild and free and awful descent. And once you fell, it was over. There was no coming back.

"Cora, are you all right?"

She nodded, eyes still closed. She couldn't look at him. It was like staring into the sun.

"Cora. Look at me. Don't hide."

She lifted her chin and blinked at him. "You terrify me," she whispered.

He raised an eyebrow. "Well, you've always struck me as an intelligent girl."

"What happens now?"

He pushed a strand of hair behind her ear and she shuddered in pleasure at the touch. His eyes flared and she immediately wanted to press her breasts into his chest again.

What would it feel like to have his hands on her? She hadn't forgotten the way he'd looked her up and down in the mirror earlier. He was such an intense man. What would it feel like to have all that intensity directed at her? To have nothing between them. No clothes. No pretenses. No years.

"Now," he leaned in and pressed his lips against hers again, the briefest kiss before pulling away, "we get Cinderella back home to sleep before she turns into a pumpkin."

He pulled back and took her arm.

"I don't think that's quite how the fairy tale goes," she murmured as he began to lead her through the crowd. Conversations stopped and eyes turned to them, the crowd parting like the Red Sea as they passed through.

Why did they all treat him that way? She glanced up at

Marcus but his face was cold as marble. If his arm hadn't been so warm and sure on hers, she might have shivered from seeing it. She glanced around at the faces of some of the crowd.

There was more than respect on their faces. There was fear.

Who was Marcus Ubeli besides the man who was turning her life upside down? Did she want to know? Or, a more disturbing question—did it matter to her, as long as in private she got to see the man beneath the mask?

She was tense-slash-giddy for the entire ride home. Sharo drove them and when a window closed between the driver and the back seat, she was sure that Marcus would kiss her again. He didn't, though. He put an arm around her and played with her hair absently during the ride home. It was silent other than the Rachmaninoff that echoed throughout the car.

She frowned when the car stopped after only a short ten-minute drive and Sharo got out and opened her door.

Marcus pulled away from her and she looked at him in confusion. "We aren't to the Crown yet, are we?" It had taken over half an hour to get from the hotel to the venue for the fashion show earlier today. Granted there had been traffic but surely they hadn't covered all that distance so quickly, had they?

She looked out the window and no, the historic hotel was nowhere in sight.

"I've arranged an apartment for you," Marcus said.

She swung around in her seat to look at him, her mouth dropping open. The penthouse at the Crown was one thing. He apparently always had that on reserve but another apartment? For *her*?

"Marcus, I can't—"

"You can," he put a hand to the small of her back to urge her out of the car, "and you will. Think of it as house-sitting. My secretary is on an extended vacation in Europe for the summer. You'll be a help if you stay here. You can water the plants."

But when Cora got upstairs, she didn't find any plants. What she did find was a luxurious, fully furnished three-bedroom apartment with a fabulous view of the park.

"This is incredible." She padded through the huge rooms. Her feet sank into the thick carpet. Marcus stalked behind her, hands in his pockets, a half smile slanted on his stunning face.

Cora stopped at a fireplace, running a nervous hand over the marble molding. An apartment like this, in this part of town, had to cost tens of thousands of dollars a month. She felt small in the overwhelming luxury.

"It's too much. I can't—" Her voice died when she met Marcus's intent gaze. He'd given her so much already.

"You can and you will. Stay here. Stay safe." He looked like he might say more, but the front door opened. A few moments later Sharo appeared. He nodded to her and handed Marcus an envelope.

Marcus opened it and glanced inside. His smile turned shark-like, satisfied. "One more thing, angel." He held out the envelope. Her hand trembled as she took it.

Inside were bills. Crisp greenbacks packed into the white envelope. The number on the bill made her knees wobble. "What's this?"

"Your pay. You told me your former employer owed you."

"They did but..." Her fingers fumbled through the thick bundle. She did a quick count. "This is too much, it's way more—"

"They weren't paying you enough. Sharo had a little talk with them, and they saw the error of their ways."

Clutching the sheaf of money, more money than she'd ever seen, much less held in her hands, her senses swam.

"A talk with them?" The big man regarded her impassively. From what she knew of Sharo, he wasn't much of a talker. Did that mean—?

"You didn't—" She stopped herself before she said, *"hurt them."* She couldn't very well ask if he'd beaten Paul up, could she? "They're okay?"

Sharo raised his chin. "They send their apologies. Wanted you to know they're getting marriage counseling. Cutting back hours at work, spending more time with their son."

"Oh. Good." Sharo did talk to them. Or, at least, they talked to him. Told him all that, and paid out well over her earnings in crisp one hundred dollar bills. She stared at the money in her hand as if it was a snake.

"See, angel?" Marcus murmured. "They won't bother you again."

Sharo was gone and it was just the two of them. He stepped closer and her world narrowed to his frame, tall and imposing, devastating in a dark suit. Her senses filled with his nearness, the five o'clock shadow edging his jaw, his delicious cologne. Her uncertainty disappeared. "You wanna thank me?"

"Thank you," she breathed, drunk on his nearness. Deep down, a little voice whispered a warning, but the rest of her was too far gone. Her heart fluttered in her chest, wild but happy. Happily trapped.

"No, baby," Marcus stopped, so close if she stepped forward, her nipples would brush his suit again. The tiny alarm bell abruptly cut off. "I meant, do you really wanna thank me?"

"Yes?"

"Then stay here. Live in this apartment. Enjoy it. And have dinner with me tomorrow night."

"Tomorrow," she whispered. His dark hair fell over his brow, softening the hard planes of his face. She swayed.

"Tomorrow," he whispered back. And he backed up, breaking her trance. She hoped he'd stay, but he only gave her that damnable half-smile and said, "Goodnight, goddess."

She was left so desperately wanting as he withdrew and closed the front door behind him. After it clicked shut, she slumped against it and lifted her hands to her lips, to her face, through her hair.

All she knew was that something huge had begun tonight with Marcus Ubeli, and her life would never be the same.

SIX

Marcus was a perfect gentleman. Cora stood in the foyer of her beautiful apartment a month later, putting on her earrings in front of the mirror, waiting for Sharo to knock on the door.

Occasionally Marcus sent his employee to pick her up. Marcus got caught up in meetings sometimes, but didn't like to be late for their outings. Sharo was a decent stand in, taking her to a restaurant, where they would serve her a glass of wine, and Marcus would always arrive soon after, smiling and full of compliments to her beauty.

A perfect gentleman, she thought again. He hadn't kissed her again, but he put his arm around her to keep her warm whenever they went on long drives through the park, or to his favored private club on the edge of the city. And when he took her to more dangerous parts of town in order to show her a friend's restaurant, he would loop her arm through his as they walked from the car into the building, and stay by her side all night. She felt safe with him.

He was generous, too. The roses in the foyer were a gift

from him. The dress and necklace she wore were other gifts. She always blushed when she got a gift—it seemed too much. But try telling Marcus that and he just shook his head and got stubborn. And when Marcus got stubborn, well...

Once, telling her that he had to miss a date because of business, he told her to go into a shop and try on whatever she liked. Sharo had followed, a silent shadow who saw everything and said nothing. Everything she touched, whether she liked it or not, arrived in large shopping bags at her apartment the next day.

She would have been exasperated—she already felt that things were so uneven between them, and every gift he gave her only made her feel that gap all the more. She didn't care about the jewelry or the clothes. Sure they were nice.

But all she wanted was Marcus.

In the end, it was why she accepted all the gifts. Because she knew it made him happy. It meant something to him, she could tell, to be able to drape the woman he cared for in fine things. To help her stand out as *his*. And that was all she ever wanted because she could barely remember a time before Marcus.

But could something so beautiful and perfect actually last? For her, Cora Vestian?

Things were just *so* good. And well...she couldn't help feeling on edge, waiting for the other shoe to drop. She couldn't help it. Her mother had built a lifetime of paranoia in her.

It didn't help that she felt sure she was being watched. Once in a while, returning home from work in the evening, she'd be coming down the street and get the feeling. She'd look over quickly, and there would be the sleek tip of a car, turning out of an alley, or parked on the street.

The windows were always tinted so she could never see inside.

At first she'd been terrified, sure it was her mother come to steal her back to the farm. But when nothing ever came of it, when the cars continued simply waiting patiently and following her movements...she couldn't help wondering. Was...was Marcus having her followed? Or was she just being totally paranoid and no one was following her at all?

It's a coincidence, Cora thought to herself as she got ready for her evening out. *You're making up something to be worried about.*

Standing in the small room that served as a foyer in front of the door, she faced the mirror one last time.

Tonight was important. Marcus had been busy lately, working early and late and all hours in between, so that she barely saw him. Their last date had been three nights ago, at a new restaurant called simply 'Nectar'. His car had met her at the animal shelter where she'd been dropping off a volunteer application and taken her straight to the place, despite her protests that she wasn't dressed for the occasion. The night started with champagne in the car and ended with them both on the rooftop of the building, looking down over the world while the band played softly for the few late customers.

"This is beautiful," she said.

"You're beautiful." Marcus wasn't looking at the city. "I think I like you in your work clothes."

She was just wearing jeans and a plain T-shirt. She tugged at the hem of the t-shirt. "You owe me for this, Marcus Ubeli."

His mouth quirked and she went on. "Dragging me to this fancy restaurant, plying me with champagne...I'm barely fit to ride on public transport in these clothes."

"I'll make it up to you," he said. "I'll buy you a dress."

She rolled her eyes and blushed like she always did. And his face, usually so serious under his dark and shining hair, had held a little half smile.

"I'd buy you all this if I could." He swept his hand over the city, glittering below them like a box of jewels. Cora giggled at his teasing. Seeing Marcus so at ease and making jokes, while he stood so close to her, she felt euphoric.

"You mean you can't?" she smiled back. "Mr. Ubeli, what will we do with you? You've been working too hard." The moonlight cupped his dark features, the shadows under his eyes evidence of long, long nights. She wanted to reach up and touch his face but she didn't quite dare.

"I've missed you," he said. Two fingers came to stroke her cheek. Her heartbeat took flight. He was touching her. And it felt— It felt— "I can't believe I have someone like you."

She stared at him and he stared back. Had he really just said that? To *her*? She knew she was infatuated with him. Any girl would be. But was it... Was it actually within the realm of possibility that he could actually feel anything back? For *her*?

But as he stared at her, she'd swear he looked just as stunned as she felt. Holy— Could it be true? Please, please, could it be true? She'd give anything, pay any price for this man to care for her back even half of what she felt for him.

And then she realized she just been standing here silently. Crap.

She spoke up, haltingly. "You've been great too. You're kind, more than generous. You've treated me like a princess." Gods, she wasn't saying this right. How could she make him understand? "I came to the city with such big dreams, but . . . every girl dreams of a life like this. You've made it come true." She looked up at him, knowing that her cheeks were alive with the heat of the moment and the cold of the wind.

Her words weren't enough. She wanted to tell him how she felt about *him*. It wasn't just gratitude for all he done. Even if he'd never given her a single thing, she would feel the same way about him. She saw how he was with everybody else. Cold. Distant. The greatest gift he'd given her was himself. He'd let her in when he never let anyone in besides Sharo.

His fingers remained on her cheek, but still as if any movement more than breathing would shatter it all.

"Cora," he whispered, and she strained to hear. The wind nearly took his words. "I want..."

"What?" she had whispered back, but there was no answer.

In the silence she'd shivered a little, and he was there, folding her into his chest, suit jacket and satin handkerchief pressing into her cheek. And he was warm, so strong, and nothing could take her away from his shelter or his heat.

"I want to keep you safe," he said. "I want to hold you, like this..."

When he didn't go on, she realized he didn't have to. It was okay if he didn't have the words. "Shh..." she whispered and closed her eyes, sinking into him.

They had stayed that way for a long time, till after the band stopped playing, and the waiters swept up, and finally they went back down to where Sharo sat in the car with a fist over his mouth to keep from yawning. She had kept her head on Marcus's shoulder all the way home, as the light on the car window softened with dawn.

Marcus had kept his promise. The dress had arrived that afternoon, with a note: *Wear it, and we'll call it even.* She had grown used to opening gifts in the weeks that he had been preoccupied with work, but this one made her gasp as she lifted it from the tissue—the fabric was luminous gray and covered over with clear beads that glinted like city lights. A small box accompanied it. It opened to showcase a necklace. The setting was shaped like a tear, two diamonds and another stone, a large red one she couldn't recognize.

So now she found herself standing in the dim light of the little foyer, allowing herself one last look in the mirror before her escort knocked on the door and whisked her away to Marcus. She couldn't wait to see him, but she wanted to look perfect for him.

The dress was lovely, soft and gray, like the stuff of clouds. The tiny beads twinkled, even though the only light in her dark apartment came from the cityscape outside her windows. She had turned out the lights in preparation to go out, and now saw her reflection in stark shadow and dulled light.

Still, her eyes were shining, and the jewels at her ears and neck flashed in the light of the city. She smiled. A happy, but pale face smiled back. She touched her cheek with cold fingers. So white, as if she'd been frightened. Patting them sharply to give them some color, she breathed in the scent of the roses.

A knock sounded behind her, and she all but jumped out of her skin. She laughed at herself as she put a hand to her chest. Grabbing her clutch, she turned to the door. She almost grabbed for the doorknob but stopped herself and checked through the peephole, as Marcus had instructed her. *City instinct,* he had told her. *Don't trust you know what's beyond your own front door.*

He sounded like her mother. But still, she humored him.

The head outside the door was bent. Frowning, she waited for it to straighten so she could see a face. It certainly wasn't Sharo; his head was shaved. The one she was looking at had a full head of hair, brown and a bit tousled, though wet like it had been raining on the streets.

Finally, the head raised. Her mouth dropped open in a silent gasp and she went cold as she recognized the face from that night at the club. The night that ended with her on her back in a car, before she escaped into the streets and the empty club where she had met Marcus.

She backed silently away from the door, fright closing her throat.

He didn't see you. He can't see you.

Still, all she wanted was to run to her bedroom and hide under the bed like a little kid. Instead, she retreated to the kitchen, grabbed her phone along with a big kitchen knife, and went into the bathroom. She closed and locked the door behind her.

Shaking, she dialed. It was a number Marcus had given her if she needed to reach him. No one ever picked up, but she had never left a message before without Marcus or Sharo getting the information.

"Hello," she whispered in the bathroom, "this is Cora." Even though she was speaking as quietly as she could, her voice echoed off the bathroom walls. Was the man still out there? Could he hear her?

"There's a man outside my door," she continued into the phone, both her hand and her voice shaking, but she gave every detail as carefully as she could, speaking slowly, like a small child. She hung up and waited.

Ten minutes later, she thought she could hear another

knock on the door. Phone in hand, she didn't move. Again, a knock. The phone rang, breaking the silence and nearly causing her to scream. She answered it with a half-strangled, "Hello?"

Sharo was at the door. It took three tries for her shaking hands to unlock it, and when she did, he came in before she asked him, ushering her to a couch with a strong hand, flipping on lights as he did. He poured her a drink and assured her Marcus was on his way. Then he went back to the foyer and she heard his deep voice, talking to what she assumed were more of Marcus's security team.

Sharo was back a few minutes later, a certain look on his face that told her that he was cautiously pleased with something.

"You okay?" he asked. She'd gotten to know Sharo a little bit over the past month, well, as much as you could get to know a gruff, silent security guard. But there was genuine concern in his eyes as he looked down at her.

"Yes," she said, smoothing still trembling hands down over her gown. "I think so."

"Two of my men were outside the apartment. They think they may have spotted him, and seen him dive down into city transport. They're still on the trail." There it was again, a look of quiet smugness that suggested Sharo was sure he'd have his hands on the man soon. "You'll never see him again."

Cora frowned. The way Sharo said it, it sounded...*final*. Not like if they found the guy, they'd call the cops.

"He didn't do anything," she said. "Just scared me, that's all." What the hell was she doing? Defending her kidnapper? She lifted hands to her temples and rubbed. "How—how did he find me?"

But Sharo's face was now impassive, and he was suddenly no longer willing to speak. A few minutes later, Marcus arrived, and she was comforted, complemented, and cradled in his strong arms. All the while Sharo watched, and Cora felt the silent, knowing glances between the man and his boss.

"Why don't we stay in tonight, babe. Go order Greek. Sharo will pick it up for us."

She left the room reluctantly, feeling the eyes of the two men on her. When she returned, they were standing close to one another, both faces were hard and strained, though she had heard no raised voices. As quiet as she was creeping back, she only heard Marcus mutter, "Don't let it happen again," before he turned back to her, a cold but gracious host.

Cora stood at the threshold of the room. She'd changed out of the beautiful gown into soft jeans and a plum colored cashmere sweater. This was the other side of the man she... the man she cared for. It was easy to let herself get swept away in the Marcus he was when they were alone together. Passionate. Tender. Sweet. But there was another side to him. A darkness.

"Give Sharo the restaurant name so he can get the food." Before the bald man left the room, Marcus added, "I don't want any delivery boy knowing where she lives." The quiet fury on his face made her pause halfway to the couch. He put out his hand to call her to him and she remained where she was.

"Marcus," she asked when Sharo had gone, "who is this guy?" Would he open up to her?

"I told you, babe. He's some dick off the streets who saw a goddess he can never touch and can't get wise." With a sigh he seated himself on the couch, staring off into nowhere, his face turned to stone.

Finally, though, he relaxed. "Come here," he said, and held out his hand again. Slowly, she moved forward and took it, allowing him to pull her down onto the couch. He cradled her as he had when they had first met, arm around her, her head against his suit jacket.

"I don't want you scared," he whispered, his lips right near her face, "Don't think you aren't safe. Nobody, I mean nobody," she felt him tense up, angry, "touches my girl."

She wanted to soothe him. She wanted *her* Marcus back. "I'm fine," she murmured. "Nothing happened."

They sat in silence for a time, and as the clock ticked, the tension left his body. Cora could feel his breathing soften. She held herself very still, like a moth trapped against a lamp; feeling the danger, unable to break away. But she didn't want to break away.

Let me in, she pleaded silently. She could handle his darkness, if he would let her be his light.

"And nothing ever will. I'll keep you safe," he said. "I won't let you out of my sight."

She remembered the gleam of the black car she spotted sometimes and frowned. "You already don't."

"What?" His voice mixed with the doorbell and she pulled away.

"It's okay," Marcus said, his hands steadying her, "it's only Sharo with the food." He mistook her anxiety and she let him, body still taut and held away from him, even though she was still so close her hair spilled over his suit.

"Cora," he repeated, and she relaxed.

"I'm hungry, go get dinner," she said, but she turned her face away from him as he stood up and went to the door.

He *was* having her followed, she knew it now. Sharo

had all but admitted it when he said men watching her apartment had followed her abductor, and Marcus's words just now... This was exactly the kind of thing she'd left her mother to get away from.

She breathed out and squeezed her eyes shut. What had she gotten herself into? Did Marcus think she didn't know? Did he think she was an idiot? Was that what he wanted, some dumb, foolish little plaything he could occasionally amuse himself with?

Moving to one corner of the couch and tucking her legs under her, she listened hard. Voices in the foyer—Marcus and another, no, two other men. Sharo? Or the other two, the ones who had been so conveniently close to her apartment? The question was: *why* was he having her watched? For her safety...or because he didn't trust her?

"You okay?" Marcus asked when he returned with a paper sack of food. Cora smiled and nodded, but it was the fake smile she always used to use with her mother. She hated it, *so* much, to use it with Marcus. But she didn't know what else to do. Everything had seemed so sure only an hour before and now...

They set out the food, and before they tucked in, Marcus asked again, "You sure you're okay?"

"Yes," the answer was shaky, but sure. She smiled again, the same fake smile. Marcus didn't notice anything was amiss, and that broke her heart a little.

"I told you, babe," was all he said, "I'm going to take care of you."

"I HAVE to get off early tonight," Cora called to the back of the shelter where she'd started volunteering. She hadn't been able to find another job without an ID and social other than a few other all-cash modeling gigs she'd gotten off of Armand's show. Volunteering made her feel less stir-crazy in the meantime while she tried to sort something more permanent out.

"Okay," said Maeve, who ran the shelter. "Start at the end and get as far as you can, cleaning. The bucket is in the closet, sponges and soap by the sink."

Cora passed two hours in silence, cleaning cages. It was hard, dirty work. Somehow, though, she felt cleaner after doing it. Scrubbing reminded her of being a kid on the farm where life was simple and full of honest, hard work. At the age of ten, it had been her job to scrub the floors of the house and to muck out the stables.

Ironic that she should be feeling nostalgia for that place she couldn't wait to get away from.

But things were so confusing here in the city.

Marcus continued to court her, taking her to the best restaurants. Sometimes she felt like he was showing her off. But that was ridiculous, he was the glamorous one. Whenever they walked into a place, people sat up and took notice. The restaurant owner would rush out to greet them, give them the best table, and check in during the meal to make sure everything was okay.

Everywhere they went, people kowtowed to Marcus, and, in turn, Marcus took care of her. He continued with the gifts, no matter how much she continued telling him they weren't necessary. He even insisted his car pick her up from the apartment and drive her to the shelter. She protested but Marcus said, "goddess," in his deep voice, amused and superior and sexy all at once, and got his way. He always got his way.

And as for her misgivings from the other night...

She frowned as she scrubbed even harder at the bottom of the cage. What was she really complaining about? That a man considered her so precious he wanted to make sure she was safe at all times?

And if he was having her followed because he didn't trust her, well, he was a wealthy man and she was a nobody. Maybe he'd been burned before. She didn't know just how rich he was but she knew he owned lots of businesses and was powerful, too. He'd only just met her. It was only smart for him to want to know if she really was who she said she was. Plus, it wasn't like she had anything to hide.

And, the question she'd finally asked herself several nights ago: wasn't he worth it? When she was with Marcus she felt like she could fly. And *oh,* when he touched her, even just the barest brush of his hand against hers...goose-bumps pebbled up and down her arms at the mere thought.

She liked him. She really liked him. She was scared to let her think about how she felt about him, it was so strong. A lot stronger than *like,* if she was honest with herself. And he was giving her everything she'd ever wanted. A new life, a new identity, one in which she could be suave and city-savvy and glamorous. That's why she came to the city, to be free of her mother. Even if Marcus helped her, protected her, okay, maybe controlled her a little, did that mean she wasn't free?

A long time later, Maeve found Cora sitting in one of the cages surrounded by cleaning supplies, one rubber glove on and the other off. Maeve had long red hair threaded with gray that she mostly kept braided. She came to check on Cora.

"Cora," she called, and Cora blinked out of her musings and glanced up. "How are things looking up here? Oh wow, you got through more cages than I thought you would."

Cora smiled. "I have experience." Cleaning cages wasn't exactly the same as mucking out stables, but the work ethic required was the same.

Cora yawned and swiped at her forehead with her arm.

"Aw, you look tired. I hope you're taking off early to head home and get some rest."

Cora shook her head. "Not quite. Marcus is taking me out to a friend's restaurant."

Maeve's easy expression dropped and her eyebrows furrowed. "I worry about you, honey. Are you sure things aren't moving too quickly with that man?"

Cora smiled at the older woman. 'That man' treated her like a queen. He could have anyone, and he looked at Cora like she was the only woman in the world. She still didn't understand it, why he'd chosen her. But he had and that was all that mattered.

Cora knew Maeve felt a matronly affection for her but it wasn't necessary. "I'm a big girl. I know what I'm doing."

Maeve didn't look convinced. "Did you see today's paper?"

Cora frowned. "No," she said but Maeve was already holding out the paper she'd had under her arm.

"I was using the paper to line the cages and the headline caught my eye. How well do you really know him?"

Cora stared down at the New Olympian Times. *Known Crime Boss Surfaces at Club.* The picture was grainy but she'd recognize Marcus anywhere.

Cora averted her eyes from the paper and scrubbed violently at the corner of the cage for a moment while she tried to gather her thoughts.

Crime boss.

Was it true?

But then she thought of how Marcus was treated everywhere they went. The bowed heads, the fearful, surreptitious glances. The power she knew he wielded, even if she hadn't understood why. And the darkness in him. If she was being honest, she'd suspected it was something like this, hadn't she? But being honest with herself wasn't her forte lately.

Because what she was feeling wasn't surprise. It was the queasy uneasiness of confirmation. She'd never asked Marcus too closely about his business because she hadn't wanted to know.

But here it was in black and white. Printed on the front page.

She glanced back at the paper Maeve was still holding out and her eyes skimmed the first paragraph. They called Marcus the *Lord of the Underworld*. She looked away again but Maeve obviously wasn't going to drop the issue so easily.

"How well do you know him?" she asked again.

Cora stopped scrubbing and tossed the sponge back into the bucket of soapy water. She scooted out of the cage and pulled off her second glove, then pushed back wisps of hair that had escaped her ponytail.

"He's a good man, Maeve."

She pulled the newspaper out of Maeve's hands and tossed it to the floor of the cage she'd cleaned. She liked Maeve, she really did. They'd hit it off ever since she'd come in to volunteer, but Cora didn't need another mother trying to tell her what she could and couldn't do.

Still, she respected Maeve. She was nothing like Cora's real mother. She wasn't pushy or overbearing and it was unfair to lump the two into the same category, so Cora reached out and squeezed the older woman's hand.

"Trust me," Cora said. "The paper always sensationalizes things. Marcus is a good man." She didn't know what else to say, but of that she was sure. He was *good*.

Maeve looked unconvinced but she nodded and squeezed Cora's hand in return. "Promise me you won't let yourself get swallowed up in him. You left home to find yourself and be free of your family." Cora had told Maeve a truncated version of why she'd left home, and she nodded at Maeve's assessment. "So don't let him steamroll over you. There's no need to rush things. And if you ever need help, remember you can always come to me."

Cora smiled in appreciation at her friend's concern. After months in the city, she did count this woman as a friend, the first she'd made apart from Marcus. Did it say something about her that the two people she'd gotten close to were both over a decade her senior, with Maeve make that two decades? Her mom had always said she had an old soul.

"All right," Cora dusted off her jeans as she stood up. "I have to go. I'll see you on Thursday."

Maeve nodded and Cora headed for the bathroom. She changed quickly out of her work clothes and into a clingy black dress with a daring slit up the thigh. She put on some mascara and lip-gloss, and headed to the front, which was a little shop for pet goods.

Sharo was waiting. "Miss Vestian," he said, holding open the door for her.

Marcus worked so much, she only got to see him every few days. But whenever they were together, it was like no time at all had passed. They picked up right where they'd left off.

Sharo drove her to the club where she'd met Marcus the very first night. Walking the steps she'd run down so fearfully gave her the oddest sense of déjà vu. She could remember the fear so vividly.

Sharo pushed through the door at the bottom of the stairs and held it open for her. She swallowed. It was just the echo of that fear that was giving her goosebumps right now. It had nothing to do with the newspaper article. Right? Right. She took a deep breath and followed Sharo through the door.

She walked back to Marcus's office, knocked lightly, and pushed the door open. And immediately relaxed upon seeing Marcus's familiar and beloved face.

He kept his office so dark his face was as shadowed as it was the first night she'd met him, all hard lines and harsh angles. But that was the air that Marcus liked to project, wasn't it? He was cold and scary to everyone but her.

...or was she just deluding herself? Was she actually special? When it came down to it, how well did she really know Marcus? She knew how he made her *feel* but that wasn't quite the same thing.

"Hi," she said shyly.

His head came up from the papers he was looking over and he paused, obviously taking her in. He did that fairly often, unabashedly checking her out and if the heated look in his eyes was anything to go by, appreciating what he saw.

He pushed his chair back from the desk and held out an arm for her, beckoning her closer.

She went. As she crossed behind his desk and stopped in front of him, she saw how tired he actually looked.

"Long day?" she asked, and he didn't reply, simply put his hands on her hips and pushed her back so that she was leaning on the desk. He gripped her hips and squeezed them, digging his thumbs in and massaging her flesh. The touch was so presumptuous and possessive, all the air fled Cora's lungs in one great gasp.

Marcus looked up at her and she couldn't read what she saw in his storm grey eyes. "Sweet Cora, so innocent," he whispered. He bowed his forehead against her middle. He wrapped his arms around her waist and pulled her against him, his face still flush with her stomach.

Her hands dropped to his hair. He hugged her with the desperation of a little boy holding onto a blanket for comfort.

Was that what she was for him—a place he could finally relax and find comfort? The thought sent an elated zing down her spine. How she would love to be this complicated man's safe place. She stroked his hair, down to his neck, massaging his shoulders, before her fingers drifted back to his hair, and he clutched her tighter.

The New Olympian Times stuck out from underneath the papers he'd been looking at. Had he been upset by the newspaper? Because maybe they'd gotten it all wrong and it was slander and—

"All right, we need to get going." Marcus pulled back and if she'd expected to see his features soft or tender, she was disappointed. He looked as calm and cool as ever.

Cora frowned but he was already standing and taking her arm to lead her out to the car.

Marcus never liked to talk much when they were in the car. He always had Sharo put on classical music and Cora got the feeling it was the one time in his busy day where he got to just sit peacefully and relax. He rarely pulled out his phone to check emails or take calls. He simply sat, sometimes with his eyes closed, most of the time just watching the city streets going by, often taking her hand like he did today. He rubbed circles back and forth with his thumb and she couldn't deny that the rhythmic motion along with the music *was* relaxing, to the point of being hypnotic.

Cora was tempted to let the relaxation of the moment and Marcus's touch soothe her fears. But she kept hearing Maeve's voice in the back of her head: *How well do you really know him?*

And it erupted out of her: "I saw the paper today. It scared me, Marcus."

He immediately went tense and pulled his hand back from hers.

"Please, Marcus. Will you tell me what's going on? Is it...is it true?"

"You don't want to know," he said. She took a deep breath and turned to look at him, forcing herself to wait for an answer even though she could see a glint of anger in his eyes. After a moment, something like a smile quirked his lips, though the coldness didn't leave his face.

"But you're my girl, so I'll tell you."

She waited through a long pause for him to continue.

"Couple of weeks back, two friends of mine decided to go in on a club. They bought the old theater, renamed it, set it up real nice. Big project like that, they needed some help. I helped them."

He paused again as if wondering how much he should share with her.

"But rumors were circling—you know, people talk. Someone thinks something's up, and the press hooks on it like it's the only story in town. There were stories going around even before the place opened. Then last night," a large sigh, "the press showed up."

She waited a moment after he stopped. "And?"

"They took pictures and jumped to conclusions. They slandered my friends and tried to shut them down. And, because they can print whatever trash they want," his jaw went hard, "it got smeared on the front page. All my friends wanted to do was open a club. Whose business is it how they run it? And the stuff they said—drugs and dirty money—none of that's been proven. Those accusations belong in court. To slap it on a front page to sell papers—that's what's illegal."

From where she sat, Cora could feel him getting angrier, though his voice never rose. She could feel it through the small distance between them, waves of cold fury, kept tightly clenched under his suit and silken tie.

"It's one thing to come after me directly. It's another to use my friends." He stared forward at the rearview mirror; he and Sharo's eyes met there.

The car glided through the streets. The windows were thick, keeping out sound, so it seemed silent, apart from the brooding classical music. Cora studied Marcus's face, afraid of what she saw there. He was distant, cold.

Without thinking, she shivered, and with a murmur —"You okay, babe?"—he put his arm around her, and they rode on with the heavy weight across her shoulders.

And, though the questions screamed inside her—*who are you? Is that really all there is to it? What do you mean, you* 'helped' *your friends?*—she found she couldn't say any more.

So deep was the silence, it took them both a moment to realize the car had stopped.

Sharo opened the door and she found herself looking up at a tall building, with many stairs leading up to its large doors.

"Go on." Marcus pushed her gently, and she dutifully climbed out.

"Is this the restaurant?" she asked, teeth chattering with

a sudden cold wind. Marcus, having stopped to speak with Sharo, came and took her under his arm and coat jacket, ushering her forward.

He gave her an enigmatic smile as they went up the steps. She could barely see beyond his sheltering arms as he pushed open the doors.

As soon as they stepped inside, humid heat rolled over Cora, lapping at her arms and face like an ocean wave. It was completely dark, though. But Cora relaxed anyway, walking into the darkness without being afraid. Marcus was at her side.

"What is this place?" she breathed.

A flashlight switched on, and the beam danced over palms and ferns, flowers and green—a whole host of growing things, sheltered in the building of glass.

"A greenhouse!" she cried, and Marcus chuckled as he came forward to show her around. They traipsed the narrow paths and found their way through the dark with only his single flashlight.

How did he know that this was exactly what she'd needed? As much as she admired the city, sometimes it got to be oppressive—so much concrete, pavement, brick, and steel, block after block in all directions. She missed growing things. She missed being able to walk out her front door and touch the earth, smell the soil, and watch the sun rise in the big open sky.

She held out her arms and laughed as her hands brushed the beckoning soft branches and leaves.

She squinted. "I see something up ahead." She dropped her arms and pressed forward.

Marcus obligingly followed with the light, until they pushed past one great frond and found a little table and some wine, lit by a silver candelabra. Going around her, he pulled out one of the chairs.

"Welcome to paradise, goddess."

Speechless, she sat quiet while he poured the champagne, and took a glass without a word.

"A toast," he said, "to our new favorite place."

She couldn't help it; she laughed. His eyes sparkled over the glass as he drank first. She was still waiting, wide eyed, when he finished. He toyed with his glass before placing it down decisively.

"You aren't like any other woman I've dated."

"Oh?" she asked. He came over to her, and she looked up at him, heart beating so rapidly she lifted a hand to her chest like that might slow it down. Would he kiss her again? Every time he did was so overwhelming and exquisite, she thought she might die of the pleasure.

"When I first saw you, angel," he said, "I knew you would be my wife."

Cora lost her breath for the second time that night. He — He did? His *wife*?

Her mind was racing a million miles a minute as he came near her and cupped her cheek.

"So lovely, so innocent. You are exactly what I've been looking for and didn't even know it." He knelt down before her on one knee. "I need you to be mine, Cora." He reached into his pocket, keeping his eyes on hers.

What was happening? This couldn't be happening. Oh gods, was this happening?

"Marcus?" she started to ask, but he opened the jewelry box, and she found she couldn't speak.

It was a ring. It was a freaking ring!

"Marry me," he said, smiling at her shock.

"Oh, Marcus," she mouthed. Her breath was gone; she

was mute. Instead, she reached forward to touch the ring. The metal was silver colored, but she knew it would be white gold. There were tiny diamonds, cut to sparkle. But the main gem was red. Mesmerized, she realized he was speaking.

"I almost got you a diamond, a real nice rock. But you look so good in red." He looked at her suddenly in such a way that she blushed. She leaned back in her chair, away from both him and the ring, hoping she could hide the fear that had pierced through her.

There was a darkness in Marcus. She still believed what she'd told Maeve earlier this afternoon. Marcus was a good man, but there was a darkness in him. Was she really ready to commit her life to a man she knew so little about? He was careful around her, showing her only the parts of himself he wanted her to see.

"So?" He prompted, after a moment of silence.

"What if I'm not ready?" She didn't know where the words came from. Dark fire flashed through Marcus's eyes, but otherwise he hid his frustration well. "It's just so soon," she hurried to say. "We've only known each other a couple of months."

"I think you're ready," he said and he stood up, towering over her, until he drew her to her feet. He moved his face close, as if he would kiss her, and she was frozen, watching his lips, "I think you want to say yes."

And then he did kiss her. "Say yes," he murmured while his lips played over her skin, kissing down her throat in the most delicious way. "Say yes."

She closed her eyes, wound her arms around his neck, and like always when it came to Marcus, gave in.

"Yes," she whispered in the darkness. "Yes, I'll marry you."

Even as he smiled and kissed her, though, a small worried voice piped up in the back of her mind. The setting was romantic, yes. The ring was beautiful. He'd expressed more of his feelings tonight than she'd ever heard from him before.

But he hadn't said a single thing about love.

SEVEN

"Now that's a nice ring," Maeve said in her quiet, matter-of-fact way when Cora came to volunteer that week. Marcus had frowned when Cora told him she'd be busy until dinner, but she was adamant to keep to her schedule. Not even planning a rush wedding to one of the wealthiest men in the city would make her bail on Maeve.

"Thank you," Cora murmured, and removed the 'nice ring,' stringing it on her necklace before donning gloves. An hour cleaning cages wasn't something most people would look forward to, but she jumped right in as if the dirty work would make her clean.

In a few weeks she'd be married. Married. To a man who intimidated and intoxicated her all at once. He came into her life, and now he *was* her life. Every part of her world belonged to Marcus.

Except this part. Was that how it would be after the wedding? Everything that was Marcus swallowing up everything Cora had been? Should she be fighting harder to retain some autonomy? But every time she was with Marcus, all she wanted was more of him.

Nothing else mattered. The rest of the world dropped away so it didn't seem like a sacrifice. And it wasn't as if he'd *asked* her to give anything up. He just slowly occupied more and more territory in her life, like a slow and not unwelcome invasion.

"Cora," Maeve called a little while later, and she blinked as if awakening from a trance.

"There's a man out here, looking for you."

Cora got to her feet so fast the newspaper scattered. The clock above her head read seven o'clock. Sharo was already here.

"Oh," a curse sprang to her lips. Maeve's brows flew up. Although Maeve wouldn't take offense at the word, she looked surprised to hear Cora use it. Cora knew she usually came off so prim and proper, and she covered her mouth with her right hand. Her other toyed with the ring on the chain.

"You okay?"

"Yes, I'm late, I'd better go."

Maeve hesitated. "Are you sure? He's kinda rough looking; I nearly sent him away. Are you sure you want to see him?"

"Yeah, it's fine," Cora mumbled, stripping off her apron. She headed out front, smoothing her hair with her fingers. She was in jeans and a t-shirt, but she'd have to change at the club.

She passed through the door that led to the pet store. Rounding the corner past a display of dog food, she stopped dead. The man had brown curly hair. It was him. His back was to her, but she recognized the man who roofied and tried to kidnap her.

Run!

Shout for help!

There wasn't a front door between them this time. They were all alone in the small shop.

But... *I'm never alone.* The wild thought comforted her even as her hands shook.

"If I scream, someone will come." Marcus still had men watching her. They kept out of sight, and she didn't mention or make a fuss about it because she could pretend everything was normal that way. So how did her former attacker get past them?

That didn't matter. All that mattered was that if she called, they'd come. She knew it. She wasn't a victim anymore. She was soon to be wife of Marcus Ubeli, the most powerful man in the city.

She crossed her arms in front of her to hide her tremor. "You need to leave and never come back again."

The man raised his hands, still facing the front. "I'm not here to hurt you. I swear. Just want to talk."

He finally turned and Cora gasped. Instead of moving back, she stepped forward. *Holy*— "What happened to you?"

The man's face was misshapen, bruises covering his face in multi-colored patchwork. She should run, or speed-dial Marcus on the special cell phone he insisted she carry. But the man wasn't making any move to come closer, so she stayed.

"Did Sharo do this?" she asked, her heart beating hard.

"Yeah," the man's words were a garbled mouthful of pain, spoken through all the bruises and swelling. "Boss don't like it when a man oversteps his bounds."

Boss?

"What?" she whispered.

"I came to warn you," he said. "Boss won't like it, but you gotta get wise. That way, you'll be ready. I done wrong and I'm tryin' to make it right. Makin' amends is what they call it. So I'm tellin' ya, you gotta be ready."

"Ready for *what*?"

The man shook his head, and groaned as if the movement pained him. It could be a trap. He could be pretending to be hurt worse than he was. She stayed back, the aisle of dog food between them. But she couldn't help asking, "Are you okay? Do you need a doctor?"

"No," the man gasped. "Listen, I'm tryin' to warn you."

"Warn me?" Her attacker was beaten, weakened. The longer she looked at him, the more convinced she was he wasn't faking it. Cora uncrossed her arms and rested her fists on her hips. "You come here after drugging my drink, trying to kidnap me—"

"It was them. It was all them. The boss and Sharo. They planned it. They laid it out. I'm down the chain, didn't hear it straight from them, but they were behind it."

"What?"

"Watching you. Scouting you. That night in the club, I saw a chance and took it. Figured the boss would be happy if I brought you in early. He wasn't happy. He had a plan—"

"The boss..." Her mouth was dry and her heart beating what felt like a thousand times a minute. "...you mean *Marcus*?"

"Yes." A car slid past the shop and the man startled, staring with the whites of his eyes.

"No." Cora shook herself. "No, you're wrong. Marcus helped me. He and Sharo protect me from...from you!"

The man jerked his head, teeth gritted. "They were watching you. They were planning to pick you up from the start. I was watching you. Those were my orders."

"Orders," Cora repeated, her head starting to throb.

"I gotta go. I gotta run. They won't like it. Once you're

in, you're in forever." He was babbling. He was crazy. He'd had a blow to the head. Multiple blows to the head.

Behind him, a long black car pulled up to the curb. Her ride was here.

She turned, but the man had gone. The door to the back was swinging closed.

Sharo found her there, still clutching her arms to her chest among the aisles of dog food. "Ready to go?" he asked, looking her up and down.

"I need to change," she said, fighting the urge to back away. Sharo seemed to sense this, and stayed close, hovering, protective.

"You can do that at the club." He turned, stiffening when the back door opened, but it was only Maeve, frowning for some reason.

"You nearly forgot this," she said in her low, no nonsense voice, handing over Cora's purse. Sharo held out a hand for it, and Maeve pulled it out of his reach. The older redhead gave him a level glance. "Excuse me."

"It's okay, Maeve," Cora said. "I trust him." She blinked suddenly, surprised at how quickly she said those words, wondering if they were lies. Gods, she needed to think.

Maeve looked at her with an unhappy expression, but gave Sharo the bag.

"Good night." Cora's small smile must have helped Maeve hold her thoughts in, but lines still formed on the older woman's forehead.

Cora survived the drive in silence. *Warn me?* She rubbed her bare arms.

Once you're in, you're in forever.

When Sharo guided her down the steps to the club where she had run to that night long ago, she didn't struggle. But the illuminated door that had once seemed like such sanctuary now felt like... Cold shivered down her back as she crossed the threshold.

Her mind felt blank. It was all too much to process. Whenever a panicked thought tried to break through, she reminded herself that that man was crazy. He'd kidnapped her for gods' sake and then had continued *stalking* her. Why should she trust anything he said?

But he'd been so beaten down, literally and figuratively. He'd said he wanted to make amends, like he was in some twelve-step program.

What if he *wasn't* lying?

A minute later Cora was alone with Marcus in his office. Mr. Ubeli. The shadows still cut across his face among the mahogany and rich carpet. Nothing had changed from that first night.

No, everything has.

"Hey, babe," he said, and leaned back in his chair with a sigh. With one hand he scrubbed his hair out of his face; the other reached out, calling her toward him. She had planned to be strong, but something in the way he pushed the dark spikes of his hair away from his eyes reminded her of a little boy, up past his bedtime. She went to him. Gods help her, she went to him.

"Long day?" she asked, and he didn't reply, simply put his hands on her hips and pushed her back so that she was leaning on the desk. His fingers stroked her arms, wrists, and hands, before retreating.

As soon as they left her skin, Cora wanted them back. She was the one who needed a twelve-step program. She was addicted to Marcus.

"Where's your ring?" Marcus's voice didn't sound cold, not quite. But his face was blank in a way she knew he wasn't happy.

"Oh," Cora grabbed the chain around her neck. The diamonds flashed in the light. The garnet was so dark it seemed to drink the light in. "I put it here so it wouldn't get dirty."

Marcus's lips pressed together, and she quickly undid the delicate chain, freed the ring, and replaced it on her fourth finger.

She wiggled her fingers in Marcus's direction. "All better. Did you think I'd lost it?" Just like always, when she was with him, everything else disappeared. She knew she'd been very upset before coming into the room, that she *still* should be, that there was a chance that man had been telling the truth—

"No." Marcus captured her hand and toyed with the slim band. His touch ignited a wildfire, racing up her arm, turning her insides into an inferno. *Oh*—

"Don't worry," she breathed out, fighting to keep her voice normal as her pulse jumped, hammering a million times per minute, "I won't forget I'm engaged to you."

"Not you I'm worried about. It's every guy who looks at you, sees an angel and thinks he can get close."

"Possessive, much?" she joked, but the intensity in Marcus's gaze seared her.

"You have no idea."

She closed her eyes as his fingertips grazed her temples, then traced down her cheeks. Her universe expanded, and it was full of Marcus. Everywhere Marcus, Marcus, *Marcus*.

And she let him, remaining still, heart now hardly daring to beat, as if even a breath might break the moment.

"I should have done this a long time ago," he murmured.

"What?" she started to say and leaned forward to hear

the answer, but at that moment he looked up, and caught her mouth with his. And then it was all over.

Every thought went out of her head, all but Marcus, and he was standing now with his arms around her, his body pressing hers against the desk.

"Marcus," she gasped when he released her lips.

"It shouldn't have taken me so long. With any other girl it wouldn't have taken me so long."

"So long to do what?" she asked, her thoughts still swirling.

"This," he said, and again his mouth closed over hers. The breath rocketed out of her, her hands flying up and hovering by his face. But she didn't dare touch him, terrified to break the spell. But she needn't have worried.

His whole body got into the kiss, closing in, dominating. His heat and scent surrounded her, flooding her with fire. Her hands gripped his strong shoulders, clutching the bunched muscle, nails digging into the fine Italian fabric as if they would scratch the smooth olive skin underneath.

"That's it, angel. Hold onto me," Marcus ordered, propping her on the desk and drawing her head back by her hair as his lips seared a brand onto her skin. His large palm cradled her head as his mouth worked down her neck. Cora let her head loll back, her body arching as Marcus pushed up her shirt and covered her breast with his hot mouth.

"Marcus, Marcus," she panted. Her body was dry tinder, a field baked in the sun all summer. One spark and everything went up in flame.

His large hand slid down her midriff, skimming over her soft skin into her jeans and panties, touching her where no one had ever touched her before. Her eyes flew open, lips parting. Only to catch Marcus's wolfish gaze as he stared hungrily into her eyes.

"So sweet. Such an innocent. Cora," he groaned against her mouth, his eyes becoming hooded as his finger swirled between her slippery folds. "You like this?"

Her eyelashes fluttered. She— It felt— She'd never— *Oh!*

"Answer me."

"Yes," she finally managed to gasp.

"That's it, my goddess," he whispered, his fingers fluttering against the sweetest spot. Her stomach was liquid and she could feel this...this insane amazing pleasurable pressure building. Oh gods she'd never felt anything like it before. How was he—? Oh gods yes, right there, like that, right there—

Her knees knocked and his breath caught. "Go over."

At his command, the tightness cracked and eased and everything poured out. Oh, oh, *oooooooooh!*

Her hand came up to stop him but, no, it simply took the plane of his cheek as if she would hold him to her, and her fingers raked through his hair, her breath coming out in a shudder as his mouth covered hers again. The shocking waves of pleasure, she'd never...*oh*—

She sagged against Marcus, breathing in the crisp linen scent as aftershocks stiffened her limbs, stiffening and releasing, stiffening and releasing.

Marcus gave her a final stroke, making her entire body shudder again, and withdrew his hand.

I've never done that before, she wanted to tell him. *Everything is new with you. I'm new with you.* The satisfied smirk tucked into the corner of his mouth told her he knew.

She ran her fingers over his perfect lips and the elegant line of his jaw. He was real, flesh and blood. Not a god. Not a statue carved by a master sculptor. He was a man.

He was hers.

Catching her gaze in his grey one, Marcus pulled out a handkerchief and wiped his hand. He folded it and pressed it to his nose, inhaling before replacing it in his pocket. Her cheeks burned.

"Beautiful." Marcus pulled her close to his body. At her height, sitting on the desk, the position pressed her soft center against his crotch. A hard length pressed there, distorting the tailored slacks. Her eyes rounded.

Marcus's thumb skimmed her jaw. "Gorgeous. Tell me you're my girl."

She didn't even hesitate.

"I'm your girl."

"You belong to me." It wasn't a question.

"Yes."

"You gonna give me what I want?"

"Yes." She swallowed, searching his eyes. "What...what do you want?"

"Everything." He took her mouth, pressing close and tipping her off balance, forcing her to hang onto him until he broke the kiss.

"But not tonight." He stroked her porcelain cheek. "You're tired." He held her quietly, her head against his chest. She listened for his heartbeat again, and soon, realized he was speaking, telling his love to her over and over again, maybe in the only way he knew how.

"I'll keep you safe, babe, you know it. You won't ever need a thing. You're my goddess, and I won't let you go—"

"Marcus," she sat up. "This is happening so fast." Didn't he realize she wasn't going anywhere? There was plenty that should have scared her off, maybe, okay scratch that —*definitely* should have scared her off. But she still wasn't going anywhere. This thing between them was too strong, too powerful. So powerful it scared her sometimes, on top of everything else. "There's no rush."

"I know you're scared, babe." Of course he knew. His dark grey eyes never left hers. "But you're with me. You're going to be okay. You can't escape, angel... This is your destiny."

Cora collapsed forward, resting her forehead against his.

"I want you," he said. "But you're so perfect. So innocent. I wanted to do it right." His fingers threaded through hers, rubbing the ring.

She sat up, suddenly understanding. "That's why you want to marry me so quickly."

He dipped his chin. He didn't want to...not until they were married. Her heart clutched at the sweetness of the gesture. She didn't know a lot about these things but she suspected, a man like him, going without couldn't be easy. But he was doing it, for her. Even now she knew he was stifling his need. She'd felt him so hard against her thigh.

"Marcus." She slid her arms around his shoulders. "I'm here. I'm not going anywhere."

"I'm not taking any chances." For a moment she clung to him in perfect silence.

He said, "From now on, you have two guards wherever you go."

"But—"

He placed a finger at her lips. "No argument. I know that dick turned up again." His face grew sober. "Sharo saw him in the shop."

She straightened. "I didn't— He didn't—" She wasn't sure what she was trying to explain so she stopped.

"I know."

Cora bit her lip. It was now or never. "He said something. He was trying to warn me."

"About what?" Marcus's face was carefully blank.

Did it really matter what that man said? He'd drugged and kidnapped her. He was obviously fixated on her, and he'd had several blows to the head. Was she really going to believe his 'warning' over everything she knew about Marcus?

Not that she really knew Marcus, but so far he'd been a perfect gentleman. And she did know him, didn't she? The things that mattered anyway.

Her eyes dropped to her lap. "Nothing. He said nothing."

Marcus trapped her hand between both of his, squeezing. "Cora, this...what we have...is new. But it's gonna last."

"I know that." And she did. Because now she couldn't imagine her world without Marcus in it.

"You know my work isn't always above the law."

"I don't know much about what you do—" she started shakily.

"You know enough."

"I know who you are, Marcus. I know that you have principles. You want good people to be safe... And bad people punished."

"That's right. I do." His grip tightened, almost painful, then it eased and he raised her hand to his lips, kissing her knuckles. "But I promise you, my work will never touch you. I'm gonna put you so high on a pedestal, you'll live in the stars."

"Lock me in an ivory tower?" she tried to smile. "The penthouse?"

"If that's what it takes." His voice was hard but then it

turned reassuring. "Cora, that man won't ever bother you again."

Her stomach plummeted, a jumble of guilt and relief. "He won't?" she whispered. *What will you do to him?* She gulped back the question. Even if Marcus told her, she didn't want to know.

"No." His eyes crinkled in a chilling smile. "Don't worry. I told you I'd take care of you."

EIGHT

They got married two weeks later in a brief, private ceremony in a small chapel near the Crown hotel.

Well, *private* in that Marcus only invited what he called the 'bare minimum' of his friends and business associates who would be offended if they didn't get an invitation. So the chapel was full to bursting with people.

Traditionally his guests would fill one side of the aisle and hers the other, but Cora only had one person to invite—the only other person in the city she really knew besides Marcus—Maeve.

Cora felt a pang thinking about her mother as she hovered at the back of the church, but it was mainly along the lines of wishing she had a normal mother who could be here, happy and joyful to give her daughter away. Instead it would be Sharo walking her down the aisle.

The only other person she even really knew there was Armand, and he was still technically more Marcus's friend than hers, though she did get to enjoy more of his boisterous personality as she had dress fittings with him. He had a line of wedding dresses so it seemed natural to go to him for her dress.

Never one to go completely traditional, Armand had picked a dress that was white with black straps and black lace at her waist. Cora wasn't picky. The dress was beautiful and it was clear Marcus approved by the look in his eye as she walked down the aisle. She wore white flowers in her hair and she positively floated the last few feet to him.

She couldn't believe she was actually here, about to marry him. He would be hers, forever.

She was so giddy, she couldn't stop grinning throughout the entire ceremony, even though the priest droned on.

And finally, the ancient priest got to the only part Cora cared about. "I now pronounce you husband and wife. You may kiss the bride."

Marcus pulled her close, cradled her head in his large hand and slanted his mouth over hers. It wasn't a chaste kiss. Fireworks exploded as his tongue stroked once, twice, three times before her lips parted and it swept inside. Heat rolled through her, running into her mouth like nectar from Marcus's lips, spilling down her neck, chest, and pooling with exquisite weight right between her legs. Her thighs clenched. Wedding bells were ringing, and every cell in her body blasted to life.

He finally released her, the cheers of the guests echoing in her ears. Sparks sizzling in every corner of her body, Cora reached out and swiped a thumb at the corner of his mouth where her lipstick marked him. Marcus gave her a wink and her whole body convulsed.

"Soon," he mouthed and she flushed redder than she already was. He turned to greet the guests, handsome face smooth and polite, but she sensed the tension, the dormant readiness in the lines of his powerful body. He was impatient with the pomp and ceremony too.

First there was the reception, an elegant affair in one of the Crown hotel's ballrooms. Cora clung to Marcus's hand in the receiving line as person after person came by to congratulate them. Some of the faces she recognized. Santonio—or Papa Santa as he liked people to call him. He ran one of the restaurants Marcus invested in. And then there was Jimmy Roscoe and his wife and their five children. Cora didn't know how Marcus knew him except that they did business together.

The rest were a blur of names and faces she didn't bother trying to keep up with. She smiled and shook hands and accepted congratulations until finally the line dwindled and they were through.

"Another half hour then we'll cut out of here, I promise," Marcus whispered in her ear as he led her out on the dance floor.

That sounded like heaven to her. She relaxed into his body as soon as the band started to play a slow, romantic jazz number. He led her expertly across the floor, smooth as spun honey.

And true to his word, half an hour later, they'd cut the cake and made their goodbyes, encouraging everyone else to stay and enjoy the party and the open bar.

They escaped upstairs.

Cora was tired after the long day but adrenaline had her feeling wide awake as they stepped on the elevator to go to the penthouse.

It was officially her wedding night now.

She and Marcus hadn't talked about it, but it was obvious that tonight would be *the night*. He'd take her virginity and they'd finally be united in every way possible. She'd truly be his, and him hers.

It was stupid, but she had the romantic notion that her whole life had been leading up to this moment.

"Oh Marcus," she sighed, leaning into his body as the elevator continued to rise. "I never knew happiness like this could even be *real*."

He didn't say anything, he just put his arm around her and pulled her into his chest.

The elevator pinged and he let her go as he strode forward and slid his keycard from his wallet and into the door.

Cora eagerly followed behind, hurrying into the penthouse suite.

But apparently she wasn't fast enough because Marcus pushed her from behind, grabbing frantically for her and shoving the door shut with his foot.

It was like he couldn't get his hands on her quick enough. He kissed her forcefully, hands at her waist pulling her into him.

Cora opened to him, her adrenaline spiking even higher as pleasure warred with fear over what was about to happen. She'd tried to learn a little bit about sex online using her phone, but the pictures that had come up—suffice to say, she'd quickly closed the browser in horror. Besides, she'd reasoned, she trusted Marcus to lead her through whatever she needed to know.

Marcus immediately shucked his jacket and yanked at his tie, but then, as if he was impatient, his hands came back to her. His hands slid down her waist and around to her backside. He squeezed her bottom and she couldn't help the groan of surprise and pleasure—having him touch her so intimately was shocking...and amazing.

Next he was tearing at the buttons on his shirt and yanking it off, then pulling his undershirt off over his head.

Cora's eyes about bugged out of her head at seeing his bare chest.

Her husband was gorgeous.

To die for gorgeous.

She knew he worked out in the mornings but...her mouth went dry the more she looked at his toned chest and the cut of his abdominal muscles, all leading to a sharp V that—

"You like what you see?" he growled and pulled her to him again, kissing her deep.

But only for a moment, because he pulled away and spun her around and pressed her face first into the wall.

She felt his fingers pulling at the laces of her dress the next moment. "Damn that Armand," he hissed, tugging impatiently. "How the hell do I get you out of this thing?"

Cora giggled and reached back to help him but he batted her hands away. Finally, she felt the dress loosen around her waist and Marcus finished by pulling down the zipper. His hands glided over her flesh as he pushed the gown to the ground and helped her step out of it.

She was left in a white strapless bra, thong, and thigh-highs. She lifted her arms to her chest instinctively.

But Marcus wasn't having it. He pulled her arms down and stared at her in that way of his, like he was drinking in every inch of her.

He lifted her in his arms and carried her to his bedroom. She squealed and circled his neck with her arms, clinging to him, but he carried her like she weighed nothing at all.

He deposited her smoothly on the bed and followed her down, kissing her and climbing in between her legs.

She groaned as he put pressure right where she needed

it. She wrapped her legs around him and ground restlessly against him, seeking what she didn't even know. Was this really finally happening? Was she actually here, in her wedding bed with Marcus? It was a dream. Things like this never happened to her. Was she really getting the happy ending?

But Marcus's lips on her felt real enough. A shudder wracked her body at his touch. The way he made her *feel...* He still had his pants on but he was kissing her and she was happy to let him take the lead.

As much as she hated to think of him with other women before her, it meant he was the one who knew what he was doing.

And now he's yours. Only yours.

She grinned and dug her hands into his hair. She *adored* his hair. It was so thick and dark. Their children would have gorgeous dark hair. Would they get his gray eyes or her blue ones? They hadn't even talked about children other than Marcus asking for her to get the birth control shot a month ago. There was so much they still didn't know about each other.

But they had their whole lives to learn. Starting tonight.

Cora's stomach flipped in joy and pleasure as Marcus reached beneath her and unclasped her bra.

When he pulled it off, she waited in anticipation for him to touch her breasts. Her nipples had hardened into little nubs and she was suddenly aching for him to touch them.

Instead, Marcus lifted her arms above her head and continued to kiss her.

He climbed off of her and moved up the bed.

"What are you—" she started to ask but he cut her off.

"Do you trust me?" His gaze had never been more

solemn and intense. It made Cora want to cover herself again but she swallowed. She'd be brave. Because yes, she did trust him, and she told him so.

"Yes."

He gave her the half grin she loved as he pulled one of her arms up and outwards. Tension rippled through her as he lifted a silk scarf she hadn't seen that was already tied to the bedpost to wind around her wrist.

What was he—? She lay still as he tied first one wrist, and then the other, to the bed. She tugged against one experimentally and even though it was silk, the way he'd knotted it, it didn't give an inch.

"Marcus," she said, brow furrowing. "I don't know about this. It's— It's my first time, you know."

"That makes me very happy to hear, goddess," he said, moving back down the bed to kiss her deep again.

His drugging kisses soon had her forgetting all her objections. Especially when he kissed down her neck and kept going. When his mouth closed over her nipple finally, she arched up into him and let out the most embarrassing moan. But she couldn't help it, it felt *so good*.

He wasn't done with teasing her, though, apparently, because he continued kissing down her body. Down to her belly button. Lower.

When he got to the hem of her white lace underwear, he dragged them down with his teeth. Cora gasped and her chest heaved as warring emotions fought for dominance—fear, exhilaration, but above all, desire.

Desire for her husband, the man she loved. Dear gods but she loved him.

It was on the tip of her tongue to confess it as he tugged her underwear and slid it down her legs, baring her to him completely.

She wasn't embarrassed or ashamed.

Because she loved him.

She wanted to whisper it in his ear. She wanted to scream it from the rooftops.

She was in love with this god of a man and she wanted the whole world to know. She grinned at him as he massaged her calf and looked up at her body.

He wasn't smiling. He looked pensive, like he was deep in his head.

"Marcus?"

He didn't answer as he pulled off her thigh-highs, then tugged on her ankle and—

Her forehead furrowed when he pulled yet another red scarf from the foot of the bed.

"Wait, Marcus." She tried to draw her leg up but he pulled her leg back flat to the bed with his inexorable strength, massaging her calf as he went.

When he looked up at her, his eyes were stormy. "You said you trusted me."

And what could she say to that?

So she let her leg go limp as he tied one ankle and then the other, until she was spread out on the bed like a virgin sacrifice.

She expected Marcus to climb up and cover her, to warm her with his body and soothe her discomfort at the position with his drugging kisses.

But instead, he left the bed. Glass clinked. Cora craned her neck. Marcus stood at the sideboard, pouring himself a drink.

"What are you doing?" She tugged at her bonds. Glass in hand, Marcus moved to the end of the bed, his face half in shadow. In between sips, his sculpted lips were set in neither a smile or a frown.

"Marcus," she called, breathless. "Please. What—"

"If only Demi Titan could see her little girl now."

What? How—

Goosebumps pebbled all over Cora's skin. She'd never told Marcus her mother's name. Much less her mother's married name. Mom had gone back to using her maiden name, Vestian, after they moved to Kansas.

But for Marcus to know—

He stepped into the light. His stone expression turned Cora cold. "Surprise, little wife." He took a long pull of his drink. "You've just married the big bad wolf."

NINE

No, no, no, no, no. This was all some big mistake. Or she was dreaming. Yes, that had to be it. It was still the night before the wedding and she was having a nightmare. This was pre-wedding jitters and her brain was conjuring the worst thing it could imagine.

"Hey," Marcus ran his fingertips up her inner thigh. "Stay with me. This is important. Don't want you to miss a thing." His lips twisted as he leaned over her. "Breathe. You gotta remember to breathe."

She sucked in air, frozen, staring at his face. His strong jaw and hooded grey eyes. The handsome warmth she loved was gone, replaced by a mask. The same hard, menacing mask he gave to everyone else—but now he was using it on *her*.

"Marcus, stop it," she jerked against the scarves binding her wrists and ankles. "You're scaring me."

"Good," he rumbled, and it was the first time since he'd tied her up that she'd seen anything resembling emotion enter his eyes. His finger trailed down her bare leg, making it twitch. Reminding her she was bound and naked. Not that she needed a reminder. "You should be scared."

He circled the bed and set his drink on the side table. Hands in his pockets, he studied her. His shadow cut over her body. "My sister was scared—when your father's goons snatched her off the streets, threw her in a dirty room and violated her."

All the oxygen left the room. Cora's ears rang, her vision dimming, narrowing on Marcus's hard face. "What?"

"They tied her up...just like this. She was a good girl. Sweetest soul on the face of this planet. She loved everybody. Never took a step out of line. And he killed her in cold blood. Your father."

Cora jerked her head and body from side to side. "No. No, you've got me mixed up with someone else. My dad died in a car accident and my mom—"

"Your mom took you into hiding when you were four years old to protect you from *me*," he sneered. "But then after all these years, what do you know, a girl who's the spitting image of Demi Titan comes waltzing back into *my* city, except instead of brunette, she's got her daddy Titan's blond hair."

Cora's mouth dropped open. No. What he was saying couldn't be true. But the look in his eye, the cold fury—the *hatred*—he certainly thought it was true.

Cora's mind raced with all he was telling her. Could it —? Had mom really hidden away for all those years to protect her from—

Cora's eyes shot to Marcus, sitting so smugly above her. Even if what he was saying was true, she couldn't imagine it, but even if it was— "I didn't do anything to you or your sister. This is the first I'm hearing of any of it."

Marcus shook his head and took up his drink, swallowing the dregs before setting it down with a thunk. "Do I look like I give a fuck?"

Cora flinched at his harsh curse. He'd never used such language around her.

"My sister didn't do anything either. I live by a Code." He reached down and cupped Cora's cheek and she jerked away from his touch. He let her.

"Under my Code, you would have been untouchable. But your family violated all that is sacred the night they took Chiara. And there's only one way for the scales to be leveled. And before I killed your father, I looked into his eyes and told him that his little baby girl was next."

Cora felt her eyes go so wide she didn't even dare blink. Her father hadn't died in a car accident. Marcus had— Marcus had *killed*— And she was—

"Are you going to kill me?" she whispered.

Marcus's lip quirked up on the side, the smile she'd loved only a half hour before. "No, angel. What fun would that be?" His fingertips skimmed her cheek. "Why would I kill you when I could keep you?" She fell into his gaze, drowned in it.

"No," he murmured. "You don't get a death sentence. You get a life sentence. Death is quick. But suffering...suffering can go on forever."

The air left her lungs. Cora panted as her body tightened, turned to concrete.

"Breathe, baby." Marcus settled a large hand on her chest. "You gotta breathe."

She inhaled, compelled as she stared into his dark grey eyes. There was something about Marcus she had to obey.

"I don't want you to hurt me," she whispered.

"I know, angel." For a second his face softened, conflicted. "I didn't want to hurt you, either."

Cora's heart leapt with hope. "But why—"

"There's an order to the universe. Everything has its place." He settled beside her, lecturing like a professor. "Everything's weighed on scales," he raised two hands, palms up. "Things gotta balance. Light and dark. Day and night. Good and bad." He dropped his hands. "Crime and punishment."

Cora's mouth worked but no sound escaped. She met Marcus's gaze and drowned in it.

"When your father," his voice vibrated under the weight of his rage, "did what he did, things got out of order. Out of place. There need to be consequences. I've been waiting for this day for a very long time."

"But *I* didn't do anything."

He looked away. "You aren't hearing me. Someone's gotta answer for what they did. I found my sister..." His eyes closed, and Cora's heart cracked. Because it was still Marcus. And the pain on his face was so real. "Her eyes were open. Her body broken. They did things to her. Things that should never be done. Angels wept..."

"I'm sorry," she whispered. It slipped out. Not apologizing for herself, but because it was what you said when you hurt for someone you loved.

He tied you to the bed! He hates you!

But she...she'd spent the last two months loving him. It didn't just disappear. She didn't know how to turn it off.

Marcus closed his eyes. He pinched the bridge of his nose, his chest rising and falling rapidly. His jaw was shadowed with stubble. Everything in her strained to go to him, to hold him. For all his power and control, Marcus was a man. Just a man. She'd seen him at his best, and at his lowest. He hid nothing from her.

Except, he had, hadn't he? He'd hid his nature in plain

sight. And she was the naive prey that had walked right into his trap.

I'm sorry. Her apology lay between them, small and inadequate against the huge debt.

He dropped his hand. He was the Lord of the Underworld once more, his expression carved from stone. Back in control.

"No, beautiful, you're not. But you will be."

He stalked out of the room. Cora shivered where he left her. Everything had turned around so quickly, she felt dizzy. She closed her eyes until soft footfalls jerked her attention back to Marcus.

Despite everything, her pulse fluttered at the sight of him, his huge bare chest dusted with dark hair.

"What's going to happen? What will you do with me?"

"Whatever I want." A shark-like smile. "You're not going to die. You're going to live a long, long time. By my side as my wife. Forever."

How could he be so cold? So ruthless? How could she have been so foolish as to think he loved her? Now her wedding night was a nightmare. So much for happy endings.

She couldn't help the tears that welled up and spilled down her cheeks.

"That's right, gorgeous. Cry for me."

That was when she saw what Marcus had picked up—his phone. He'd turned on the camera and was aiming it her way. Red rage bloomed in her head.

"No."

"Yes." Marcus backed away, like he was framing the perfect shot. "We've got to have some wedding photos to send your side of the family. It's the least we can do considering your mom and your uncles couldn't make it to the wedding."

Her *uncles*? She didn't even know she *had* uncles.

"Stop." Her begging was muffled as she hid her face in her arm. "Please stop."

"Look at me," he ordered. "Cora." His footfalls stalked closer. "This is happening."

"No." Think, she had to *think*. This was still Marcus. Inside the man, the monster, there was a powerful attraction to her. Maybe she could find an inkling of the Marcus who cared.

A hand closed around her wrist like an iron shackle. She resisted.

"Cora, I'm not going to ask you again."

Her bones melted. She let him pull her hand away. He looked down at her and her body flushed under his scrutiny.

"You're sick," she bit out. Anything to deny her body's pull to him.

"I won't take the pictures, if you submit to me."

Her laugh wracked her body. "How? It's not like I can run away."

"I'll drop the camera if you submit to me. And act like a wife."

"You mean like I love you?"

He inclined his head.

The cracks in her heart dripped poison. "I did love you, you know. That wasn't a lie."

"I know."

"Was everything you said to me...was it all an act? Was it never real?"

He didn't answer.

"Fine. I'll do it." she raised her chin. Pretending to be brave. "It's not anything I haven't done before."

He was switching off the camera when he swung back to her, his normally grey eyes went black. "Excuse me?"

"Oh, did you think I was a virgin?"

He came back and covered her knee with his hand. He squeezed and her breath stuttered, betraying her. "I don't think you're a virgin," he told her. "I know you are."

She raised her chin. "I've had guys," she lied. "Lots of them."

He shook his head. "You're a terrible liar."

"It's true."

Marcus moved over her, his large body stretching head to toe with hers. His cologne mixed with the crisp linen scent of his white dress shirt. She was naked, he wasn't, but coiled power rippling through him was visible in his taut muscles and the endless depths of his eyes. Heat crackled between them. "Lots of guys, huh? I'll have to make you forget them."

His touch seared her as it always did. Her legs trembled and she blinked at him, searching his face for any semblance of the man who took her in and cared for her.

And then she remembered his callous smile as he'd aimed a camera at her.

"I hate you."

His eyes crinkled in a cold smile that didn't touch his mouth. He tutted. "Is that any way to talk to your husband, wife?"

"Don't call me that."

"Wife? That's what you are."

Her head jerked negative and his expression darkened. "Yes." His hand rested on her tensed chest, sliding up to collar her neck. "My wife. Better or worse," his gaze roved over her, his eyes gunmetal grey. "Rich or poor. Sick or healthy. Till death do us part."

She closed her eyes at his mocking version of their vows. He was going to humiliate her, hurt her, and her body didn't care. It responded to Marcus and warmed at his touch. Her heart thrummed and lungs strained. She panted as if she'd run a marathon.

He reached for his belt buckle. Cora's eyes were wide before, but now they swallowed up her face, flashing white. Her entire body shuddered. Why had she let him tie her up? Stupid.

But she'd believed he loved her.

He never said it. So why did you think it?

Because he asked her to marry him! What other reason could he have had? Apparently revenge for crimes committed more than a decade ago that she hadn't even known about.

"You told me you'd take care of me." Her voice was small, plaintive.

"I did." His deep voice dripped promise. "I will."

"Please," she gasped, knowing it was pathetic to beg but still unable to believe there was nothing of the Marcus who'd held and kissed her so tenderly left inside the cruel man sitting before her now. "Don't touch me."

"No?" His lips twisted. "You don't want me to touch you?"

"No." But he was touching her, barely, stroking the side of her breast. It felt so good. She never wanted him to stop. "You want me to stop?" he asked as if reading her mind.

"I—"

"You like it when I touch you."

Her thighs pressed together. She whimpered. His fingers never stopped stroking, stroking...

"Admit it," his voice deepened, rolling over her senses. The room fell away.

"I'm going to touch you whenever I want, wife. And you're going to like it."

"But...you hate me." She was ashamed of how her voice cracked. And even more ashamed that she was leaning into his touch. But he was so familiar. And his touch felt like a comfort, even now.

"Hate never stopped anyone from feeling pleasure."

Cora's eyebrows knitted together. What did that mean?

Marcus's dark hair brushed her belly. He dipped down over her body, and as if the last terrible fifteen minutes had never happened, he kissed down her stomach again. His cologne washed over her, smooth and sweet.

Her elbows and knees softened, her stomach flip flopping. Cora stared at his shining head. His mouth was warm on her cool flesh and then his hands were there, gripping her hips like she loved so much. Oh, *oh!*

She couldn't help the noise that escaped her throat and he paused.

"You gonna fight me, angel?"

She should fight. She should shout 'yes' and try to wrench out of her bonds, do whatever it took to escape.

But his tongue touched the smooth plane of her stomach and something inside her snapped. She wasn't prepared for it and her muscles clenched at the sudden shocking rush of pleasure. Golden liquid gushed through her, pouring from her belly and filling up her pulsing center until it overflowed. She felt her own moisture on her legs and her face flamed with embarrassment.

"I guess not," Marcus chuckled. He pulled back and she knew he was admiring the wetness flooding the space between her legs. "Shame. I would've enjoyed a fight."

Tears immediately cascaded down Cora's cheeks.

His fingers trailed over her pale skin, bringing a rosy

flush to her chest. They trailed down, over her quivering belly to sink into the wetness. Cora gasped and tugged at the wrist bands. Marcus's eyes narrowed, but he kept stroking her. Her hips rose, jerking in time to his come-hither movement.

"You know, you can stop this at any moment."

What? Was he serious?

He twisted a finger in her virgin hole. Her feet dug into the bed and her abs tensed as she lifted herself into his hand. Her body pulsed around his fingers as he cupped her.

"Just tell me. Say, 'stop.'"

What was his game? She could stop at any moment? She could—

"Stop," she mouthed but no sound came out.

His fingers stilled but her hips kept rocking. Cora clenched her teeth. She wanted him to touch her. She wanted...

Marcus raised a brow. She whimpered. Her hips tilted in invitation.

"Poor wife. So confused. Do you want me to touch you? Do you want me to kiss it better?"

To Cora's horror, she nodded.

Marcus bent his head to taste her. Her legs spasmed, her body sighing into his mouth.

Stop, she screamed in her head. *Stop.* But when she opened her mouth, still no sound came out. His mouth worked over her mound, detouring to her slick thighs, nuzzling her labia, nipping at them with his teeth. She stayed silent, other than her moans.

What was happening? He'd given her an out. Why hadn't she taken it? He hated her. He'd only married her to get revenge. But his caresses, his kisses, they didn't feel hateful. They felt familiar. They felt like *Marcus*. The man she... The man she loved.

That man's not real. He never was.

But for a second, she wanted to pretend. She wanted to pretend that he'd never said all those awful things. She wanted to pretend this was their wedding night as it always should have been, and he was kissing and worshipping her because he adored her.

So when he kissed lower and urged her thighs open, she let him.

His mouth touched her most intimate place. She squealed in shock and shame and— And *pleasure*.

"Marcus," she murmured, meaning to ask him to stop.

But he began to suckle at the top of her sex and his finger dropped to explore, teasing at places she herself had never touched.

She never even used tampons, so to feel someone—and not just someone, to feel *Marcus*, oh—

And the things he was doing with his mouth—

Cora heaved shocked gasps, in and out, tossing her head back and forth because it was the only part of her body she could actually move. She grasped onto the silk scarves. She needed something to hold onto, something to ground herself as the wild, shocking sensations rose higher and higher—

Oh gods, she didn't know what to do with— If this didn't— Where was this all going—

"*Ohhhhh!*" Her squeal faded to a high-pitched whine as pleasure rocked her body, as suddenly as if she'd been shocked by a jolt of electricity. She felt it to the tips of her toes as her legs went rigid. For two counts of her heartbeat, it was all perfect.

And then it was over and Marcus was crawling up her body.

She blinked back to the moment, trying to get her bearings.

Marcus. Who wasn't her beloved after all. Who'd only married her for revenge.

But would he still make love to her now?

He was straddling her body and she could see his...his sexual member. He'd pulled it out of his pants. Veins stood out on the long shaft. It was darker than the rest of his body and pulsing.

And it was huge. *Huge.*

Was he going to try to stick that inside her?

Even as horrible as things stood between them, with the way he'd made her feel, would she object?

Yes, her mind said. Her heart on the other hand... It was pathetic, she knew, to want any part of this terrible man. And yet—

But Marcus wasn't trying to stick it in her, it looked like.

No, he was taking his long, thick shaft in hand and rubbing it up and down. Ruthlessly. Viciously.

Cora should look away, she knew.

But she'd never seen one. And to see Marcus so naked, not literally but figuratively— She looked up his taut stomach and into his face, only to find him looking down at her.

She couldn't read what she saw in the half-second before he lowered his gaze to her breasts. Cora didn't look away, though. She continued watching his face as he pleasured himself.

He gave himself over to it, that much was clear. In this one thing, at least, he either didn't bother with keeping up his mask or he simply couldn't. Cora saw a million things in the vulnerable, longing scrunch of his brow—or at least she thought she did.

It made the pleasure that had barely subsided in her rear up again. Her hips jerked involuntarily, looking for friction. But Marcus was too far away, all but straddling her breasts.

He continued to work himself for several more moments and then threw his head back.

Cora's face jerked down when warm wetness splashed her chest. She looked on in astonishment as spurts of white cream erupted from the head of his huge shaft as he tugged it more mercilessly than ever.

When he'd finally emptied himself, he looked down at her, his chest heaving. He reached down and rubbed his seed all over her breasts, squeezing her nipples as he went.

Cora shuddered, so turned on and shocked by the entire thing. Did people normally do this in bed or did Marcus see this as some sort of punishment? It all felt so good.

Marcus climbed off the bed. "You like that, don't you? Then make sure to smile for the camera."

"Wha—?"

But Marcus was already snapping pictures with his phone. Pictures of her naked body, smeared with his —with his—

The blood left her face. "You said you wouldn't!"

"Naïve little Cora. All's fair in love and war."

"Really I don't even need this." He dropped the phone on to the bedside table. With a dark smirk, he pointed to the corner where two walls met the ceiling and held a dark shape of a second camera, its tiny bright eye blinking red. "Video makes so much more impact than photos, don't you think?"

Cora bit her lip, unwilling to give him anything after how cruel he'd just been to her. He laughed, and it wasn't a nice laugh. This really wasn't *her* Marcus. That man had truly never existed.

If she needed any more proof, him leaving her all alone in the room, tied up with his seed drying on her chest certainly did the trick.

TEN

Marcus stood in the small dark closet he used as his security room, sipped his drink and stared at nothing. On screen, his new bride struggled in her bonds. Her beautiful hair fell over her face, a sheaf of wheat spilling over the pale palette of unmarked skin.

He'd just cum, but he was harder than ever, ready to conquer, to plunder. She was right where he wanted her, bound and helpless, a virgin offered up as a sacrifice to appease a monster. Which she was—a virgin and a sacrifice.

And he, the monster.

She didn't deserve this. The second his Shades had spotted her, he'd had them monitor her every move. She didn't so much as sneeze without him knowing. She looked like her mother, but acted nothing like Demi.

He had to see it to believe it. But at first he couldn't stand to look at her. He sent Sharo instead, Sharo, whom he regarded as a brother.

"Well?" he'd asked when the big man returned to report. "What's she like?"

"Kind. Naive, but hopeful. Sweet." Sharo didn't have to

say it, but Marcus heard the silent commentary. *Just like Chiara.*

The gods gifted him the perfect revenge, wrapped up in a lovely package. So lovely, he didn't want to destroy it. How the gods must be laughing. He had the means for revenge but, for the first time in sixteen years he didn't want to take it.

Oh, he wanted Cora. When he laid eyes on her, he was undone. The flick of her eyelashes, the flutter of her fine boned hands, the shy smiles he drank in like a man who'd crossed a desert. She was the oasis he didn't know he craved.

On screen, she tossed her head back and forth, the fragile column of her throat taut as she called out for him. Her skin shimmered like mother-of-pearl where he'd spilled his seed. And gods, when she'd come, the pleasure so obviously foreign to her...

His dick curled up to his belly, aching to take her. When he'd spewed his seed all over her beautiful bare breasts, he hadn't been thinking of revenge. He'd been lost in her. The taste of her sweetness still drugging his senses. Unable to look away from her half-mast eyes hazy with lust even though she'd just come. She wanted more, and fuck him, but he'd wanted to stay there all night and give it to her.

He'd barely managed to force himself from the room after smearing his seed all over her chest, marking her as his like a barbarian.

He forced himself to finish his drink, savoring the bitter dregs. Even now, the thought of having her at his mercy, separated only by a wall, absolutely thrilled him. All that innocence at his fingertips. He would've enjoyed corrupting her, keeping her tied to his bed, even if she wasn't his enemy.

These momentary misgivings would fade. A king had to be ruthless in order to maintain control. He'd long ago accepted that he was a necessary evil.

He had her. He would keep her. Time would fade her beauty and warp her innocence.

He'd dreamed of this day for years and he wouldn't let anything ruin it, even a foolish thought of last-minute sentimentality. Revenge was a heady draught, wine made from pomegranates. Sweet with a bitter edge. He'd drink as deeply as he could.

And then he'd pour the rest down Cora's throat until she choked.

ELEVEN

"Marcus," Cora shouted for the millionth time. "Marcus!"

She dropped her head back to the mattress in frustration and humiliation. He'd just left her here, tied to the bed. She had no idea how long it had been. She'd fallen asleep for a while and she could see morning sunlight peeking through the Venetian blinds on the window. And she had to of been yelling for an hour straight with no response. Was he just going to leave her here?

"Stupid," she hissed, her throat aching and dry as she slammed her head back into the mattress. Her other bodily needs couldn't be ignored for much longer, either.

How had she gotten herself into this mess? But it wasn't like she could claim ignorance. Her mom had warned her about how dangerous the world was.

She's over-exaggerating, Cora always told herself. *She's paranoid.*

Or maybe she knew exactly what she was freaking talking about.

You're only in danger because she lied about who she was. About who Dad was.

Cora looked up at the fancy texture on the ceiling, her eyes searching out patterns. Looking for meaning where there wasn't any. Story of her life.

If Mom had only told Cora *why* she was keeping her so isolated instead of ordering her around and forbidding her from taking a step off the farm, maybe they could have worked together. But no, Demi Vestian always knew best and God help anyone who told her different.

And consequently, Cora had walked right into the lion's den without even knowing it.

"Stupid." But this time it was directed at her mother. Why couldn't she have trusted her own daughter?

Cora looked up at the hand where she'd been slowly working at her ring. It was difficult to take off a ring with only one hand.

Difficult but not impossible.

She swore she'd lose her shit if she had to wear this mark of his ownership one more second. She'd fought her whole life to be free and she wasn't giving up now.

She bit her lip as she finally managed to wiggle it past her largest knuckle, and finally off, into her hand. She gave the rope as much slack as possible on that hand by straining all her other limbs, before she flung it as far as possible to the far corner of the room. She smiled as it got lost among the greenery in the corner.

"That was poorly done, wife."

Cora's head swung toward the door, her mouth going dry. Well, drier than it already was. She was parched.

She yanked at her restraints. "Let me free."

Marcus wandered over and propped a hip on the bed. His large hand encircled her ankle and slid upwards, leaving a tingling trail in its wake. Cora fought the response but her body apparently didn't know any better. Her limbs weakened and her stomach flipped, reacting to Marcus as she always did.

"Are we ever truly free?" Marcus mused, stroking her thighs. She hated the liberties he took with her body. Hated and loved it.

"Freedom..." He looked toward the window. "It's an illusion. From the minute we're born we serve a purpose." His face turned back to her, his eyes cold. "We play a role. The gods design our lives and we are merely pawns."

Cora fought the urge to roll her eyes. It was such bullshit. "You don't believe that."

Marcus's hand trespassed closer to her throbbing core and she jerked her leg as far as it would go—almost a whole inch. She didn't know what she was angrier about, the fact that he was touching her or her own response. No, it was more than anger. She was furious. She couldn't remember ever being more furious in her entire life. He thought she was meek and pliable and that she'd be terrified of him and do whatever he said. Well he had another thing coming.

"You think you are a god," she spat. "Rich, powerful, handsome—"

"Handsome?" he raised a brow.

She ignored him, or tried as hard as she could while his fingers grazed her pussy and her body released a shot of heated serum. She bit back a groan and focused on keeping her voice steady. "You think everyone else is a mere mortal you can toy with."

"Hmmm," he considered this, his fingers tracing arcane symbols on her inner thigh.

She gritted her teeth. "Stop touching me."

Marcus seemed amused. "Why? Because you hate it? Or because it makes you feel too good?" He leaned in, his hands taking further liberties. "You belong to me. You know it. Your body knows it."

She hated him. *Hated* him. She didn't belong to anyone but herself.

She spat in his face. He jerked back, mood broken. The only sound was her harsh breathing.

She regretted it immediately. It was stupid. She was letting her anger make her reckless. She should conserve her fight and wait for the most likely chance of escape. But he'd offered her paradise and brought her to hell. And anger felt so much better than letting that hurt in.

He pulled a handkerchief from his suit coat pocket and wiped his face.

"Be careful, wife. I've killed men for lesser offenses."

And there it was. She'd shut her mind to the warnings and fooled herself. She'd defended Marcus, insisting he was a good man no matter what the papers said. No matter how Maeve tried to warn her. But now he told her the truth. He had nothing to hide.

She believed it now.

Marcus was a murderer. She was married to a monster.

But when she said it out loud he only smiled.

"You're finally beginning to see things clearly."

"It's true, then. All the things they say of you." She ought to be feeling a lot more fear in this moment. But she was so off kilter, all of this so surreal, the fear didn't penetrate.

Marcus shrugged. "You'd think they could come up with a more imaginative title than Lord of the Underworld. But rest assured, my Shades and I are the shadows that hold back the chaos in the streets of New Olympus."

"More like you profit off it," Cora muttered furiously. She knew she should stay silent, she knew it. But for him to stand here and pretend so sanctimoniously that he did what he did for any other reason than money was just—

Marcus tilted his head at her and she saw his jaw flex, but he said nothing.

"How long are you going to keep me like this?" When he still didn't reply, she tugged on the scarves. Her wrists would bear red marks for a while. "You can't keep me tied up forever."

"Can't I?"

Cora furrowed her brow. "I guess you could. But why?"

"Until you learn your place."

"My place? As what, your wife?" She slowly worked it out in her head. "A trophy on display to prove your power over the Titans?"

Marcus shook his head as he shrugged out of his coat jacket. "Maybe so."

"You're nuts." He loomed over her, dark and beautiful in the low light, removing his cufflinks and rolling up his sleeves. At the sight of his forearms, sleek and strong and dusted with dark hair, her core clenched. It was almost enough to distract her from her rage.

Almost. "If you think I'm going to forget what you've said, what you've done to me..." She clenched her teeth.

"You know how many women would kill to be in your place?"

"What, tied to your bed?" she scoffed.

He raised an arrogant brow. Why was he so handsome when he was mocking her?

"They can have you. I don't care." She turned her face away, keeping her expression blank.

"I could have them," he agreed. "A different one every night. If I wanted to tie them up, they'd beg me."

"Wow, I'm so impressed by your manly prowess," she

deadpanned. "Do you keep notches on the bedpost?" She twisted to look up at the headboard even as her stomach twisted at the images his words conjured, imagining Marcus entwined with another woman.

"You'll learn to watch that smart mouth of yours," Marcus muttered. "And what was it you said before? Rich, powerful, handsome...most women would settle for one outta three. Lucky you."

His hand dropped to her thigh. "You're the one I want. As soon as I saw you, I knew that I would have you. Here, like this." His voice deepened and despite herself, her inner muscles contracted. Marcus trailed his rough fingers over the thin skin of her inner thigh. "I knew I'd be the one to break you. We'll have such fun, angel, you and I."

She fought to hide the way her breath hitched at his touch. *Why?* Why was she still so attracted to him?

"Stop touching me," she gritted out. She couldn't think with his hand between her legs.

The gentle touch became a strong grip, solid and claiming. Her body liked that, too. "You're mine. Bought and paid for."

Every word out of his mouth only made it worse. She wasn't a whore. "That's not how it works," she spat, still fighting the pull of her body towards his with everything she had in her.

"Isn't it? I spilled blood for you, Cora."

She flinched at that and her body momentarily cooled. "The man who roofied me." The one who'd come to the dog shelter to warn her, his face mottled with bruises. *Don't think about that.* If she went down that trail, she'd start screaming.

There had been so many warnings and red flags. But she wouldn't listen, would she? She'd explained every one of them away, she'd been so blinded by Marcus. And now... "That man, he's dead, isn't he?"

"He put his hands on you. No one harms you and lives." The words might as well have been carved in stone.

"No one but you." A wave of tiredness swept through her. "What do you want from me?"

"Your submission."

Never.

She glared at him.

He bent forward and the light cupped his face. His gaze raked her naked flesh. "Your total submission. Instant, utter obedience. Your training starts now."

"Training?"

"You won't act like a wife, fine. You're still my property."

"What does that—"

"If you want off of that bed, you're gonna have to get familiar with crawling."

Her skin prickled and her chest felt hot, the fury burned hotter and hotter. "Go to h—"

"First things first," he cut her off. He pulled an item she couldn't see out of the bedside drawer, something that clinked. "You won't wear my ring, you can wear this." He held up a piece of thick leather attached to a long, glittering chain.

A collar.

"You're out of your mind," Cora whispered, staring aghast at the collar.

"On the contrary." He leaned close. So close she could smell the aftershave she used to love. But his face? His face was nothing like that of the man she thought she knew. "I've been waiting a very long time to see my enemies crawling at my feet."

She shook her head. What did he—? "I'm not your enemy," she whispered. "I barely know you."

"The sins of the father shall be visited upon the sons. Or daughter in this case. The sins of the father, Cora."

He caressed his hand down her cheek and she yanked away. Echoes of the fury and the new terrible, terrible sadness warred in her chest. She'd never had a chance with Marcus, had she? He'd always see her as her mother when he looked at her. The thought made her want to throw up. Because that meant it really all had been a farce.

How had he managed it? Kissing and touching her all those months? Holding her hand and looking into her eyes when she wore her mother's face that he so despised?

She shut her eyes. This wasn't Marcus. The Marcus she thought she knew was dead. Or worse, he never existed. She couldn't appeal to this man's humanity. He had none.

"You said you'd take care of me." It escaped anyway, a heartbroken whisper.

"I will. I will take care of you. Submit to the collar, Cora."

It was no use. She needed to harden herself, like he had. Gathering her reserves, she spat, "Go to hell."

"I see you need more time to consider your predicament. I'll come back when you're ready to assume your place."

He was almost to the door when Cora called out, "Wait! I'm sorry. Please." Even she could hear the desperation in her own voice. "I... I'm thirsty. And I need to go to the bathroom."

She closed her eyes. *It doesn't matter. They're just words.* Words didn't mean anything. And if groveling meant she could get free of being tied naked, spread-eagled to a bed, certainly she could survive a little indignity.

Because that was the key word to focus on—survive.

She'd been strong enough to survive everything her mother put her through. The years of isolation. The punishments. The emotional manipulation.

She'd survived and come out stronger.

But Marcus.

Would she be able to survive Marcus?

A shudder went down her spine even as she forced herself to look up at him and lock gazes when he peered down at her in return.

"I hate you." It popped out but this time he didn't pull back, he only chuckled. It was so wrong, hearing the same sound she used to adore, now, here in these awful circumstances, as he lifted her hair and secured the collar around her neck.

"I had this made special for you." Eyes holding hers, he clipped on a chain and tugged. Heat singed Cora's cheeks. Followed by terror. She had to get out of here. He'd just put a *collar* on her. No sane man did that. He'd *killed* people.

She couldn't stand being here another second. She had to escape.

He untied her wrists.

Steady, she whispered to herself. *Be smart. Think this through.*

But her heartbeat fluttered like a rabbit being chased down by a predator.

Run.

Marcus moved to the bottom of the bed, the chain tied to the collar around her neck clinking as he went. It didn't look like he had the best grip on it. He wasn't even looking at her as he untied her ankles.

Run.

The second he had her left ankle untied she exploded off the bed and bolted for the door.

Run!

Only to be jerked painfully backward by the collar around her neck. She choked as she was wrenched off her feet onto her ass. Coughing and gasping for breath, her hands flew to the collar.

"Ah ah ah," Marcus walked around front of her, wagging a finger calmly. He wasn't even holding the leash. He'd looped it around the headboard and that was why she'd been yanked backwards so unforgivingly.

"You really do want to be tied to the bed again, don't you? I guess we'll try this again later."

"No, no! I'll be good! I promise."

It had been fight or flight—the impulse was too strong, and she'd known there was no way she could fight Marcus. But some monkey part of her brain had thought, maybe, if she was untied, she'd be fast enough to make it to the door—

"No!" she screamed when Marcus grabbed her by the wrist and shoved her back down on the bed, landing on top of her with his body.

She thrashed to get him off but it was no use. He was twice her size and before she knew it, he had tied her collar to the headboard in a way that choked her unless she lay very still.

"Careful," he murmured. "Don't want to damage that pretty neck."

This time he took the time to pull out real, heavy leather cuffs for her wrists and feet. He soon had her wrists bound. Oh gods, no. She bit her lip hard as she fought back tears while he spent a moment stroking the red lines on her skin from her struggle with the scarves. No, he would not see her cry.

She clung to the anger and tried to stoke it again. Like a fire. Like a shield. She tried to let every ounce of hate pour from her eyes and kicked out when he grabbed her ankles. But it was no use.

Within five minutes she was spread-eagled again, this time tied more securely than before to the bed.

"We'll try this again in an hour. You'll learn to play by the rules, little girl. One way or another."

She let out a furious grunt, glaring at Marcus.

He only chuckled again as he left the room.

It took long minutes for her head to clear but finally she forced her breaths to even out. Just like she used to when mom would lock her in the cellar.

She would get through this. She'd lived through one indignity after another with her mother, hadn't she? And all because she could taste her future freedom. She'd lived in that imaginary future and let it nourish her for years.

This was just another momentary setback. But she'd escape this bastard—and not by trying to make a run for it the first moment she was free. That had been stupid. No, it would require cunning and planning and maybe even—she swallowed hard—it might even require playing along with Marcus's sick little twisted games.

No, next time she wouldn't run. She'd be the sweet little terrified girl he expected. And then when the time was right, she'd make her escape, steal out of town and eventually make Marcus Ubeli rue the day he ever thought to trap her in the first place.

TWELVE

An hour later, Marcus was back sitting at the edge of the bed, holding out a glass of water with a straw in it. He'd already taken Cora to the restroom and then reattached her collar to the headboard. He'd been prepared for her to make another run for it but she merely followed his instructions with her head bowed.

She was more subdued than she'd been during his last visit. He didn't know why he was disappointed not to see the fire in her eyes. It made his cock rock hard every time she talked back with that smart mouth of hers. And even more determined to get her to submit.

She sucked greedily at the straw.

"Not too fast or you'll get cramps."

She glared up at him. Ah, there it was. He didn't bother hiding his grin. He never imagined how much he'd like having her helpless, completely dependent on him.

Normally women were nothing more than a form of stress relief. Useful for a night's indulgence, but rarely brought back for a repeat performance. If they were, it was only because they were convenient and knew the score. He didn't need the hassle or a possible pressure point his enemies might use against him. He wouldn't make the same mistakes his father had.

But Cora was something altogether different. And he still wasn't sure how he felt about that.

"Careful," he murmured as she choked on the water. His stomach tightened as she coughed and gasped in a gulp of air, finally regaining her breath.

His entire body had been coiled, ready to turn her around and pound her on the back. What the fuck? He should enjoy the sight of her sputtering, her eyes watering.

Instead, relieved, he wiped her mouth carefully and helped her sit up to drink the rest. She stiffened but let him handle her. The feel of her warm, lithe body in his arms turned his erection painful. He had to take a moment to compose himself under the guise of setting the water glass aside.

It wasn't supposed to be like this. He had her right where he wanted her. But instead of crushing her and teaching her the merciless lesson he'd intended, he was coddling her.

Taking care of her.

It had been a problem from the beginning. Dating and courting her hadn't been as painful as it should have been. He'd taken himself in hand every night, and gotten off imagining Cora looking up at him, eyes wide and innocent and so very trusting.

Even now, he wanted to unbuckle the collar, check for marks, and soothe her sore skin. And somewhere along the line, he decided to *train* her to obey, being careful to insure she'd bend and not break.

Because even though she was his enemy, he didn't want her totally broken.

Oh yes, the gods were laughing. And Marcus was the butt of no ones' joke. He was meant to be ruthless in all things. Especially revenge. So he would turn his heart and flesh to stone, harden himself to her pleas and wide eyes, and take the pound of flesh she owed by virtue of her birthright.

Behind him, Cora sighed.

Don't ask. You're not supposed to give a damn.

"What?" he bit out.

"I'm just wondering. Do I have a tattoo on my face that says 'victim'?"

His brow wrinkled and he turned around to look at her. "What's that supposed to mean?"

"You're not the first person to take advantage of me. Oh no. There's a pattern here. I came to the city to escape it. But look what a great job I'm doing." She scoffed humorlessly. "The Donahues, then the guy who—"

"You won't ever have to deal with them again," he said before thinking.

"Oh right. You did something to the Donahues, didn't you? Threatened them. Or whatever. Still," she rocked her head back and forth, as far as the collar would let her. She wasn't looking at him. Her derision was reserved for herself. "It's always the same. I thought it was just my mother, but I'm sensing a pattern. And the common denominator is me."

Marcus forced his fists to unclench and his forearms to relax. She'd been hurt before. Why did it make him so angry? It shouldn't affect him one way or the other.

"It started with my mother, and now you—"

"What about your mother?" he interrupted.

"—you all think you can control me. And I let you. I'm

so weak. I don't want to be weak anymore." The last part came on a whisper, as if she was speaking to herself.

"What did your mother do?" Marcus forced himself to remain calm. He didn't know much about Demi other than that she'd grown up in foster care and had no family to speak of, then she married Karl Titan at 22 and had Cora a year later, her only child.

Cora scoffed, eyes to the ceiling. "What didn't she do? She locked me in the basement, held me against my will. Kept me on the farm like it was a prison. She wouldn't let me leave even for school or to socialize. Then there were the times she'd get physical, slapping or punching me if I ever stepped out of line, not to mention all the verbal abuse."

Cora shook her head. "I don't even think I've ever said it all out loud. But I was as trapped as...well, as trapped as I am now." Her mouth twisted in a mocking semblance of a smile. "She did it all to *protect* me, of course. That's what she'd tell you, if you were ever on speaking terms."

"She hurt you?" A storm brewed in his chest. The thought of Demi slapping or beating his Cora... Because she *was* his. His jaw clenched and his vision narrowed the way it did when he had an enemy in his sights. No one else had the right to put their hands on what was his.

Cora looked at him a long moment. "I survived it, Marcus." She said it so matter of factly. "I'll survive this, too."

He was doing it again. Forgetting she was the enemy. "Of course you'll survive. You'll live a long miserable life, I'll make sure of it." No one would hurt her. No one but him.

She sighed. "Did it ever occur to you that I'm just like your sister? An innocent, caught by circumstance."

"You're nothing like my sister," he bit out again. "She died, and all the good in me died with her."

It felt good to finally tell her the truth. And it was a good reminder of why she was here and the mission he'd devoted himself to since he discovered Chiara's broken and bloodied body. His jaw hardened.

"That's not true." Cora strained forward. "There is good in you. I told Maeve so because I believe—"

"That's enough." Time to teach her her place.

He unlatched her chain from the headboard and held it firmly. She made no protest when he led her out of the room.

He ought to make her crawl. He'd intended to humiliate her in every possible way. But it just didn't...feel right at the moment.

He still wanted it. Badly. To see her on her knees before him—his cock went steel just at the thought. But there was something about her willing submission, that moment when she finally gave in, the feisty spark still firing in her eyes—he was quickly becoming addicted to it.

In fact, he hoped to see it in just a few moments.

She allowed him to lead her to the table, a heavy wooden piece long enough to seat twenty where they could eat with a view of the city glittering before them.

A table set for one.

A cushion lay beside his chair. He felt the moment she saw it and recognized what it meant.

"No." She tugged away. "Uh uh."

Marcus waited, holding her leash firmly, pleasure unfurling in his stomach. It was wrong to be enjoying her training this much but after all these years of self-control, it was the one impulse he couldn't seem to deny himself.

"This is the price," he reminded her. Food already sat

on the table, plates covered by silver steam covers. The food smelled delicious and he could only imagine how it tormented her. Her stomach growled, an undeniable argument. She had to eat.

He watched the internal fight play out on her face.

And then finally, beautifully, she went to her knees.

Triumph sang through his chest. "Good girl," he murmured as she settled on the cushion.

She bristled. "I'm not your pet."

"Aren't you?" The chain clinked as he drew her forward. She waited, chin by his knee, as he removed the steam covers, releasing mouthwatering smells in a rush of steam. If he thought about how close her mouth was to his cock, he wasn't going to make it through the meal.

Instead, he tried to concentrate on a small forkful of omelet and lifting it to her mouth. She glared daggers at him. But then she opened her mouth and ate.

"See," he said after a few minutes feeding her. "This can be nice."

"This is fucked up," she muttered after swallowing the last of the omelet.

He patted her mouth with a napkin. "The Cora I knew wouldn't cuss like that."

She gave a saccharine smile. "Then you shouldn't have killed her."

His cock twitched painfully in his pants.

"Are you done? Full?"

A quiver entered her voice. "Yes." She watched him carefully, like prey would a circling predator. It ought to have disturbed him, how much he liked the image.

Enough waiting.

He rose and pushed the food plates to the floor before drawing her up. He set her on the table and splayed a hand on her chest, pressing her down. "Lie back. I want to look at you."

With a whimper, she tensed, but let him push her to her back. He propped her legs open and reseated himself. He had a full view of her private parts...everything. She was delectable. Her scent intoxicating. His breath puffed over her folds and he saw her shiver. She tried to close her legs, but his shoulders nudged them open.

Her beautiful virgin pussy. Wet and glistening for him. He licked his lips, his erection painful now. More than anything, he wanted to stand up, rip off his buckle and plunge into her wet depths. The thought of how tight she would be tormented him. He could barely sleep last night and he'd had to take himself in hand twice more before finally entering her room again this morning.

He traced her plump labia with his forefinger. "Tell me, do you touch yourself often?"

She looked stubbornly at the ceiling but her cheeks flamed pink and as he began to probe inside, even more heated juice spilled onto his fingers.

"So ready for me," he murmured.

She cursed him under her breath.

His fingers bit into her thighs. "Excuse me? What was that?"

"You heard me." He also heard how her voice quavered.

"I don't think you understand the nature of your situation. This," he covered her pussy with his palm and didn't miss the way she squirmed against him. So responsive. It drove him insane. "This is mine."

"So is this," he shoved two fingers in her mouth. Her eyes widened. "You eat when I tell you, speak when I tell you, kneel when I tell you. And you don't talk back. If you need to learn the lesson, I'm happy to teach you." He removed his fingers, wiping them on her midriff before burying his face in her cunt.

She squealed and her legs went tense around his head before relaxing and flopping open a moment later.

The sounds that came from her throat were fucking indecent. And the way she tasted. Ambrosia. The gods wished they could have feasted on her.

But she was his.

All his. Only his. Forever his.

And he was going to take her and make her his wife in every way possible so she never forgot it.

He thrust his chair back and stood up. "Stay here. Don't move."

His condoms were in the bathroom. She'd gotten a birth control shot before the wedding, but he wasn't taking any chances. The fact that he could even think straight enough to remember was a damn miracle. But he'd sworn never to bring a child into this fucked up world and not even Cora's magic pussy was enough to make him forget that most basic tenant of his life.

He stormed out of the room, only barely keeping himself from all out running. Finally, he'd sink his cock inside her. Maybe it would finally quiet the insanity she created in him. Yes, once he had her, her siren pull would ease. He'd be able to think clearly again. He could go back to the original plan.

He grabbed a condom from the box in his bathroom, on second thought grabbed two more, then turned to head back toward the dining room.

He'd imagined it a thousand times, what it would feel like to finally sink balls deep into her delectable pussy. And now he was only moments away from—

But Cora was scrambling toward the front door, chain

in hand, all but tripping over her own feet in her haste to get there before he got back.

Marcus was across the room in four strides.

She screamed when he locked his arms around her from behind. So tight he probably knocked the breath out of her, but he didn't care.

She thought she could run from *him*? She thought she could escape?

She flailed and slammed her elbow back. Fuck. He couldn't help the, "oof" that escaped his mouth. It hurt. But he didn't let her go. He would never fucking let her go. And soon she'd realize it because it was a lesson he wouldn't let her ever forget.

But then she just went insane in his arms.

"Help! Help!" She kicked out and connected with the white column that held the statue she'd admired when he first brought her to the penthouse, a million years ago. The statue hit the ground and shattered. But she didn't stop flailing, kicking and scrambling and thrashing.

"Fuck," Marcus cursed. Cora kept screaming as he carried her to the bedroom.

"Be quiet," he ordered, holding her down with his weight. "Cora. Be still!"

She froze at his barked command. He lay a hand on her heaving midriff, calming the storm. "Are you hurt?"

She looked at him like he was the crazy one.

"Lie still and let me make sure you didn't get glass in your feet." He released her and examined her bare legs. He wanted to shout at her, *what the hell were you thinking*? But he knew what she was thinking. She was trying to get away from him.

And now a shard of glass had embedded itself in her calf. Who knew what the state of her feet were. A sick feeling twisted through his stomach. He hadn't protected her. Scowling, he pulled it out. "I need to clean this. Will you stay on the bed?"

When she stared at him, he sighed. Without a word, he shackled her leg to the bedpost. It was a much longer chain, but still secured fast.

She wouldn't have gotten hurt if she'd just listened to him. He went to the bathroom and returned with a first aid kit. She jerked a little when he cleaned the tiny wound, but lay quiet and blinking as he bandaged it. He held his breath as he looked at her feet, but there wasn't any more glass. He breathed out a relieved breath.

"You need to stop fighting me. You could have really hurt yourself."

Her jaw hardened and he realized that the words had come out with more bite then he'd intended. Well, she could get over it. Things would only go one way in this marriage. His way.

Her next words only proved she didn't understand, though. "If I stop, will you leave me alone?"

"No." He closed the kit with a decisive click. He met her gaze and underneath the stubbornness, he saw her. The her she never had learned how to hide. Vulnerable. Beautiful. Precious. "I told you, Cora," he finally said more softly. "I'll take care of you."

Cora's brow furrowed like she didn't know what to make of him. But he could see it in her eyes. She wasn't resisting him, even when she said, "I can't do this." She jerked her foot, testing the shackle's hold.

"You can," he murmured. He knew how strong she was. But he needed to show her there could be strength in submission, too.

"You fight me, but you don't want me to leave you

alone." He leaned closer and she closed her eyes, like she was letting his deep voice wash over her. "Let go, Cora. Just let go, and let yourself be mine."

He slid a hand up her thigh and her breath shuddered out of her. Her leg was tense under his touch, but she didn't move.

"Let me show you," he murmured. "Let me give you a taste of what it'll be like. I can be a kind master."

Emotion rippled through her at the word *master*, her body inadvertently responding to him. Instead of disgust she felt desire. Even with eyes closed, her face betrayed her.

"We can do this the easy or the hard way. It's up to you." He kept stroking her leg. "Imagine what it would be like. To not fight. To not have to be strong. To let me keep you." His voice deepened, relaxing, hypnotic. "I can keep you safe. No one will touch you."

She stirred a little at that. "No one but you."

"But you like it when I touch you. We've established that. What makes you think you wouldn't like the rest of my rule over you?"

A little sigh. Her body stretched before him, flushed and perfect, made by the gods to be claimed and plundered by him. She was open and compliant as he touched her, clay in his hands. Even though he'd hardened himself, he felt the strangest stirring.

What if—? What if it could be like this? Days with her on his arm, by his side, and nights with her yielding to him?

He wouldn't just *be* the most powerful man in the world. He'd *feel* like it, too. Everything he'd built, everything he'd done, all the shit and grit and sin he'd waded through for years... what if it could all be for her? Innocence put on a pedestal and guarded like the precious thing she was. His wife, his trophy and reward.

He just had to mold her...

Slowly, he shifted and seated himself on the bed where she could still reach him, even with the chain. "Come lie over my lap."

She blinked at him, brow furrowed. Uncertainty warred with curiosity.

"Now, angel," he said, still gentle. "Or it'll be worse for you."

She moved, crawling over the bed to him, and he hid a smile. He'd read the signs right. She wanted to fight, but her instincts told her to submit.

He'd show her she wasn't fighting him as much as herself.

His cock hardened as she draped her lithe body over his legs. *Later.* He'd relieve himself later. Right now, he needed to focus on her.

"What...what are you doing?" Her voice was small and uncertain.

"I'm going to teach you a lesson," he said in a soothing voice, rubbing her pert bottom. She shifted and he squeezed harder a silent order to be still. She obeyed right away, letting her light weight collapse on his hard thighs. His cock rose in his pants, brushing her belly. Every breath she took, he felt.

Gods, this might kill him.

He focused on massaging her ass and the backs of her thighs, working out knots. Preparing her for punishment.

"That feels good," she mumbled.

"That's right. Be a good girl and I'll make you feel good. There's no need to fight. You won't win."

She gave a little huff, but kept still. He rubbed the place between her legs and she jerked, her shoulders tense.

"Easy," he soothed like she was a wild horse. "Let me make you feel good."

He felt the moment she decided to surrender as she finally relaxed into his touch. She'd pushed the boundaries as far as she could and now, tired of fighting, she could submit. He withdrew his fingers and she gave a gusty sigh.

"I'm gonna spank you now," he told her firmly, "and you're going to take it. You know why you're being punished?" he paused, but she remained silent. "You ran from me. You can't do that, Cora. You'll only end up hurt. I can't protect you if you don't obey."

"I'm never going to obey you." A defiant whisper. The last of her resistance.

"You will. I'll teach you." He squeezed her right cheek hard enough to press a white patch on her bottom, outlined in red. He smacked her left cheek lightly, enjoying the ripple through her firm flesh.

His palm clapped down harder, one cheek and then the other. She wriggled and he gritted his teeth against the torment of stimulation to his leaking cock. He was in charge. He would not lose control and rut her like he wanted to, so badly. Not until she earned it.

He weighted her legs down with one of his, holding her with a large hand in the small of her back. After a token struggle, she gave up, her body growing loose and languid, accepting of each swat on her bare ass.

As far as spankings went, this was a light one, enough to sting but not enough to bruise. Marcus didn't miss the hitch of her breath or the slight shift of her hips as he spanked close to her pussy. He used his leg to split her thighs apart, and saw with satisfaction that her folds were glistening.

"You're doing so well," he purred. "Submitting. Taking your punishment. Such a good girl."

She didn't answer, but he didn't need her to. The slick serum leaking between her legs, dampening his slacks told him how she really felt. But hadn't he known all along? There was an undercurrent to the undeniable attraction they had for each other. He dominated and she obeyed. They'd cleaved together in the easy dance, her yielding power, him taking it, since the first moment they'd met.

If she wasn't the enemy, Marcus would say she was his missing half. Only she could make him whole.

But she was the enemy, and he knew better than to succumb to her charms. He'd mold her and master her until she knew her place—at his feet—and his inexorable rule over her. The small voice that told him it would be better if she freely came to him to submit... He shook his head against the thought. That was weakness and had no place in his reasoning.

Cora whimpered and he palmed her right ass cheek. Her pale skin was flushed, warm to the touch. He'd spanked her with increasing intensity and she'd accepted it.

Part one of the punishment was over. Time for part two.

His hand slipped between her legs, finding the slick furrows on either side of her clit and stroking. She writhed and he weighted her down, his fingers never pausing in their rhythm.

"Stop fighting," he said. "Just enjoy it."

"I shouldn't..." Her words were slurred like she was drunk. Drunk on endorphins. Drunk on him.

"Do you want me to stop?"

An endless pause before she answered in a clearer voice, "No."

Marcus allowed himself a satisfied smirk.

He eased his grip on her, giving her freedom to wriggle away if she wanted. She stayed still and he rewarded her, strumming her like an instrument, her gasps and moans a music of his making. He played her to perfection until she stiffened and gasped and came, soaking his hand and his crisp white shirt cuffs.

"Good," he praised her. "So very good."

But he wasn't done. Once wasn't nearly enough to get his point across. And he couldn't keep his hands off her flesh even if it was.

He rubbed her pink bottom and shifted his leg off hers. She didn't move though, and didn't protest when he spanked her again, round after round interspersed with rubbing her needy flesh until she came and came and came.

The third time she forgot herself and moaned loudly and wildly as her orgasm hit, which only drove Marcus to demand more of her. By the fifth, she was exhausted and mewling her release but it was all the sweeter, watching her sweat-dampened face, all confusion and fight faded to sweet, sweet surrender.

Her legs splayed open freely and she pressed her bottom against his hand even when he wasn't pleasuring her. In this moment she was his and his completely. And he'd never felt more like a king.

It wasn't until after, when he stood over her limp and sated body, that he realized his mistake. That every gasp and inadvertent squeeze of her cunt on his fingers was a link in a chain, locking him to her as securely as he'd tied her to his bed.

He waited a long time, watching her sleep, too hard to think straight, too tangled up in her to leave.

THIRTEEN

Cora jerked out of her dream. A nightmare. She'd stood at her wedding, said her vows, and then Marcus turned into a monster and carried her off. She'd screamed and reached out to the wedding guests for help but Armand and all the rest only sipped their drinks and laughed.

She squeezed her eyes shut again and rolled to her side. Something tugged her ankle with a clink. The chain.

It wasn't a dream.

The wedding. The wedding night when he'd filmed the whole thing and been so cruel... But then he'd changed again. He was so tender after she'd broken the statue. Then the... punishment.

It had been humiliating to be taken over his knee like that, but she told herself she was allowing it because she needed to get underneath his defenses. Trying to make a run for it again had been just as stupid and useless as the first time.

She just needed to outsmart him. To play by his rules for a little while. Give him what he wanted and gain his trust. Already he'd made her leash longer. He couldn't keep her here locked up forever.

He wanted her as a trophy and what fun was a trophy if you couldn't show it off in public? If she played his games, maybe he'd give her more and more leeway, and then she could make her escape once she had a real shot at it.

The problem was, once his 'punishment' had started...

Her eyes all but rolled back in her head as she remembered. At first it was just a confusing mix of pain and pleasure while he spanked her.

But then...it went somewhere else entirely. She didn't even know how to explain it. It was like she'd floated off the ground while still being in her own body. Like a timeout from real life where she didn't have to worry about anything except sensation. And pleasure, oh, the *pleasure*. She hadn't even known it was possible to come that many times.

She gave over her body to him, leaping off a cliff and knowing, just absolutely *knowing* that he would catch her.

What the hell was that about?

Her cheeks heated and her stomach went liquid at the memories. Every time he touched her, she melted.

She scrubbed her hands down her face and looked out the window. She didn't know how long she'd napped. It looked like it might be nearing sunset.

She slipped off the bed, testing her new, longer leash. The chain let her go to the bathroom, if she sat with her foot outstretched. How generous.

The shackle around her ankle didn't have a lock to pick, as far as she could tell. Same with the collar.

You won't act like a wife, fine. You're still my property.

She clenched her teeth, shaking off memories of the confusing pleasure. Fuck that. Just because he could play her body like a violin didn't change anything.

"Yeah, I said 'fuck,'" she said, looking around the room. "Get used to it." Her mother taught her good girls didn't swear, but where had being good gotten her?

Tied to her bed on her wedding night.

She spent long minutes testing the strength of the chain and the bedpost securing it before giving up.

She glared up again at the camera in the corner, red light still blinking at her. "I'm hungry," she announced. She was only a little bit hungry after the filling breakfast earlier, but she had the feeling it was a request Marcus wouldn't ignore. He seemed to have a thing about taking care of her physical needs. She'd bet that in a minute, Marcus would enter and tell her whatever humiliating task she had to perform for food. And she'd do it.

Submit. Survive. Escape.

"Any day now," she muttered, flopping back on the bed. She was still naked. Her new husband seemed to like her like this. Helpless. Naked. Chained. The sick fuck.

She ran her hands over her arms and then her chest. She'd gotten through her first day of marriage. What would tonight bring?

More of the same, no doubt. He would come for her and she would bend, bow and scrape. She couldn't help it. Something in her responded to him. He held all the cards, but she'd do anything to stay in the game. So yes, she'd bend. But she wouldn't break. She'd remain her own no matter what he did.

No matter how many times he called her, "*Mine.*"

Long minutes passed and he didn't come. Was it because he knew she was trying to exert some small control over the situation? She crossed her arms over her chest but she couldn't help her thoughts from straying where they always did. His body strong and beautiful as a god's, powerful, all consuming. Thinking about it, her breath came faster and her nipples pebbled.

How could she resist his power over her?

Stroking her right arm absently, her wrist brushed her nipple. Heat shot from the tight bud to her awakened core. Whenever Marcus walked into a room, her body came alive.

Maybe she could... No, she shouldn't...

But what if she did?

She bit her lip. And then, easing back, she opened her legs. The first graze of her fingers was like the coming of spring, warmth breathing over the land. The heat unfurled and bloomed with a thousand petals bursting open. She'd never dared touch herself before. Her body was a secret garden and only one man held the key.

Fuck that. Her finger dipped into her wet channel, spreading silky slick over her inner folds.

Why had she waited so long to do this? This wasn't shameful or indecent. It felt—

"Ohhhhhhh," she groaned, her legs tightening, her eyelids fluttering closed. The pad of her finger found a spot that sent electric sparks through her.

Forget Marcus, she could please herself.

On second thought, *Marcus...* His hard face filled her vision, silver eyes flashing, the points of his cheeks tinged red with anger and arousal. *Mmmm,* yes, right there.

Her back arched as her finger circled her clit. So good.

She blinked languorously—

"Marcus!" she yelped and scooted back, giving herself room to sit up.

Her husband loomed over her.

"Enjoying yourself, wife?" There was a world of tension in the word 'wife.'

"Actually, I am." Her voice came out an airy squeak, with nothing of the defiance she intended.

He followed her, a storm cloud dark with barely controlled violence. He gripped her wrist, brought it to his lips. He held her gaze as he sucked her fingers into his mouth.

She whimpered, pressing her thighs together. Who was she kidding? The pleasure brewing between her legs was a volcano now compared to the flickering flame of her earlier arousal. Marcus cleaned her essence off her fingers, tongue curling around each delicate digit until she closed her eyes, dizzy with pleasure.

His left hand cupped the place between her legs. "This belongs to me. You feel pain and pleasure only at my command." For a beautiful moment, the heel of his hand grazed her clitoris. A shockwave rolled through her.

He released her and it was gone. Cora bit back a moan. Her body throbbed, mourning the loss.

"Well, excuse me, lord and master." There was her defiance. Apparently losing out on an orgasm made her cranky and unhinged her brain from all survival instinct, because she kept snarking. "I didn't realize you were going to take over all my body functions."

"Everything, Cora. All of you belongs to me."

She swung her legs over the side of the bed. "Well in that case, *your* stomach is hungry. Feed me."

He moved to the bedpost and crouched next to the chain. His body blocked her view, so she didn't see how the mechanism worked.

Next time. He had to slip up at some point.

He returned with the chain in hand and gave it a thoughtful tug. "I'll feed you. But you'll still be punished for touching what belongs to me."

"How are you going to punish me this time? Tie me up? Humiliate me? Spank me? Oh wait, you've already done all that."

"You think this is the worst that could happen?" he wound the chain around his wrist, tugging her upwards.

She came to her feet, quivering at his closeness. She wanted to rage at him, to beat his chest and scream and rip out his heart like he'd ripped out hers. The rest of her wanted him to touch her, strong and sure and gentle, satisfying the hunger that beat inside her.

He drew her up on tiptoes. She gave him her best glare, but she was caught and at his mercy, a fish on a line.

He opened his mouth to say something and her stomach growled loud enough to echo through the room.

Marcus closed his mouth, amusement glimmering in his silver eyes. "Hungry?"

"Already told you I was." She could fight him better with a full belly.

Dinner was much the same as breakfast. Her on the cushion at his feet. Him feeding her filet mignon bite by delicious bite. Sometimes he didn't use the fork. He made her suck the juices off his fingers.

And she did it, becoming wetter and wetter each time, especially when his thumb lingered in her mouth, caressing her bottom lip and dragging down her throat to her chest where he plucked at her nipples.

She moaned helplessly, so riled up she was sure that he could make her come with only a few swipes of his fingers. Or better yet, his tongue.

When dinner was finished, he didn't lift her up on the table like before. And when he took her back to the room, he merely reattached her chain to the bed.

And then.

He.

Left.

"Wait," Cora said, "where you going?

He turned at the threshold and looked back at her. "Miss me already? Do you want me to stay?" There was a hungry wolf in his eyes as he asked it.

"No," Cora said automatically. "I hate you."

"Well, your wish is my command," he said, completely solicitous. The next second, though, the wolf was back, all predator. "But if I so much as see your hand brush that pussy that belongs to me without my say-so, believe me, you will not like the consequences. You'll wish for the days when you were merely tied to the bed." The ice in his voice sent a shiver down Cora's spine.

She lifted her chin and glared at him. "Get out if you're going to go. I can't stand to look at you another second."

His mouth lifted in a half smile. "Beware what you wish for, little girl."

And then he was gone.

FOURTEEN

Cora rested on the heavy cushion, leaning against her husband's leg. Above her head, on the desk, the keyboard crackled as Marcus typed.

This wasn't what she thought her honeymoon would be.

Walking around naked, posing for her husband, letting him lead her with a collar and chain like a pet? Curling up on a cushion at his feet and dozing the day away. At night she slept with a chain leashing her to the bed. She didn't dare complain in case he decided to tie her up completely again.

She didn't even know what day it was. Maybe five days since the wedding? Six?

Several times a day, sometimes after a meal, sometimes out of the blue, he'd press her to the floor or lift her onto his office or dining room table or the floor. And then he'd toy with her and lick her and tease and torture her...all the way until she was *riiiiiiiiiiiiight* on the edge of coming.

And then he'd stop and go back to whatever he'd been doing as if nothing at all was the matter. Always with the threat of tying her to the bed again if she dared touch herself to finish off what he'd started.

She was so damn stir-crazy and horny and on edge, sometimes she wondered if it might be worth it. Just once. If only she could come just *once*.

She didn't know how he'd done it. Sex wasn't anything that had even been on her radar until Marcus.

But ever since she'd felt his hands on her body and experienced the kind of pleasure he could wring out of her...it was like those drugs they said you only had to try once or twice to become addicted.

Well, she felt addicted to sex now...and she was still a virgin! What would it be like if they finally...?

She swallowed and glanced up at Marcus. Even worse, she had a horrible suspicion that her addiction was Marcus-specific.

Above her head his fingers flew on the keyboard. He wanted her next to him, kneeling on the cushion while he worked. Curled up at his feet like she really was a pet.

The second day he chained her to his desk, she got vocal. "How long are you going to keep this up for? You can't just chain me like a dog wherever you go. I'm a person, damn you."

No response.

"Hey, I'm talking to you." She'd shoved his legs underneath the table.

He responded then all right. He gagged her and cuffed her hands behind her back and that was how she spent all of day two until bedtime. Other than the three times he'd driven her to the brink of orgasm and pulled back at the last possible second, leaving her so wanting she was glad for the gag because in that moment she would have begged and pleaded and promised him anything if only he'd please, *please* finished what he'd started.

Thankfully she'd gotten herself under control by the time he released the gag before bed, and all she wanted to do was scream in his face. Scream and kick and punch and scream some more. But she bit her damn lip because after a day going out of her mind with boredom and the devastating bouts of pleasure stopped just short of orgasm, she was beginning to get the picture.

This was about power.

And him letting her know that she didn't have any.

Day three was little better. She spoke up a few times. "Can I at least have a book to read? Paper to draw on?" She wasn't an artist by any means but even doodling would feel like extreme intellectual stimulation at this point.

She'd already examined every inch of his penthouse office by this point, counted every one of the 113 books on his bookshelf—most of them dry looking business and accounting books with a small section of Stephen King novels—and spent hours looking for faces and shapes in the artfully spackled drywall.

Unsurprisingly, there had been, shocker, *no response*.

The daytime chain he allowed her was slightly longer than the nighttime one. She could sit up at his feet while he worked at his desk. Another thing she was grateful for and furious at her own gratitude.

One thing was clear, Marcus Ubeli was a master manipulator. He had been from the beginning.

Today she sat at his feet, her mind stewing.

She was angry, bored, frustrated, and so, so horny.

She sighed and ducked her head, examining the fraying edges of her manicure. She thought she was so fancy, going to the spa, getting ready for her wedding. If she could send herself a note, she would've told herself to ditch everything and run.

Not that the old Cora would believe her. She'd believed in fairy tales, in handsome businessman meeting a beautiful, young woman and falling in love. Sweeping the girl off her feet. A wedding of her dreams and life of wedded bliss.

She should write the authors of those fairy tales and tell them they were full of shit.

She wiggled to get into a different folded position. Her legs kept falling asleep. Marcus didn't speak, but rested a hand on her collar in silent warning to be still.

"This sucks," she blurted.

The keyboard went silent. Oops. Marcus was scarier when he was still, a shark sensing blood in the water. She'd poked the bear. Oh well, too late now.

"I'm bored."

"You expect to be entertained?" Grown men would go mad with fear if Marcus spoke to them like that. She stared at the carpet and said nothing. Because he'd spoken to her. Finally, after days of silence, he'd finally spoken again. She thought she'd overexaggerated the low sinful timbre of his voice in her head but, no, every syllable was a rasp that went straight to her sex.

A click and Marcus pushed the closed laptop away. Then she was up, tugged and lifted onto the desk, facing those scary grey eyes. Marcus ran his hands over her arms, studying her bare breasts.

He didn't look angry or annoyed. More, thoughtful. He stroked her hair back from the collar, sifting a corn silk lock between his fingers. Heat bloomed in her, rising to her cheeks, making her dizzy. A few simple touches and her body primed itself for him.

From the smirk etched around his mouth, Marcus knew it.

"Time for your punishment," he told her, and pushed her legs apart.

"Marcus—"

He propped a finger at her lips. "Quiet, angel."

Her eyes widened. He hadn't called her angel in a while. Well he hadn't called her anything considering he hadn't been speaking to her, but *angel* hit her in her solar plexus. Which was so, so, stupid.

But then he was touching her and the world went hazy. He took his time, palming her knee and positioning her thighs wider, treating them to tiny strokes that seared her core. He inspected her often like this, and she submitted. She was always wet, and when he stopped, she always undeniably wanted more.

She shook her head, unable to reconcile the ugliness of her situation with the beautiful things he made her feel.

"Poor neglected pussy," he mocked, swiping his thumb over her folds gently. She'd object to the tone, but didn't want him to stop. Maybe, since he was talking to her again, it meant he'd finally stop torturing her. But she didn't dare ask out loud. No, her begging was all silent.

Don't stop. Keep touching. Right there—

"Close?" His long eyelashes flicked up to her face. Her hips danced and his left hand steadied her. He leaned in, pinning her left leg under his elbow as he bent his head close—so close— He was— Oh—

His tongue swirled over her slick skin, finding the needy points, soothing them, increasing the ache. Her hips bucked and he chuckled, hot breath puffing over her sensitive flesh.

"Marcus," she wanted to grab his silky hair and tug him close but didn't dare. "Please—"

A few more licks and she was so close. So close—

Marcus scooted back in his chair.

No!

And lifted her back to the cushion at his feet.

NO!

He meant to leave her unsatisfied *again*.

She glared at his shiny black shoes underneath the desk. Her jaw locked. He pulled the laptop to the middle of the desk and started typing again, like nothing at all had just happened.

Cora's fists clenched. He could toss her away so easily. He made her mad with want but he was Mr. Unaffected.

Marcus saw her family as strong. These uncles Cora had never known about.

But Marcus saw her as weak, merely a pawn to play against them.

It didn't matter that she didn't even know her uncles. Or her father. Her father who had killed an innocent *girl*.

That was the blood running through her veins. A murderous father and mother so overprotective, it bordered on abusive.

Cora scoffed. Who was she kidding? It had gone over the border on more than one occasion. All the time, in fact. She hadn't even known how abnormal it was until she got out into the world and learned how other people lived.

And now here Cora was, falling back into her same old patterns. Head down, yes ma'am, yes ma'am, whatever you say, Mom. Except replacing her mother with Marcus. Better to follow the rules than endure the punishment.

Cora shook her head and looked down at herself.

The chains might be new but the slavery wasn't.

She thought she could change. She'd sworn she *was* changing. Had changed.

But here she was again with her head bowed down, waiting for someone else to decide her fate.

And then she got a crazy idea.

An absolutely fucking absurd idea.

She looked towards Marcus's legs underneath the tall desk and felt like giggling hysterically. Well, he certainly wouldn't be able to ignore her existence if she...

Images flashed in her head of Marcus walking around the bedroom each night after he'd showered. He liked putting his body on display for her. She thought back to the past few days and the hungry way he'd lapped at her sex. He hadn't been indifferent then. It wasn't just to 'punish' her. Even now, she could see his cock straining against his dress pants.

Cora's insides tingled thinking about it all.

Thinking, that was the problem. Or rather, *over*thinking.

So she decided to stop. Thinking. Overthinking. All of it.

It was time to take action.

She crawled underneath the table.

Between Marcus's legs.

She'd been married for over a week and hadn't even gotten to touch him. To touch *it*. So she reached for his belt buckle.

He jolted in his chair when she made contact and began to undo the buckle. But that was all. He didn't say a word or move to stop her.

Was this a game of chicken? Who would flinch first?

It wouldn't be her. Not because she had nothing to lose. She had plenty to lose still. She wouldn't flinch, though, because she was actually curious to see this through.

Curious and afraid, but that was nothing new.

So when she finished with the belt, she quickly moved to unbutton and unzip his pants.

The audible hiss he expelled above her? Now *that* was gratifying.

Here was power. Was it a fucked up way of getting some back? No doubt. Wasn't stopping her.

She reached into his pants and slid her hand between the slit in his boxers.

In a sudden motion, his strong hand came down and clenched around her wrist.

She took a page from his book and ignored him, saying not one word.

He was thick and round and firm in her grasp. Soft over steel. It was dim underneath the desk but she could still make out the basic shape of him.

And her eyes went wide.

It wasn't the first time she'd seen it. But seeing and touching were two different things. And the way it hardened and grew in her grasp—

Her gasp escaped before she could muffle it.

As quickly as his hand had taken hold of her wrist, he released her. Interesting. He was going to allow her to continue her explorations.

Was it because he was male and it was true what they said, that no man would turn down sex? But he'd had her at his mercy for a while now and other than that first night, she hadn't even seen him take himself in hand.

Because sex was about power to him. Did he still think he had the power in the situation just because she was the one on her knees?

Even the thought infuriated her.

She would show him. She was not a pawn in somebody else's game. She was a motherfucking player.

So, pushing all other thoughts out of her mind, she went up on her knees and took the bulbous tip of his sex into her mouth.

"Gods," he choked.

Cora smiled and licked all around the tip. It was curiously salty and a little bit bitter. She grasped the bottom of his shaft with both her hands—he was large enough it took both—and took more of him into her mouth.

He leaned back in his chair and widened his legs further. She saw his stomach flatten and heave as she started to work him, in and out, in and out, just the head.

She'd never done it before, but she'd read. She'd read a lot. First in her romance books and then, as her wedding day neared, everything else she could get her hands on, well, apart from the Internet which still scared her. But plenty of women's magazines had lengthy articles on the art of giving your man the perfect BJ and Cora employed every tactic she'd ever read about.

Spelling out the alphabet on the very tip of his...his *cock*, right where she felt the tiniest slit. Bobbing up and down with her lips over her teeth, making sure to pay special attention to the ridge of his crown while still rolling the flesh of his shaft up and down. And every so often, taking him deep, as deep as she could manage without choking.

When she decided to employ yet another tip, reaching down and tugging on his balls, he shoved his chair back and pulled himself out of her mouth.

Cora fell forward onto her hands, looking up for the first time into his face since she'd begun. She wasn't sure what she expected to find there but it was better than she could've hoped for.

He did not look cold. He did not look distant.

There were two spots of color high up on his cheekbones, accentuating the sharp cut of them even more. His eyes were wide and his nostrils flared with every heaved breath. His heavy cock jutted out from the front of his unzipped pants and Cora couldn't help but stare. She'd just had that in her *mouth*?

What the hell had she been thinking?

She swiped at her mouth with her forearm and above her, Marcus let out a low growl like an animal might.

Definitely not disinterested. Or indifferent.

Oh shit.

Marcus reached for her and she scrambled back but he shoved the table out of the way. Shoved. The. Table.

The next thing she knew, he was bent over and unlocking the chain attached to her collar. He gathered her up in his arms and he was carrying her.

Okaaaaaaaay, so this was unexpected.

"Marcus," she whispered.

He didn't respond. What he *did* do was carry her to his bedroom.

He laid her out in the center of his bed and he followed after.

For the first time in days, he looked her in the eyes. It was stupid, but her breath caught. His gorgeous, intense, demanding eyes. He still didn't say anything, but he held her gaze as he slid his hand down her stomach.

He caught her chin and her eyes searched his. She had no idea what he was thinking. What was he thinking?

"Undress me," he hissed.

She swallowed and nodded. Her fingers found the buttons of his expensive Italian shirt. *Steady, steady. Just breathe.* Ignore the solid plane of his chest. Ignore the tiny jolts of electricity zapping her every time her knuckles brushed him. Ignore the stutter in his indrawn breath, the demanding length poking her bare thigh, promising pleasure and pain when the time came to tear her open.

This was it. She knew it was. There was no more waiting, no more teasing, no more half measures.

The white shirt fell away, revealing strong forearms. He helped her peel off his undershirt and then—

Dear gods above. Faced with a wall of smooth, firm muscle, olive skin dusted with a little dark hair, she swayed on her knees. She knew Marcus was strong, but hadn't contemplated the acres of muscle under his tailored suits. Now, half naked before her, he was just so...big. His head towered over hers. Her hands couldn't fit around his upper arm.

He caught her wrists, drawing her close. His head ducked, his lips caught hers for a hard, claiming kiss. His erection dug into her thigh until she swiveled her hips, pushing her throbbing parts into the satisfying length of him. She was a virgin, never had anything inside her, but she wanted it. Oh how she wanted it...

When Marcus broke the kiss, her lips were throbbing, swollen.

"This," his big hand slid over her bottom and squeezed. "Is mine."

She nodded frantically, tears pooling in the corners of her eyes. She wanted him to take, to own her. She needed it.

Marcus let out a groan that told her he was as undone as she felt.

"No one but me, Cora. No one touches you but me."

He laid her down, hands catching her hips. "Spread for me, baby."

She propped her legs apart. He dove between them, dark head working.

No. Her head flew back. No, no, no.

The gleam in his eyes did it. *YES*. She flew apart. Finally after so many days of teasing. But it wasn't enough, there and then gone too soon. She needed more. She needed so much more.

And there he was, still watching her, so focused, so single-minded. Her hands lifted to his shoulders as he moved over her body. She couldn't look away as she felt him reach down and position himself.

He was preparing to enter her.

To *enter her,* enter her.

She swallowed and unwittingly, her fingertips dug into his shoulders.

But he paused, his voice strained and gravelly. "You say no right now and I stop."

His eyes searched hers back and forth.

Say something. Tell him no. Hell fucking no. What was she even doing?

Earlier... Sucking his... That was about taking her power back. But this? Letting him... Who had the power now?

But the look on his face, damn him, she was right back where she'd been the moment she was walking down the aisle toward the man she loved with all her heart. His features were gentled and there was something raw in his usually hardened face.

Another manipulation.

But damn it to hell, instead of saying no, she nodded her head yes.

And he was there, pressing in at her most intimate place. Fear struck. She remembered how huge he was. He'd split her in two.

But he shook his head ever so slightly like he could sense her fear. And while he didn't stop, no she could see he wouldn't, couldn't stop now that he had begun, he pushed forward slowly, carefully.

Cora felt it the moment he came up against her barrier and so did he. Cora could see it in his eyes. He didn't stop, though, and she didn't want him to. She nodded again and he pushed forwards. Her hip twitched and there was a sharp pinch before her flesh gave way. He sank deeper. She closed her eyes and clutched his shoulders.

"Look at me," he demanded.

Why? *Why?* He knew what she was giving. She'd been a fool to think she could ever wrest any power away from this man. He was an unstoppable force and to him she was nothing but a wildflower, here today and paved over tomorrow.

"Cora, give me your eyes."

Her throat stung as she opened her eyes. She felt the tears as they rolled down her temples and into her hair.

Marcus's sharp eyebrows were drawn together, his huge body looming over her small one, as he worked himself inside her, inch by inch.

Her breath caught as he probed the tight fist of her inner muscles. "Easy. Open...open for me."

Her hands clawed his back, caught his strong shoulders, and hung on.

"That's it," his breath tickled her ear. "Hold tight to me."

The pressure grew. She gritted her teeth, ducking her head to hide in the curve of Marcus's throat. He was a rock, immovable. She was the ocean, ebbing, moving around him.

Slowly her body opened, her legs softening even as the pain swam through her.

"Yes. Yes, that's it, beautiful. Give yourself to me."

"Marcus," she rasped. Tremors ran through her head to

toe. His hips melded with hers as he invaded her. When he stopped, fully rooted, thrills ran down her sides. Her chest rose and fell, nipples hardened to diamond points.

Marcus held himself over her, his arms taut by her face. His head was bowed, dark lashes casting shadows on his cheeks. His lips moved slightly.

If she didn't know different, she'd guess he was praying. She felt like praying too. They were fully merged, his body towering over hers, protecting and claiming her.

This was what heaven felt like.

She'd never felt more connected to another human being.

The pain ebbed and he began to move. Slow rocks at first, nudging further into her inner sanctum, trespassing boldly. The strong ridge of his manhood rubbed a delicious part of her and Cora raised her hips, seeking more.

"Cora," he rasped, and there was a world of possibility in her name. Her fingers passed over his face as if she were blind and wanted to memorize the cut of his features. In this room, this dark womb, she would forget all the hurt he'd done her.

"Marcus," she turned her face up to his. He dragged his lips over her mouth, her cheek, the corner of her eye, giving her silent, bruising promises as his body reaped pleasure from hers. He made a prolonged, male sound, pushing deeper. His eyes were closed, his face intent as if he'd found something important, something beautiful he'd longed for, but never hoped to experience.

Yes, she prayed. *Marcus, come back to me.* He groaned again, the muscles in his back turning to steel under her stroking hands.

She felt it. For the first time, she understood how the

entire act worked in harmony, every part of his body so perfectly made to bring pleasure to every part of hers.

He was made for her.

"Oh gods," she cried out. "Oh...oh...*oh! Marcus!*"

Her chest thrust up and out and she clung to him, her fingers in his hair as the climax hit, bright and beautiful, and so, so right. Yes, *yes*. This. *Him*.

A thrust, two, three, and he rooted himself deep and stayed there. She held on and hoped she read the signs right.

After an eternity, he pulled out. She hissed, her insides protesting.

"You all right?" he searched her face.

"I'm good." Her legs were noodles, her muscles over-stretched. She'd be sore tomorrow.

"That was...thank you." She shouldn't thank her captor. But this was Marcus. He'd come back to her for a moment and for a moment, it was beautiful.

"Yes. You did well." He parted her legs and studied the stains on the sheets. Watery blossoms, evidence of her virginity. She covered her cheeks. She shouldn't be embarrassed, but it seemed more intimate. She'd bled for him. Her blood mingled with his seed.

But then something seemed to come over his face and he turned away from her. Long seconds ticked by. Finally, his back stiffened and then he looked over his shoulder.

"Not bad, for a virgin." She flinched and met his mercury stare, horror rising in her as he said, "I know I'll watch the recording of this many times. And I think your uncles will really appreciate Part II of the wedding video, especially when you screamed my name and came all over my cock."

With a dark smirk, he nodded toward the corner camera.

The blood left her face. No. Not after all this. They couldn't be back to where they'd started. She'd seen the way he'd looked at her when he was deep inside her. She'd seen it in his *eyes*...hadn't she?

The pain twisting her guts felt like that first night all over again when he'd first betrayed her.

But she didn't say a word or speak up for herself as, without another word, he left the room.

FIFTEEN

Well, that had not gone according to plan.

Not the sex and not his cruel comments afterward. It was a lie about the cameras recording. He always turned the cameras off whenever he was with her.

And gods knew he thought about taking her virginity. Thought about it all damn week and for the months before. But this last week, fuck, every time he teased and tasted her, every time his cock grew painful in his pants, all he could think about was finally taking her and making her *his*.

But he was training her and training meant discipline. Patience. Making her crave him and pleasing him above all else.

He just hadn't expected— He never could have prepared himself for—

He hadn't even worn a condom. And if he had it to do again, he would have done it the same way. She'd gotten the shot almost a month ago and fuck, feeling her virgin pussy, nothing between them, with how she clenched like a vise around him—

He scrubbed a hand down his face and watched her on

the monitor even though he was disgusted at himself for doing it. Every second he wasn't in her presence, he found himself glued to this damn screen. She was supposed to be obsessed with him, not the other way around.

He was about to shove his laptop screen shut when he saw her back start to shake.

Fuck. She was crying.

She looked so tiny in the big bed.

He dragged a hand through his hair, remembering every moment of when she'd taken him into her body, so hot and tight—she'd gripped him like a vice—eyes wide, without guile—

Like an innocent. She was a virgin. He'd known she was, but knowing and experiencing were two different things.

And when her orgasm had hit, milking his climax out of him at the same time, she'd looked at him like he was a god himself, like she'd worship at his feet forever and give him her submission along with her whole self and her soul, too.

The problem was, he was terrified he might have been looking at her the same way.

So he'd shut it down and reminded them both of who they were.

And now she was crying.

Marcus wanted to hit something. She wasn't playing by the rules. This wasn't how it was meant to go. None of this was going according to plan.

His phone rang once, loudly in the otherwise silent room. Marcus snatched it out of his pocket, never more glad for the distraction.

"What?" Marcus barked.

"We got a situation," Sharo's voice rumbled.

"Don't tell me I gotta come down."

"You gotta come down." Sharo confirmed.

He gave a sharp nod even though Sharo couldn't see him. Maybe getting out of here was exactly what he needed. He needed to get his head together, that was for damn sure.

"Be there in twenty." Marcus hung up and stood. He went to his bedroom and dressed in quick, practiced movements.

He meant to leave right then and there. But, without fully intending to, his feet took him to Cora's door.

Leave. You only did what had to be done. She's the enemy.

He stood frozen for several more moments. And then he quietly opened the door.

Cora was laying down now and he walked to the bed. He didn't know what he meant to say when he got close, but then he saw it didn't matter. She'd cried herself to sleep.

She was beautiful in repose, but then she was beautiful no matter what she was doing. Sleep didn't erase the furrow of distress on her brow. Was she dreaming of him?

His eyes squeezed shut. *Sentimental idiot.*

Still, he couldn't leave without giving her something. She'd be sore when she woke. Even though it had been her first time, he hadn't taken it easy on her. The least he could do was give her the means to take a bath in peace.

He ran a hand gently down her calf and when she didn't wake, he undid the ankle cuff and freed her from the bed post.

"Sleep well, wife," he murmured. She didn't so much as twitch.

Without another word, he turned and flipped the lock he'd had installed outside her door as he left. Then he strode for the front door and soon he was in his Bentley, his driver speeding toward the Styx.

No, tonight had not gone according to plan.

But nothing with Cora ever had. She was never supposed to show up in his office that night, bedraggled and beautiful. She was never supposed to flash him that trusting, adoring smile afterwards, day after day after day.

He'd made a new plan, of course. Marrying Demi's daughter had struck him as an even better means of revenge than the simple kidnap and ransom he'd initially intended.

It all served the same purpose: to draw the Titans out into the open and make them pay for their crimes. Cora's father had been the one holding the knife, but his brothers had been there, too.

Marcus had waited a long time for his vengeance but he would have it now.

None of the remaining Titan brothers had children. Cora was the only heir. Demi would go to the brothers. She had no choice, no power on her own.

And if he could make her suffer in the meantime, imagining the horrors he'd visit upon her daughter? All the better.

But there was still no sign or word from any of them.

And today he'd crossed a line he didn't know how to come back from.

Innocents ought to be spared.

Marcus lived his life by a code and that was its bedrock. He mired himself neck deep in shit doing what had to be done because at least when he was in charge, he could make sure that only the guilty paid.

But it was never meant to touch the innocent.

Like his sister.

Chiara was beautiful. Delicate and pale, her head in the clouds all the time, she'd never seemed to fully inhabit the same grimy reality as the rest of the world.

And that was as it ought to have been.

What should never have been was finding her bleeding out on a dirty mattress in a filthy crack house where the Titan brothers had taken and discarded her.

His parent's death, he'd understood. His father had started as a lowly immigrant shopkeeper, and built an empire. Vito Ubeli had faced injustices and fought in the face of it, and built an army to protect the weak. That didn't mean he wasn't brutal, and one day found death at the hands of an enemy he'd crushed. And when he'd died, his son Marcus was meant to assume control.

But Marcus was only fifteen at the time and he'd waited, thinking someone more qualified would take the lead in his stead. In another year's time, his sister was dead. He'd never forgotten the lesson: strike first and strike fast, and seize any power to be had.

He was a necessary evil to hold back the chaos.

He watched the city lights fly by as they drove. East of the city, the streets grew narrow together. Marcus had his driver stop at an alley way too small to fit a car into.

"Cover me," Marcus said, after scanning every corner of the intersection.

"You sure?" The man in black also looked suspiciously down the alley.

A door opened in the side of one building and Sharo's unmistakable silhouette stepped into the pool of light.

"Wait for me. Should be under an hour," Marcus told his soldier, and got out of the car.

"Picked one of our men up tonight, late to a drop," Sharo said. "Went looking for him and found him in a bar on the *Westside*."

Sharo emphasized the name of the territory between New Olympus and their sister city, Metropolis. Like

Marcus ran the Underworld of New Olympus, the Titans ran Metropolis. And the Westside was currently a no man's land where Marcus still battled for the same control he enjoyed over the rest of New Olympus.

"Said someone stopped him and took his shipment, so he was hiding out, trying to figure out how to tell us."

"You believe his story?"

As usual, Sharo's face held no expression. Lesser men cracked after an hour staring into the mask of rich, midnight skin and fathomless eyes. *Like staring into the fucking abyss,* Roscoe, one of the capos, would say.

"His story doesn't add up. And there's been suspicious activity on his route before, which is why we had eyes on him. We think he handed over the goods to our old friend's out West, but got them to cash him out and make it look like a hold up."

"If it's our old friends," Marcus used the euphemism for the Titans, his blood heating, "then this driver isn't just passing on goods. He's feeding them information."

The two men walked through the warehouse, passing by rows and racks of garments, until they reached stairs to the basement. The air reeked from the stench of the fabric dyes and detergents. The chemical smells did a good job of masking the scent of blood.

Sharo paused at the foot of the stairs. "Got the boys to soften him up a bit. He doesn't know I'm here."

"Alright," Marcus said. "We play it like we did with that last switch—what was his name? The Frenchman."

"Le Mouchard," Sharo pronounced perfectly, and stood aside, letting Marcus lead the way through between the dye vats to the cleared space where they'd tied the snitch up.

A few men all in black stood around a wretched figure

blindfolded and hanging from the ceiling so that his feet barely brushed the floor.

The Shades were Marcus's soldiers, loyal enforcers who ran his massive empire. They were recruited young off the streets, trained in a central facility, and given every opportunity to rise through the ranks. *You can tell a leader by the men who follow him,* Marcus's father had told him time and time again.

The Shades all nodded to acknowledge their leader and Marcus let himself almost grin, before slipping into character.

"What the fuck?" he shouted, and his voice rang out in the empty space. The snitch, a doughy man in a stained wife beater and khaki shorts that had seen better days, started shivering. Sweat ran down under his blindfold, into his sparse beard. Marcus knew the Shades had worked him over a little bit, but left nothing more than painful bruises. His blood had yet to flow.

Marcus directed his false anger around the circle of Shades. "I ask you to bring him in for questions and this is what you do?"

"Fuck, sorry, boss."

"Cut him down. For fuck's sake. Now."

The men scrambled to bring a chair and loosen the ropes that held the man suspended from a few exposed ceiling pipes.

"Give him some water."

Marcus sat in the chair that was provided for him and continued to study the traitor.

"Take that fucking thing off." He nodded at the blindfold. "This isn't an interrogation. This how you treat my employees?"

A Shade handed Marcus a bottle of water and the boss waited until the blindfold was cut away.

The man before him was breathing heavily, trembling with relief. As soon as the filthy scrap of cloth was gone, Marcus leaned forward, filling the snitch's vision.

"Here." Marcus handed over the water bottle, and rested his forearms on his knees, studying the snitch.

"T–t-thank you," the traitor said. "I thought I was a dead man."

"Marty, right?"

The man nodded.

"I'm Marcus Ubeli."

"Yessir, I know you, Mr. Ubeli." The man took a sloppy swig of water, holding the bottle with shaking hands.

Marcus smiled. "I remember you. You took that gun shipment up to Eyrie, when the suits were putting in check-points at the weigh in stations up and down 95."

"Yeah, yeah, that was me."

"You took back roads around all the points, and when a local cop stopped you at two am, you told him you were looking for a place that was open so you could take a dump."

"Right, that's it," the man guffawed half-heartedly, his beady eyes darting around the room at the silent circle of Shades.

"That was good thinking." Marcus raised a finger and shook it at Marty. "Real good."

"Thank you, sir. Can I ask—"

"No muss, no fuss, no questions asked," Marcus cut him off, and the man fell silent. *Bingo,* Marcus thought. "So what happened to my shipment?"

"Your shipment?"

"Yes, Marty, all the goods that go in the back of your

truck belong to me. I'm ultimately responsible for them, so if there's a break in the chain, I need to know about it."

"Uh...I told them, sir, and they didn't believe me. Someone took it."

"Someone? Do you know who?"

"No, fuck, I'd tell you if I could," the man's voice strained with sincerity, and he never broke eye contact. A sure sign he was lying. "They wore masks."

"Of course," Marcus motioned towards his water bottle. "You need another of those?"

"What?" the man stared at it like it had sprouted from his hand, then took another swig. "No, I'm good. Thank you."

"Marty, I hope you don't mind if I keep you here, talk to you some more. See, I have to figure out where this shipment got to, so I can go and retrieve it. I need your help to do that. You willing to help me?"

"Of course, yeah." The man wiped his mouth, but couldn't stop his eyes shifting around the stone-faced enforcers surrounding him and Marcus.

"It may take a while. You want me to get a message to someone who's waiting up for you? A woman or something?"

"Uh, no, my wife, she's used to my late hours."

"Alright." Marcus glanced around the circle of waiting men. One Shade, looming over Marty's right shoulder, cracked his knuckles, massaging his beefy hands. With a subtle shake of Marcus's head, the thug backed down.

Interrogation of a suspect couldn't be done with force. The man would give false information, would say anything to stop the pain. Manipulation led to much more reliable information. Befriend someone, and they will tell you what you want.

Every time.

"Thanks for helping me out, Marty. I appreciate it. And I have a beautiful woman waiting for me in my bed, so I'm sufficiently motivated to finish this."

A chuckle ran around the circle and even Marty's features relaxed.

"So here's the thing that I don't understand," Marcus leaned forward in his chair. "Why didn't they kill you? I mean, that's what I would do. Shoot the driver, take the goods, dump the body."

Marty mopped the sweat from his forehead. "Uh, I don't know."

"You don't know. Lucky break for you, though. Seeing as you're breathing and not dead in a ditch."

"Look, I ran over something, drove a mile and the rig, she was pulling weird, so I stopped to check it out. The car came out of nowhere and these men jumped out waving guns. They had me outnumbered."

"Of course." Marcus closed his eyes. "How many men?"

"Don't know how many, saw two waving guns, another on the other side, maybe two in the back. They got me out and on my knees and told me not to move. Thank the gods your guys were looking out for me."

"Why were you on the back road and not the Ape?" Marcus mentioned the Appian Way, the main artery out of New Olympus.

"Thought I knew a quicker route."

"Even though your orders were to meet up at the abandoned rest stop on the Ape? I'm told you went ten miles out of your way for this shortcut."

The man licked his lips. "Listen, I know it looks bad. I know it looks like I was headed to Metropolis."

Marcus's eyes narrowed but he didn't interrupt.

"But I ran over something and I didn't want the load at risk. If I had an accident, fuck, the suits would be all over it. I didn't want that to happen so I took a shorter route. I mean, it's been years and the Titans ain't done nothing—"

"The Titans? I thought you said you didn't know who jumped you."

"I don't, I mean, I just guessed. They're your enemies."

"That's also a little out of their way to pick up a shipment, but the road you chose was wooded, secluded. Not a bad place for a meet."

"Or an ambush." Marty corrected.

Marcus let the silence stretch. Marty nailed his story airtight, maybe was briefed by the Metropolis gang. The Titans were nasty fuckers. If Marty was dealing with them, maybe there were balls of steel under his worn khakis.

Time for a crowbar.

"Listen, Marty, it's getting late. I'm a man who values my time; I'm sure you're the same way. So I'm going to tell you: I already sent someone to your house. Sharo, you know him? Big guy. Doesn't say much. His fists do the talking, although he's a keen hand with a wet saw."

"Oh gods." The man's pasty skin went white.

"They call him the Undertaker. Kinda cliché, I know, but it gets the point across."

Marty's mouth flapped open like a dying fish, but no sound came out. Marcus kept talking.

"Anyway, Sharo's not a big fan of waiting, either, and he's standing in your wife's bedroom now, watching her sleep. In a minute I'm going to text him instructions, and what I tell him depends on what you say."

"No! Not my Sadie." The man fell forward out of the chair, onto his knees. "Please, please, don't hurt her. I'll tell you."

Marcus nodded. "You have two minutes. Start talking."

TEN MINUTES LATER, Marcus walked back out to the stairwell where Sharo was waiting.

"Fucking Titans," Sharo growled.

"Send out a patrol. Shipment's long gone, but maybe we can still track it, be ready next time."

"Already done. We're bugging up the rest of the goods. If another trucker flips, we'll have ears inside."

Marcus rubbed his stubbled jaw as if he could wipe away the night. "This is the second incursion into our territory this month," he said. A man's broken cry echoed out from the metal dye vats behind him. "After all these years, they're finally making their play. It's got to be because of her."

Cora's mother. She must have gone to the Titans and plead her case just like Marcus had known she would.

Sharo nodded.

"They're not gonna stop. Not until we end it." Sharo's midnight skin shone even in the shadows.

"It's about time." Marty's screams rang out again, and Marcus headed for the stairs. "Tell them to turn the fans on. Drown out the noise."

SIXTEEN

When Cora woke up, her head felt thick, her eyes swollen. What time was it? It was dark out. The last thing she remembered was giving into the tears half an hour or so after Marcus left. She'd swiped them away as fast as they fell, furious at herself. How had she let herself feel anything for that selfish, monstrous, unfeeling—

Wait, something was wrong. It was the middle of the night and she wasn't sure what had woken her. She frowned as she swung her feet over the side of the bed.

But then it hit.

The weight around her ankle. It was gone.

She frantically turned on the bedside lamp.

Holy shit! She lifted up her ankle. And then laughed in disbelief.

The weight around her ankle was gone, along with the chain leading to the bedpost.

She'd done it. She'd earned his trust. Or was this another test?

She waited ten minutes, occasionally calling out Marcus's name, but got no response. Biting her lip, she got on the bed, spread her legs, and touched herself, knowing that if he was in the apartment and watching, that would definitely bring him running.

Still, nothing. He wasn't home.

It was now or never.

She scrambled to the door. It was locked.

But after her mother locked her up, she'd vowed never to be stopped by a locked door again. She'd practiced for hours and hours after studying online videos—it was one of the first things she'd done as soon as she got free of the farm.

She went to the bathroom and grabbed a few hairpins. A few minutes scratching at the lock and it clicked. She backed up, barely daring to believe.

But when she turned the knob, the door opened.

Think, she had to think. She grabbed a plain t-shirt and jeans from the closet. Clothes Marcus had never let her wear the whole time she'd been here. And shoes. She needed shoes. The fabric scratched her skin. She'd grown used to being naked.

How long had she been in here? A week? More?

She pulled her hair into a ponytail and let the door creak open. Maybe he posted a guard, anticipating her escape.

But no. There was no one in the penthouse. She crept into the open room, barely daring to believe it. Marcus never left her alone for long. The gods were smiling on her, giving her a perfect chance to escape.

Too perfect, the little voice said, and she hushed it. Marcus expected the locked door to hold her. She'd outwitted him for once.

Before racing out the door, she grabbed a coat and buttoned it to cover the collar and leash she still wore. She didn't have time to figure out how to undo it.

She put her hand on the doorknob and paused. Someone had cleaned up the statue she'd broken. A giant bouquet of flowers sat on the column instead.

She preferred the statue.

Not that it mattered. She was never coming back here.

She pulled open the door and escaped into the night.

SEVENTEEN

"Are you okay?" asked a female officer two hours later, checking in on Cora where she waited in a windowless room inside the police station.

Cora was huddled on a chair with her knees to her chest, arms wrapped around them. She looked up at the sympathetic looking woman. "I asked for someone to come cut this thing off of me an hour ago."

Cora held out the chain connected to the collar around her neck. Her voice sounded slightly hysterical even to her own ears but she couldn't help it.

After sneaking out of the hotel, she realized she didn't have a place to go or anyone to help her. Marcus had confiscated her phone that had Maeve's number programmed into it, but even if Cora still had it, she wouldn't have wanted to bring the older woman into this. People were scared of Marcus for a reason.

So Cora had found a cop and asked to be taken to the station. They were the only ones she could think of who actually could help her.

It was over now. She was free. So why was she still so on edge?

The woman's eyes went wide. "Oh my gosh, of course. I'll be right back with some cutters."

The door shut behind the woman and Cora couldn't help immediately getting up and going to check the doorknob. It wasn't locked. Cora pressed a hand to her heart, willing it to slow.

You're being paranoid. These are the good guys.

But she was still on Marcus's turf. As soon as she'd blurted out everything that had happened ever since her wedding day to the policeman at the front desk, he brought her to this room. Fifteen minutes later, a superior officer, Captain Martin, had come and she'd reiterated her story more slowly.

"Please," she begged. "Marcus is a powerful man. You need to transfer me to a station that's further away. We are still on his turf. He has soldiers, I don't know how many. You probably know more than I do. What if he attacks the police station—?"

"It's all going to be okay now," said the kindly police captain, a man in his mid-50s with more salt than pepper in his hair, as he patted her hand. "You're safe now and we won't let anything happen to you. Ubeli isn't foolish enough to attack a police station. That's not how his kind works. Now you just rest up while I make some calls and we'll see about a more permanent situation for you."

But Cora hadn't been able to do anything other than pace back and forth in the small room and then finally curl up into a ball on the chair while waiting for any news. Whenever she shifted on the chair, she was reminded of last night. Of what it felt like when Marcus had finally...

Taken the last of your innocence.

She still felt it now, the bowling ball tearing through her guts when she realized it had meant nothing to him. That he still only saw her as a means of revenge. She would only ever be her father's daughter to him. So she'd run.

By now Marcus would have come home to the apartment. He'd have found her gone. The cameras in the room would have shown her picking the lock and escaping. He'd also probably deduced that she couldn't have gotten far, especially if she'd been caught on any street camera footage.

It was probably only a matter of time before he tracked her to the police station.

She pressed her fingers to her face. What was she going to do? What the *hell* would she do if the cops couldn't—

She jumped out of her skin when the door banged open again. But it was the female policewoman with what looked like bolt cutters.

"This might be overkill," the woman said apologetically, "but I know it will get the job done."

"Fine by me," Cora said. "I want this thing off my neck."

The woman nodded. "I'll be careful."

She slid the cutters between Cora's neck and the leather and with one firm snip, the leather collar came free and with it, the chains clanked to the floor. Cora cupped her neck. The bare skin felt strange. Not that she wanted the collar back, she just—

The cop was watching her.

Cora forced a smile. "Thank you. Just...thank you."

The woman put a hand on Cora's shoulder and squeezed. She bent over and picked up the chains attached to the severed collar. "I'll get these out of your sight." With that, she left the room.

And Cora was back to waiting, waiting for she didn't know what. Her new life to begin, she supposed.

It wasn't five minutes before the police captain entered again, carrying a folder. Captain Martin sat at the table across from her. Cora forced herself to drop her knees so that her feet were on the ground. She'd taken off the voluminous coat but now she shivered even though it wasn't especially cold. It was Captain Martin's face. He didn't look like he had good news.

"What is it? Is something wrong?"

"I don't think I have to tell you that Marcus Ubeli is a dangerous man."

Was this guy kidding? "Yeah, I figured that out when he locked me in a room for over a week with a collar around my neck. You don't have to convince me that he's a bad guy. Preaching to the choir."

"Good, good," the police captain said. "Then you'll be happy to testify against him in a court of law."

"What?" Cora shoved back from the table and stood, holding her hands up. "What are you talking about?"

"Well you've come in here with a pretty fantastic story," Captain Martin said. "We've been trying to nail Ubeli for years on racketeering, drug trafficking, money laundering, you name it. But kidnapping and captivity will make for one hell of a story, especially if you have any insights into the rest of his business dealings."

Cora was shaking her head the entire time he spoke. "I don't have anything to do with that. I want to get out of here. Right now. I want one of your guys to drive me as far west as you can take me and I'll disappear." She held her hands up again. "I don't want anything to do with Marcus Ubeli. I want to forget he even exists."

"Well, that's not likely to happen, seeing as how you're married to him. But if you work with us—"

"I'm not going to testify!" Was this guy nuts?

The captain's eyebrows scrunched together. "So maybe your so-called captivity wasn't as unwanted as you're calling it. You know lying to the police carries a penalty of—"

What the fuck? "I didn't lie to you! I wasn't lying about being kidnapped. Well, I mean, at the beginning, I thought it was the start to our honeymoon. But it all changed when he—when he— How dare you even suggest that I wanted what he was—" She pressed her hands to her head. "I didn't want to be there with him. Not like that. But I don't want to testify..."

"If you're worried that he'll get to you, punish you for talking to us—"

She flinched at the captain's choice of words. *Punish.* That's exactly what Marcus would do. Punish her in the most delicious way possible. Make her submit to his will and make her like it. "I'm not afraid of that..." Okay, she was. Because if she stayed to testify, there was no way Marcus wouldn't find a way to get her back.

She jumped to her feet. "I want to get out of here."

"Mrs. Ubeli—"

"Don't call me that," she snapped.

The captain's face hardened. "You want to see what sort of monster you married?" He opened the file and photos spilled out. Bodies splayed and bloody, eyes open, faces contorted in fear, frozen in the moment they realized their oncoming death.

She recognized one face. The curly haired man who'd roofied her. He'd said he was following orders. He'd tried to warn her.

Now he was dead.

I'm gonna take care of you.

"This is what your husband does," the captain ranted. "This is how he conducts his business."

"Do you have proof?"

"No. That's why we need you."

Light dawned. Cora scraped the photos up with her fingernails and stacked them into a pile. "You want me to testify against him somehow. Say he did these things and confessed to me."

Excitement flickered in the captain's eyes. "Yes."

"You want me to lie."

He said nothing.

This city is a beast, Marcus told her once. *Innocents fall and the criminals go unpunished.*

"My husband doesn't think he's a criminal," she told the captain quietly. "He thinks he's dispensing justice." Even when he didn't want to. There were moments when they were together, where he hesitated. He could've destroyed her for what her family did to his sister. Instead, he'd...

"That's what the cops and courts are for."

The police do nothing. They're either corrupt, or have no power. And here was proof. The captain wanted her to lie on the stand. She wasn't about to give her freedom up in order to satisfy some police captain's wet dreams of glory in capturing a notorious crime boss.

She just wanted to get the hell out of here.

"If you testify for the DA, we could get you what you want. Set you up with a new life. New identity. Ubeli would never be able to touch you. You'd be safe. Free."

"You mean witness protection?"

He nodded. "Federal marshals would have your back. You could live somewhere nice and sunny, all year round. Pick your paradise."

Cora's eyes wandered to the mirror that covered one wall. She looked tiny. Pale with shadows under her eyes, her long hair snarled. Who was she to try to stand up against the Lord of the Underworld?

She closed her eyes, not able to bear looking at herself anymore. There were no good choices. She wasn't a little girl anymore, shielded in her mother's controlling arms. The world wasn't a pretty place and she had to face it.

"No. I won't testify."

Captain Martin didn't say another word. He simply picked up the folder he brought in with him and strode from the room. The door shut behind him with a heavy *clang*.

Cora laid her head in her arms on the table. What now? Would they not even help her if she wasn't willing to testify against Mar—

But she hadn't even finished the thought before the door was pushing open again.

And there stood Marcus himself. "I must say, wife, choosing not to testify against me is the first smart thing you've done all day."

EIGHTEEN

"Marcus," Cora sucked in a breath, her heart hammering like a bird in a trap. She backed away, putting the table between her and Marcus. Her mouth opened to scream, but she thought better of it.

"What are you doing here?" she croaked. Did the police know he was here?

Marcus tilted his head to the side, a cold smile curling his perfect lips. Despite everything, the sight of him hit her in the ovaries.

They were back in this cruel game where he was the hunter and she was the prey. She retreated as he paced forward, stopping when her back hit the wall. Cornered.

"Did you think the good officers of this precinct wouldn't notify me of my missing wife's appearance? Cora," he put a hand over his heart in mock concern. "I was so worried."

Ice trickled through Cora's veins. The police? He even had the *police* in his pocket? Was it just this local department or how high up in the city did it go?

Marcus put his hand to her neck and she closed her eyes, preparing for him to squeeze.

But all he did was rub his thumb across her collarbone. "What have you done with my adornment, wife? It was a wedding present, after all."

"What are you going to do to me?" She licked her lips, and heat flared in Marcus's gaze.

"What I'm going to do now is take my wife home." Her nipples hardened at his proximity and the look in his eye. Her crazy body responded to him as always.

Nothing stopped Marcus from getting what he wanted, and he wanted her.

He took her wrist in an unflinching grasp and pulled her toward the door. She tugged at him, more out of habit than outright defiance, and he paused.

"If you make a fuss, you won't be the only one who pays." He didn't look back at her and didn't have to. He wouldn't just punish her. He'd punish the cops in the precinct who helped her. Maybe the captain deserved it, but the lady cop who'd been kind to her didn't.

Cora didn't protest as he pushed open the door and pulled her firmly out. His presence rolled over her senses and everything else receded.

Oh no. He was taking her back with him. And she was letting him. Before, submitting to him was a game she'd played in her head. She always swore to herself that sure, she'd submit—in order to get his guard down. And if she enjoyed it sometimes, well that was all the better, because she'd be more convincing to Marcus that she was harmless.

Escape had always been the ultimate plan.

But there was no escaping Marcus. Today had made that more than clear. There was no place to run and nowhere to hide where he wouldn't find her. At least not in this city.

So what did it mean that she went with him now without even trying to fight? As they walked through the police precinct, the halls were eerily quiet. Was she supposed to just accept this as her fate? To give up all her dreams of freedom?

While the precinct had bustled with people on her arrival, now there was no one to be seen as he walked her down the hallway. Seeing the abandoned desks made it all sink in—just how powerful her husband was. She'd never had a chance.

She swallowed hard against the choking emotion as Marcus pushed through a set of doors Cora hadn't seen before, that led to a side alley.

Sharo stood waiting by the car. If he was surprised to see Cora, his face didn't show it. He merely opened the back door like always. Marcus didn't acknowledge him. No, his focus seemed to be all on Cora as he marched her directly to the backseat and urged her none too gently into the car.

She wrapped her arms around herself and scooted to the opposite end of the bench seat the second he let her go. His presence affected her no matter what. It filled the car, like the subtle scent of his cologne. A sweet ambrosia, drugging her, dragging her under.

She wanted to try the other door, to open it and run as fast as she could. But no doubt it was locked, and even if it wasn't, Sharo would be able to easily chase her down. She wasn't in the mood to lose the last ounce of dignity she had remaining.

Marcus was silent on the short ride back to the Crown hotel. Again he grasped her wrist instead of her hand as they exited the car and made their way through the lobby. Cora felt all eyes on her. The way he was dragging her after him, no doubt she looked like a chastised schoolchild.

She hung her head so that her hair obscured her face. But only for a moment because what the hell did she have to be ashamed of? She lifted her head and squared her shoulders, glaring down anyone who looked their way. It wasn't her who ought to be ashamed, it was everyone else who allowed themselves to be under Marcus's thumb.

If she shouted that Marcus was keeping her against her will, would any of these people even bat an eye?

What could they do even if they did, though? Call the police? A lot of good that would do.

They were in the elevator, now, Marcus and her, ascending to the top of the building. It felt like only seconds later that the *ping* sounded and the elevator doors opened again. She was right back where she started. And everything was worse. So much worse. Her heartbeat began to race.

She wanted to ask Marcus again what he had planned for her punishment, but no. She kept her back straight and her head up. She'd handled everything he'd thrown at her so far.

And if he ties you to the bed again? Fucks you slowly? How long before you break down and beg?

In spite of herself, Cora's entire body trembled as Marcus pulled her over the threshold into the penthouse.

She'd submitted before because she could justify it as a means of eventually gaining the upper hand and escaping. But now? Now if her enemy made her cry out his name in ecstasy, there was no excuse. There'd be no way to rationalize her actions in her head next time.

No, if she submitted to Marcus again, it would mean

facing the truth she'd long been denying—that some part of her liked it. Craved his touch and his dominance.

Her mind immediately tried to reject it. No. Never. She'd never—

"Welcome home," Marcus said sardonically, letting the door slam shut behind them. Cora jumped at the noise. Marcus didn't let go of her wrist.

"Marcus, I—"

"I don't want to hear it."

"But—"

"Silence." The barked word was like the crack of a whip.

He tugged her to the living room and pointed to the couch. She sat on the very edge of the cushion, body tense and feet not quite touching the ground, waiting like a student called into the principal's office. But the seconds stretched to minutes and judgement never came.

Marcus paced away, pulling off his jacket and removing his cufflinks. He looked back once as he rolled up his sleeves, exposing his forearms, lean and hard and dusted with dark hair. Cora's breath caught, but he only strolled to the side bar. Glass clinked and he returned with a glass half full of amber liquid. He offered it and she shook her head, but when he didn't move she finally accepted it. He strolled back and poured another glass for himself. He took his drink to the window and stood sipping, his profile outlined in shadow.

In the silence, her nerves were screaming. *What would he do to her?* The waiting might kill her.

Cora raised her own glass but stopped when she breathed in the alcohol's cloying scent.

"Just get it over with." Her voice broke the airless quiet.

Marcus turned and regarded her. She set her glass down on a side table with a solid click.

"Punish me, yell at me, whatever you're going to do." She folded her arms around her middle. *Don't let him in. No matter what.* He wanted to enslave her just like Mom had for all those years. She said it out loud to remind herself he was no different. "My mother locked me in the cellar. I guess getting tied up in a bedroom is an upgrade."

Marcus's gaze darkened. He ambled over, his casual stroll at odds with the fierce intensity on his face. The focus of a hunter intent on his prey.

She couldn't move, trapped in his regard. Not even when he stepped so close her knee brushed his.

No. You want to be free. It's all you've ever wanted.

His hand went around her neck, collaring her with warm, hard fingers.

Her pulse hammered under his palm. She closed her eyes against his gorgeous face. But she couldn't shut out the warmth of his hand or the way her body completely relaxed at his commanding touch. Why? Why did he affect her like this? She was so confused; she didn't know which way was up.

"I had to try," she blurted when silence became too heavy to bear.

"I know." His thumb stroked her chin in a semblance of tenderness.

"So do it." She tried to sound strong but her voice wavered. "Whatever you plan to do with me. Do your worst." And she looked him straight in the eye. His eyes were dark, almost black.

He dropped his hand and took a seat opposite her.

Her breath stuttered out of her. He savored his drink

and observed her like she was a piece of art he owned. "Do you know why I'm training you?"

Because you're a controlling madman? she wanted to bite out. But he'd told her the first night why he was doing all this. "Because you delight in torturing me."

"Yes." He swished the dregs of his drink. "There is that. But ultimately, Cora, I keep you so you're safe."

She laughed. She couldn't help it. "You really believe that, don't you?"

She shook her head, rubbing her tired face. "You do all these awful things in the name of peace. You tell yourself Olympus is dangerous and that you're the only one who can hold back the violence."

"It's true. No one else is strong enough."

"You think you're the city's savior."

"Not a savior. An emperor."

Of course. She could totally see him standing on the Senate steps. Handing out laurels. Sending out troops. Conquering nations, torching cities, enslaving the enemy and sowing their fields with salt.

"It's better to be feared than loved," she quoted Machiavelli. Marcus in a nutshell.

"Do you, Cora? Do you fear me?"

"Yes." Her answer was barely a puff of air.

He cocked his head, looking pleased. "And what about love?"

"What about it?"

"You said you loved me."

"That was before. Now I know the real you."

He stood and pulled her to her feet. "I've been too lenient with you. I let you off the leash and you betrayed my trust."

Had he really thought she wouldn't run if given half a chance?

"You'll never be free. But now you know the boundaries of your cage." He leaned close, his scent washing over her, a mix of subtle cologne and scotch. "There's nowhere to run to, Cora. I will hunt you down. You belong here, at my side. Forever."

Her breath hitched but he wasn't done. "So why not stop fighting it? Let yourself go. Let yourself be mine." He backed up and she wobbled. His presence was a force and when it was gone she felt the loss.

"Now, strip." With that order, he left her.

Submit. Obey. Escape. That still was her ultimate plan.

But that required submission, didn't it? And Marcus wouldn't be satisfied with anything less than total control of her body and command over her mind. She was losing herself and the scary thing was—she liked it.

It's okay. A small voice told her. *He's bigger, faster, stronger than you. You may as well enjoy it.*

And if she didn't obey, no doubt he'd strip her himself. So she shucked off the jeans and shirt along with any sense of normalcy. Her skin pebbled in the cool room.

When she was down to her bra and panties, Marcus returned, box in hand. He set it down and put his hands in his pockets, nodding at her to carry on the show. Face tight, she stripped out of the rest. It wasn't like she had anything to hide. Today was the first time she'd put on clothes since the wedding.

But still, she waited, chest heaving, as he studied her. Eventually he came to her side, running a hand down her back and sides like he was examining a horse he wanted to buy. She couldn't help a shiver of desire when he cupped her ass. She remembered her last punishment all too well.

"Are you going to punish me?"

Bent halfway through his examination of her quivering thighs, he tilted his head up. "Do you want me to?"

Her answer stuck in her throat. What would she do to ease the weight of anticipation?

His words rang in her ears. *Let yourself go. Let yourself be mine.*

She didn't trust him. *Couldn't* trust him. At least not with her heart.

But her body? The thought about what it might be like if he took her back to that perfect, ecstatic place where she could finally, *finally* escape her own head and all the confusion and noise. Where she could just...*be.*

"Yes," she said, suddenly decisive. "I want you to punish me."

Something flashed in his eyes, gone in an instant. He raised his chin. "I think, wife, I may have underestimated you."

Her heartbeat pounded in her ears. Was it possible to surprise him? To challenge him and make him regard her as an equal?

Marcus opened the box he'd brought and lifted out a heavy collar. Metal, silver, stainless steel and linked to a leash. So much for being his equal.

Smirking, he drew her before a giant mirror with a heavy gilt frame. He positioned her in front of it and held her still with hands on her hips.

His lips found her ears. "What do you see?"

"You, me. Us."

"I see a submissive."

A ripple went through her body. He held her up with an iron arm around her waist when her legs would buckle.

"Such a shame we have to be enemies. Circling each

other, round after round, fight after fight. We were made for each other."

"Don't," she whispered, feeling close to tears. She was raw, wrung dry. His tender words were arrows. She could withstand his cruelty, but not his soft, soothing voice, spinning a story of destiny. After all, who could fight the Fates? Why even try?

It's just your body. It doesn't mean you're giving him your mind. Or your heart. And he can do such *lovely things to your body.*

"Give yourself to me, Cora." He raised the stainless-steel collar. She closed her eyes just before the click.

"Mine," he breathed, then he tugged on the leash, forcing her head back, forcing her to look him in the eyes.

At the same time he dipped a finger inside her. She gasped, her walls clenching in pleasure at the invasion. She was already wet. She had been from the moment she stepped back inside the penthouse.

His strong fingers twisted, probed, and tested her inner walls, the whole time his thumb teasing circles around her clit. Her body sprung to life for him as it always did.

"You're beautiful."

His gaze swallowed her whole. Everything was Marcus. His thumbs chafed her nipples lightly. She let her head drop in surrender as he worked her body to the peak.

"That's it. That's my good girl. Give yourself over to me and I will give you everything."

As her hips began to rock and pleasure bloomed, she stood again on the precipice—the devil whispering in her ear and the whole world spread at her feet.

His palm ground into her sex and her orgasm rose, brilliant and devastatingly beautiful, a bright sunset unfurling through each limb, rosy and tinged with gold.

At the last moment, though, he took his hand away. She cried out but didn't move. It was right there. *So* close.

"You want to cum?"

"Yes." More than that, she needed it.

"Then crawl, Cora. Crawl for me."

He moved to crouch several feet back, holding her leash out of the way. She was a needy knot of limbs.

"Come, Cora," he beckoned. "Crawl to me."

For a long moment, she froze. Here it was. The crawling. But as she watched him, she saw it for what it really was: a choice.

To do it meant to submit to him completely. Voluntarily. To crawl not because he'd shoved her forcefully to her knees but because she wanted all he had to give her.

And in the end, the choice felt so simple.

She sank to her knees. Because this final decision meant she didn't have to do any more deciding or worrying or justifying. Life shrank down and became so simple.

"Yes, beautiful. You've never been more beautiful. Come to me now."

All tension left her, body and mind, as she gave herself over to him. The storm in her head finally quieted.

She wanted it and she didn't have to be ashamed anymore. She wanted his eyes on her slinking form, her swaying hips. She wanted to seduce and delight him. And the way he looked at her...like she was the most beautiful thing he'd ever seen, his face the picture of a man obsessed. Yes, *yes*. Nothing had ever been more right.

She crawled eagerly.

"There," he murmured when she reached him, positioning her so her chin was high and back arched, pushing her bottom in the air. Her body shuddered at the touch of his hand as it ghosted across her backside. "All the way to the bedroom, goddess."

So she crawled, ass swaying, eyes lifting occasionally to see Marcus's glowing gaze tracking her progress, all the way to the bed.

She'd barely gotten there when he was reaching down and tugging her to her feet.

"It's time for your reward." His voice sounded strained like he could barely manage to get the words out.

But the next second he was back in control of himself, always in control. He loosened his tie, stripping with smooth movements. He shucked his shoes, shirt, pants and boxers and paused, unwittingly posing in the half light. He was naked and she was lost because here was a god in human form.

Wide shoulders, strong chest tapering to lean hips, powerful thighs. Either he worked out every morning or performed some magic to make his muscles strong and sleek, even and well formed. He could've been a statue carved by a master, but at the sight of him a sculptor would lay down his tools and weep at the perfection that defied reality.

Yet for all his otherworldly beauty, he looked like a man, coarse hair dusting his hard thighs and chest. He looked like a ruler of old. He only needed a crown. If the people wouldn't give him one, he'd take it.

And he was hers. He said she belonged to him, but it went both ways, right? He could've handed her over to an underling, or made Sharo punish her. But he would never allow another man to touch her. He wanted her for himself. She'd wanted a sign that she meant something to him—was it here all along, inherent in his possessive nature?

She could only hope. Because she was becoming lost to him.

"Lie back and spread your legs."

She wanted him inside her now. She wanted to throw her arms and legs around him and grind their bodies together. She wanted him frantic with need for her, to know for certain that he was as lost as she was.

But instead she did as he said, laying back on the bed and opening eagerly to him.

He took his time arranging her, pulling her to the edge of the bed, angling her legs just right. Damn his control. But it was all worth it when he finally climbed over her.

"Hands above your head."

She lifted her hands. Anything to move him along. But she should have known that nothing could hurry Marcus. That was the point, wasn't it? For her to give in to him completely. His way. In his time.

And when he finally, finally entered her, the first slow drag of his cock had her right at the edge again, her previously denied orgasm revving right back up.

He pushed into her and she held her breath, her body tightening. Everything in her focused on the slow, fluid glide of his cock entering her, easing the ache and stoking it at the same time. She lay there quivering, an empty vessel waiting to be filled.

Her legs and back tensed, nipples hardening and toes curling as Marcus's thrusts drove her towards orgasm. He moved over her, the snap of his hips driving her further up the bed. She caught his shoulders, gripping and petting the bunching muscle, such magnificent power under her palms.

He paused and slipped his hands under her bottom, large palms cupping her back cheeks and drawing her close. The new angle made his pubic bone graze her clit and she bit back a moan. Fuck, she was close, her climax like a freight train, rushing towards her, an inexorable force about to hit—

He stopped. Pulled out. Stepped back and surveyed her heaving flesh like a piece of furniture.

"Marcus. Please."

He took himself in hand, fisting his cock with her own slick as lubricant. He watched her with hooded eyes. "Touch yourself. Pull your nipples."

She plucked at her breasts, obeying instantly. Anything to bring him back. Anything.

Pleasure surged through her, but it wasn't enough. Without Marcus, it would never be enough.

"Punishment," he reminded her, and horror bloomed over her. He was taunting her, touching her, teasing her. He'd fuck her forever and never let her cum. He knew her body and mastered it.

"Please," she whispered. "I need it." He didn't chastise her so she continued. "I need you. Marcus, please."

"All fours."

He'd barely given the command before she scrambled into place. Head up, back arched, bottom upturned, just like he'd taught her. The bed creaked under his weight and then—

He slammed into her.

Yes!

His hips drove into her in delicious rhythm. A tug on her throat told her he'd taken hold of her leash. He was being gentle, but reminding her she was owned.

"My beautiful darling, how well you beg." Another beautiful stroke. And another.

Her orgasm blew up like a bomb, a silent explosion, a billowing mushroom cloud against a sunset. Her limbs weakened, body wracked with aftershocks of the orgasm she'd been dying for.

She ended up bowed, head resting on her forearms and bottom in the air as he battered her from behind. At last he growled and finished.

When he tugged her up and led her to the bathroom, she clung to him with her arms around his waist. She stood as if in a dream. A trance, a reality that mirrored the life she wanted, as if her world had turned upside down but she found she could live in the reflection. In fact in this moment, she wanted to live there forever.

Marcus took her into the shower and turned on the heated spray that soothed every part of her.

"You did so well, goddess," he murmured as he washed her body, slowly, inch by glistening inch. His own cock jutted out from his body, hard again, but he didn't make a move to satisfy himself, or make her do it. He cleaned every inch of her, even shaved her legs and mons. Meanwhile she felt like she was floating, like she'd never step foot back on the ground while he cared for her like she was a precious treasure. Precious to him.

When he dried her off and propelled her towards the bedroom, she felt drowsy. Her body was languid, her thoughts sluggish. He'd put her under a trance and she didn't want to wake. So it was good when he took her back to bed and tucked her in. He sat beside her and then leaned down, pressing the sweetest kiss to her forehead. He lingered there long moments, his head bowed over hers like he was in prayer.

As she sank off to sleep, the image remained in her head, him bowing like a supplicant even though she was the one who'd just given her submission.

NINETEEN

So this was...different.

Cora sat at the table with Marcus for breakfast later that week. Yes, *at* the table, not under or beside the table at Marcus's feet.

She shook her head and took another bite of her eggs.

Marcus was reading the paper, apparently completely oblivious to her. He hadn't said a word to her this morning, not even when he'd set her plate on the table opposite his instead of on the floor.

It was a first. The last few days, even after he'd put away the chain, the plate had still gone on the ground.

She hadn't known how to feel about that. Was he rewarding her for her submission in the bedroom? Or had he just finally realized that, duh, there was no point in chaining her if she'd be scooped up if she tried to leave the penthouse anyway?

But that would've been true all along, so the chain had been more about humiliation and subjugation than actually keeping her trapped. So, did he consider her appropriately cowed after the police station and the...the crawling?

Her face heated even at the memory.

Or maybe *this* was the fucking point, to have her constantly questioning and second-guessing, and even third-guessing herself so she never knew which way was up. Because while every time he took her to bed, dominant and demanding, so often he took her to that place of ecstasy beyond thoughts, just *feeling*...in the morning she woke to find her brain firmly in command again.

And her brain didn't know how to deal with what her body so welcomed. Marcus. In control. His will ruling every single minute of her life.

She dropped her fork to her plate with a loud clatter and sat back in her chair, crossing her arms over her chest.

Marcus finally dipped his paper to look at her, but only for the shortest moment.

"We are going out tonight. So shower and shave."

What?

"What?"

He lowered the paper enough to look at her again, his expression unreadable. "If you don't, I'll do it for you."

"Fine," she snapped.

"A stylist will be here at four. Be ready by then."

"I don't have anything to wear."

"She'll bring the dress."

"Where are we—"

"Enough," he cut her off impatiently.

She clenched her teeth mutinously. But if he was telling the truth... And he was actually going to take her out of the penthouse... Well, it wouldn't kill her to play by his rules for another day.

~

SHE SHOWERED. She shaved. And at 4 o'clock, a knock sounded on the door. Marcus opened it to a thin, fashionable man pulling a suitcase and a rack of what Cora assumed were dresses in black hanging garment bags.

"Don't speak to her," Marcus ordered abruptly. "I'll choose the dress."

Cora glared at him, feeling her cheeks heat. Was this what it would be like all night? Him humiliating her in front of whoever it was they might see, wherever it was they were going?

She took a deep breath in and let it out slowly. It didn't matter. Her pride didn't matter. She could *behave.* And she wouldn't be stupid like last time.

She wouldn't run down the street on her first opportunity out of the penthouse crying for help. No, she had to play this game smart. If Marcus wanted her to be a puppet on a string, she had to pretend to dance.

But that didn't mean that she couldn't still use tonight to learn all she could and to seek allies and opportunity.

So later, she smiled sweetly at the stylist who nodded at Marcus, obviously intimidated if not outright afraid, and gestured toward the master bathroom. "If you come this way, we can get started."

Three hours later, she was made up, her hair teased and curled and sprayed into a sleek updo with curls cascading over one shoulder.

Marcus had chosen a red dress, far more daring than anything she would have ever chosen for herself. The front was modest, but it draped daringly over her shoulder, exposing her back so that the stylist had to use tape to make sure none of her derrière would be exposed.

She stared at herself in the full-length mirror, even more

bewildered feeling than when she'd looked at herself on her wedding day.

She looked sophisticated and worldly. Far more than she felt. She was a farm girl from Kansas.

She shook her head. No, that wasn't true. Not anymore. She wasn't the wide-eyed girl who'd first ridden the bus into the city three months ago. Not after Marcus.

Still, she wasn't... She turned and looked at the daring dip of the back of the dress in the mirror, and saw Marcus coming up behind her.

Her breath caught at the sight of him.

Marcus in a tux was... Terrifying. Formidable. Drop dead gorgeous.

He came right up behind her. She gasped when his hands came swiftly to her neck and watched with bated breath in the mirror as he used the small, oddly shaped key to unlock the collar around her neck.

She could only guess at what the stylist had thought of it. The clunky stainless steel had obviously not gone with the elegant look but as per Marcus's instructions, the stylist hadn't said a word.

Marcus tossed the collar to the bed behind him and produced a large, square velvet box from his suit coat jacket. He sat it on the dresser beside the mirror and opened it, still silent.

What was he—?

"Are those dia—"

"Yes."

Cora's eyes went wide as he lifted the delicate diamond studded choker to her neck. Chill bumps raced down her body as he lifted her hair. His fingertips graced her skin as he fastened it at the back of her neck.

The one-inch thick interlaced diamond necklace

sparkled, even in the dim light of the room. It was made of what looked like hundreds of smaller diamonds along with larger diamond studded in a central pattern.

It must cost a fortune.

Cora couldn't help her hand lifting to touch the spectacular piece of jewelry but she stopped herself at the last second from actually making contact, dropping her hand again. She swallowed hard and the diamonds glittered with the movement.

"Why?"

"So everyone will know you are mine."

Cora nodded. Finally an answer that made sense.

"What if I lose it somehow? Or the clasp breaks and I don't notice it fall off, or—"

"It won't fall off. Now, I trust you won't manage to lose this again, either."

He pulled out another box, this one smaller and familiar, and opened it.

It was her engagement ring and her wedding ring that she'd thrown across the room that first night. Had it only been two weeks ago? It felt like a century.

Her eyes flew to Marcus's in the mirror but his face was stone. Impassive.

She took the rings out of the box and slid them on the fourth finger of her left hand.

After she had, Marcus put his large, cool hands on her bare shoulders, eyes meeting hers in the mirror.

"You will not embarrass me tonight. You will act like a proper wife."

"Because gods forbid anything sully your sterling reputation?" The barb was out of her mouth before she could help it.

Marcus was not amused.

He slid his hand from her bare shoulder over to her throat and for the first time all day, she saw a fire stoked in his eyes.

He put no pressure on her throat around the choker, but kept his hand there.

And in demonstration of how much Cora was not the simple farm girl from Kansas anymore, the sight in the mirror and the feel of his commanding hand there had her tingling in all sorts of ways, none of which were fearful.

She might not be an innocent anymore, but she was assuredly just as foolish. Because her heart squeezed at his touch, too.

She turned away from the mirror and strode for the door. "I assume our chariot awaits."

SO YES, the stylist and the dress and the necklace should have tipped her off. But Cora still wasn't prepared when Sharo let them off in front of a red carpet. It was a gala with an Actual. Red. Carpet.

It was a charity gala, Cora would learn over the course of the next hour as Marcus took her arm and she was blinded by camera flashes as they walked the aforementioned red carpet into the Elysium hotel ballroom, the only hotel in New Olympus fancier than the Crown.

Cora tried to keep her eyes from bugging out of her head when she saw famous actors, actresses, musicians, and politicians mingling all around them.

Marcus strode through the crowd without batting an eye and Cora did her best to keep up with him. He'd stop occasionally and make small talk. And he was charming.

Charismatic even. He introduced her around, his hand always at the small of her back.

Cora had officially entered the twilight zone. Marcus was smiling. It was obviously a show he could put on at will, but still, she'd forgotten what his full smile looked like. The dimple. She'd forgotten about the devastating dimple.

Was this what he had been like when they were 'dating'? But no, after twenty minutes of watching him, she realized it wasn't. She didn't know if she felt better or worse that he hadn't taken the energy to be this full, false self to draw her in, or if it meant she'd been able to see slightly more of the real him from the beginning.

Or maybe she still had no idea who the hell the *real* him truly was.

After he'd met whatever quota of social engagement he felt was appropriate, he led her to view the auction items that had been donated for the charity gala. All sorts of things were up for bid: Paintings. Box seats for popular sports teams. Dinner with the mayor. A helicopter tour of the city. Theater tickets.

The theater tickets were the only thing to tempt Cora. She promised herself as soon as she had any disposable income, she'd go see a show.

"Anything catching your eye?" Marcus asked. "Maybe a handbag or two?"

She rolled her eyes and set the flyer down about the hottest show on Theater Row. "Nobody's around now. You don't have to keep up the act."

"Did you just roll your eyes at me?" The question was quiet and slightly incredulous.

Cora gulped as she looked up at him and her tongue snuck out to lick her lips. That zinging sensation was back in her belly at the intensity she saw on his face. Stupid girl. Stupid girl.

A gong sounded and everyone around them started to move out of the auction area but Marcus kept staring at her.

Cora's hand went to the necklace around her throat, stroking the glittering gems. She pointed her chin at the retreating crowd. "I think that means dinner is about to begin."

Marcus stood unmoving for another long moment before giving a sharp nod, taking her arm, and walking so stridently to join the flow of people that she had to lift her skirts in order not to trip as she followed him.

They were seated at a large round table with ten other people. Marcus glanced at their seating cards and at those beside them. His face went dark, and he promptly switched them with two from another table.

Cora wasn't sure he was allowed to do that but who was going to stop Marcus Ubeli?

Cora sat down and smiled awkwardly at those already seated at the table but Marcus didn't sit beside her.

"I'll be right back," he murmured before stalking off to the side of the room to talk to someone. Cora watched him go and get into a discussion with a man. That man called over another man. Marcus pulled out his phone and quickly texted someone.

Why was she staring at Marcus? She had her own agenda.

She looked around the table and smiled at the two other couples seated there. "Hi, I'm Cora. It's so nice to meet you."

The two women at the table exchanged a glance before looking back to her. "You're married to Marcus Ubeli?" asked the one a couple of seats away from her, a pretty redhead whose male companion had to be at least forty years older than her.

Cora tried to keep her smile genuine. "Yes, two weeks now. Still in the honeymoon stage."

"How nice," said the redhead in a tone so patronizing, Cora gritted her teeth.

She glanced back at Marcus and saw that he was now talking with three people. Two men and a woman, a blonde who had her hand possessively on his arm, her body angled into his in a way that brought Cora's breath up short.

It was an intimate touch. An invasion of space unless... Unless you knew the person very well. Intimately so.

"Cora, darling!"

Cora swung her head around in time to see Armand heading her way. He leaned down and gave her two kisses, one on either side of her cheek. He stepped back, beaming at her.

"Look at you. Absolutely stunning, my love. I must talk Marcus into letting you model the dress I'm working on. No one else could do justice to the signature piece. I designed it with you in mind."

Cora flushed as Armand plucked the two seating arrangement cards beside her, handed them to an assistant who was trailing him and sat down beside Cora.

"So what do you think of your first gala?" he asked, raising his arms flamboyantly. "Does it live up to expectations?"

"I didn't really have time to make any expectations," Cora said, "I didn't know we were coming here until we arrived."

"That beast," Armand said. "You look stunning."

Cora glanced over at Marcus again. The woman was

still there and she'd moved closer, if such a thing were even possible.

"Ugh, that woman is a witch."

Cora jerked her head back at Armand who'd obviously noticed her looking at Marcus.

"You know her?"

"Unfortunately."

When Cora stayed silent, Armand obviously took pity on her.

"She's an executive at one of the big telecom companies in New Olympus."

"They dated?"

Armand lifted a hand and waved it in a so-so gesture. "I'm not sure I would call it that."

"For how long?"

"Off and on for maybe a year or two."

"Then what happened?"

"The rumor mills said she wanted more. Apparently he didn't." Armand raised his eyebrows significantly.

"How long ago was it?"

"I guess they broke things off maybe two months before you got to the city."

Cora reached for her glass of water. After a long swallow, she thumped her glass down, almost sloshing water onto the tablecloth.

"She's old news, honey. He's only got eyes for you. I've seen the way that man looks at you."

Cora barely stopped herself from scoffing. If Armand only knew.

And what the hell was she doing wasting energy thinking about this anyway? Cora turned to Armand, angling her back away from Marcus. Tonight was about developing relationships. And yes Armand was Marcus's friend... Or maybe they had some business together? Cora didn't know what a crime lord and a fashion designer might have in common but still, Armand was a start. The more information she had, the better.

"So, tell me how you've been. How is the line doing? And the spas? You've opened a chain of upmarket spas, right?"

"Ugh, they've been running me ragged. I thought being an entrepreneur and being my own boss meant I got to set my own hours and sleep in. Ha! I work from dawn till dusk and still never get to half the things on my to do list." He leaned in. "Probably doesn't help that I party from dusk till dawn." He winked.

Cora barked out a laugh, startling herself. How long had it been since she'd genuinely laughed? It felt good. It felt really good.

Cora reached out and gave Armand's forearm a squeeze, letting go almost as quickly as she touched him. But her smile was genuine when she said, "It's good to see you, Armand. Really good to see you."

"Armand," Marcus's deep voice came from behind Cora. She jumped in her chair and craned her neck to look up at him. He set a hand possessively on her shoulder before sitting down beside her.

"How's business?" Marcus asked and Armand transferred his attention to him.

Cora watched Marcus. Had he seen her touch Armand? Was he mad at her about it?

But Marcus seemed at ease. More at ease than he'd been all night, relaxed back in his seat and sipping from a glass of bourbon he'd picked up from somewhere as he and Armand chatted about the newest spa Armand had opened. Unlike with other people Marcus had chatted with tonight, he and Armand seemed genuinely friendly.

Waitstaff came around and collected cards asking which entrée they'd like, and Cora excused herself to the restroom.

Marcus stood up at the same time she did and his eyes skewered her. She heard his unasked question.

She leaned up on tiptoe and whispered in his ear. "Let me guess, you have thugs guarding the ballroom and I'll be snatched up and taken back to the penthouse if I take a step out of line?"

Marcus wound a hand around her waist and pulled her up tight against him. His breath was hot on her ear as he answered, "Something like that. I expect you back within ten minutes. If you don't, I will come looking for you. Or one of my...thugs will." When he pulled back, the corner of his mouth twitched.

He gave her waist one last squeeze and let her go. But Cora could still feel his touch long after she'd walked away from the table toward the restroom.

She went to the bathroom, relaxing only when she closed the door to the stall. What was she doing? Had she actually felt *jealous* of that woman out there? When what she was meant to be doing here was trying to find a way to escape?

She dropped her face into her hands but lifted it again quickly. She couldn't afford to muss her makeup. She rolled her eyes at the ridiculousness of her situation.

Talk about a gilded cage.

But sitting on the toilet wasn't going to get her anywhere. So she flushed and opened the stall, heading for the sink. She was so in her own head, she didn't even really notice the woman who'd opened the door as she began to wash her hands.

"So, you and Marcus Ubeli."

Cora looked up and her eyes widened at seeing the elegant blonde had stepped in the door. The same woman Marcus had been talking to earlier.

"I have to say, bravo. I thought that man would be a bachelor for life. He always did like his fuck toys young but I never imagined he'd go and marry one."

The woman advanced and stood at the mirror beside Cora. She settled her clutch on the bathroom counter and pulled out a tube of lipstick. Her dress was black, the lipstick fire engine red. She looked to be in her mid-30s. She was stunning, refined, sophisticated. The kind of sophistication that came from experience and not a fancy dress.

Cora couldn't help staring at her as she began touching up her lipstick that already looked perfect.

The woman's eyes slid back to Cora. "Well, aren't you a quiet little mouse." She put the top back on the tube of lipstick and closed her clutch with a *snap*.

Cora still didn't say anything. It wasn't like she could defend her relationship with Marcus or would even want to. He didn't mean anything to her. She hated him.

"Really? Nothing to say? You know he and I have been lovers for years? I was supposed to be seated beside you but you saw how upset he became. It's still so raw between us. We fight like cats and dogs and then we make up passionately, that's how it's always been. But trust me, he always comes back to me."

The woman looked Cora up and down, eyes narrowing, obviously waiting for a response to her cattiness.

And it wasn't that her words didn't make Cora feel small and little. They did. This was not her world. She didn't know the rules to the games these people played, Marcus least of all.

And suddenly she had the strongest longing to be back at the farm where everything was simple.

If only she could go back in time. Her mom wasn't really *that* bad. And it was nothing Cora couldn't handle now. She wasn't a child anymore. She could stand up for herself now.

After a day like today... And everything with Marcus...

If only she could go back to a life of rising when the sun came up, spending her days on the land, and sleeping after a hard day's work.

She'd do anything to go back to that.

The woman looked like she was going to make another snide comment before dismissing Cora completely, when Cora reached out a hand. "Can I borrow your phone?"

"What?"

"Can I borrow your phone? I forgot mine at home and there's someone I need to make a call to."

The woman's eyes narrowed in confusion but she opened her clutch and slid out her phone. "If you use it to text something to Marcus pretending to be me, he'll see right through it."

Cora just stared. The petty games these people played. "I'm not texting or calling Marcus." Cora snatched the phone out of her hand and stared at her. "Do you mind waiting outside?"

The woman snorted an amused laugh and sashayed to the door. She looked over her shoulder once as she grabbed the door handle. "I'll be waiting right outside when you're finished."

Cora nodded distractedly, already dialing.

She glanced underneath the stalls, but the restroom was empty apart from her.

"Hello?"

Cora closed her eyes and leaned back against the counter at hearing her mother's voice.

"Mom."

"Cora!" A clatter sounded over the phone. "Cora, where are you? Where is he keeping you? Are you okay? Tell me where you are and we'll be right there. We'll kill that son of a bitch."

"No, mom," Cora frowned. "I'm fine. It's okay. I thought maybe we could—"

"Where are you? I swear that bastard will never hurt you again. We'll make him pay. I'll cut his heart out of his chest and we'll go back home where no one can ever hurt you again—"

"Mom!" Cora spun around and slapped a hand on the counter. "Listen to me for a second. I'm fine."

"Tell me where you are," her mom all but shouted.

"Right now, at a gala at the Elysium hotel. And the rest of the time he's keeping me at the Crown. Why didn't you tell me about dad? And what he did?" She hadn't meant to ask it, but it popped out.

"Because you were never supposed to be part of this world. It was always supposed to be you and me. Just you and me. And that's how it will be again. We'll kill that son of a bitch and—"

"No," Cora said, irritated and angry. "I don't want you or my uncles to hurt him." As soon as the words were out of her mouth, she realized they were true.

"What?"

Cora stared at the floor and lifted a hand to her forehead.

Gods, she was fucked up. Because it was true. She didn't want Marcus hurt. And what that woman had said earlier, it had bothered her. She *had* been jealous.

And as nice as farm life sounded...she couldn't go back. It was too late for that. What she'd begun with Marcus, whatever this was, she had to either see it through or get out of it on her own.

She looked at herself in the mirror. And now the woman reflected back didn't look like as much of a stranger anymore. She looked pale but striking. The jewel tone red of the dress made her skin look luminous.

"He's gotten into your head." Her mom stated it icily.

Cora couldn't deny it. Why wouldn't she want all the retribution her mother was promising otherwise?

"We haven't been able to get into the city but we're working on it, baby. We're coming." Her mother's voice was so ice cold that it sent a chill down Cora's spine.

Cora had heard it like that before, usually before a punishment, one of the bad ones.

"I have to go, Mom. I can figure this out on my own. I just wanted you to know I'm okay."

Cora hung up the phone before her mom could say anything else. And she strode to the door, opened it and all but slammed the phone down into the beautiful blonde's hand.

It had been stupid to take it and stupider to call her mother. Even hearing her voice brought it all back.

The slaps if she burned the bacon at breakfast. Being shoved to the ground and locked out of the house if her mind wandered off and she was late returning from the fields. Denying her meals if Demi thought she was getting too thick around the middle. The daily barrage of demeaning words and name-calling.

Yes, Marcus had put a collar on her. But he'd never once hit her. He didn't call her names and if he continued allowing her freedoms like this, getting out of the penthouse, maybe even going back to volunteer at the shelter—

So because he's the lesser of two evils, suddenly he's your knight in shining armor?

"You know," the woman whose name Cora still hadn't learned, lifted an eyebrow at her coyly. "Marcus can be adventuresome in the bedroom. The next time he and I get together, it could be fun to have you as the third in our ménage à trois."

Cora glared at her. "You can go fuck yourself."

She strode back toward the table where Marcus was sitting. Marcus stood like he meant to pull her chair out for her but she jerked it out roughly before he could and sat down hard, keeping her eyes firmly forward at the auctioneer and not looking his way.

Champagne had been served around the table and Cora grabbed her glass and tipped it backwards. It was bubbly and cool and in spite of the bite, she drank it all the way down. She reached for the untouched glass in front of Marcus but he swiftly put his hand out and stopped her.

She glared his way. His eyes darkened and locked with hers in response. He did not look happy.

Well fuck him too. She gave him a saccharine sweet smile. "Oh darling, I'm so thirsty," she said loud enough for everyone else at the table to hear.

"Have my water, sweetheart," he replied, handing her his water goblet.

She narrowed her eyes at him but accepted the water. She'd get her hands on more champagne later. If there was ever a night to get drunk, this was it. She didn't care that she was only nineteen.

Suddenly, Marcus lifted an auction paddle she hadn't even realized he had in his lap and called out, "$50,000."

There were gasps from all around them and Cora sat up straighter, suddenly looking back and forth from the auctioneer at the front of the room to Marcus.

"Well folks, that's one expensive set of theater tickets. Do I have any other bids? Didn't think so. Sold, to number forty-six."

Cora's mouth dropped open. Did he just—? Her head swiveled back to Marcus.

"What did you do?"

He gave her his characteristic mouth twitch. "Donated to charity."

She stared at him as the auctioneer went on to rattle off the next item.

She was left to stew in her own head about the evening, her mother, the woman in the black dress, and most of all, Marcus. She came to few conclusions about any of it other than the fact that she was very confused and probably couldn't trust her own judgment.

The auction finally finished and dinner was served. Armand chattered in her ear about city gossip and others around the table made polite conversation. When the subject of Marcus's donation came up, a reckless hair struck Cora.

"I'm not surprised," Cora said, smiling at Marcus. "Marcus supports all sorts of charities. It's one of the reasons we fell in love. He loves the fact that I spend so much time at a dog rescue shelter down on 35th and Thebes." She turned her smile towards Marcus. "Isn't that right, honey?"

His eyes narrowed but he nodded. "Yes, I've always admired your generous spirit."

"Oh really?" said a man from across the table, leaning in in obvious interest. "I don't know if I said, but I work for the New Olympian Post. Everyone is always curious about the elusive Mr. and now Mrs. Ubeli. I'd love to get a story on the charity."

"No," Marcus said at the same time Cora clapped in apparent delight and said, "Yes! That'd be wonderful."

Marcus's head swung her way and she continued smiling at him. "Oh come on, darling. You're such a respected businessman about town." She lifted a hand to straighten his tie even though it was already perfectly straight. "It's natural that there's curiosity about you."

Cora looked back to the reporter. "Come by this Tuesday. I'll be volunteering then."

Underneath the table, Marcus's hand clapped on Cora's thigh. She turned back to him and gave him a glittering smile. "Maeve will be so delighted to share the shelter's story."

Marcus smiled coolly, his eyes hard, before changing the topic. His hand, however, was still very much engaged, as it slid under the slit in the side of her gown up her inner thigh.

Cora had to hide her gasp by taking a quick sip of water.

Marcus's hand didn't stop there, though. With one hand he ate his smoked salmon and with the other, he continued his path up her thigh until he was nudging her panties aside and then, *oh—*

Cora's fingers went white knuckled around her fork as he thrust a finger inside her. Right there at the dinner table. In a room with hundreds of people. While she was wearing a designer gown and Marcus chatted with another man about the current state of the stock market.

How dare he—

Oh. *Oh—*

The pleasure quickened her stomach, sharp and surprising. She sank back in her chair and opened her legs as wide as the dress would allow.

No. What the hell was she doing? She couldn't—

Oh! Two of his long, thick fingers explored her now, in and out, stroking through her folds and up to her clit before pushing inexorably inside her again.

It was wrong. So, so wrong for her to be enjoying this.

Her chest rose and fell sharply as pleasure radiated throughout her body, warm lapping waves. She clutched her water glass and bit her bottom lip to keep herself from crying out. Oh yes. Oh *yes*. Right there. Just like that.

It was coming— *Oh!* She wanted to throw her head back and close her eyes. But none of them could know what he was doing to her. She didn't even want to admit what he was doing to her. His fingers worked her even more furiously.

The climax hit soft at first but it spread, wave after wave, radiating out from her center. A lightness so pure and freeing she wanted to hold onto it forever. The things Marcus made her feel... The things he made her feel—

He kept stroking her through it, more languidly now as she rode the crest, riding it and riding it and riding it—

He clutched her entire pussy in his large hand and massaged it as the waves subsided. A tremor rocked her body that she couldn't help and her eyes flew open. Shit, she hadn't even realized they dropped closed but the pleasure had been all-consuming.

His hand retreated. She almost gasped at the loss.

Marcus pushed his chair back from the table. "If you'll excuse us," he said crisply. He held out a hand to Cora. "Darling?"

It was not a request, Cora could tell by the fire burning

in his eyes. Her hand trembling, she lifted it and took his. He pulled her up from the table, his fingers interlocking with hers. Cora briefly shot a wobbly smile in the direction of everyone at the table. Armand looked back knowingly. Oh God, had everyone at the table realized what was happening?

Marcus didn't say anything as he pulled her through the crowded tables and Cora didn't dare either.

Out of the ballroom, they went. All the way to the coat check.

"Your ticket number, sir?" asked the attendant.

"Do you know who I am?" Marcus asked.

The attendant's eyes widened and he swallowed. "Yes sir, Mr. Ubeli, sir."

"Give us the room," Marcus demanded. "Twenty minutes."

The attendant pushed open the half door he stood behind and scurried out without another question.

Cora shook her head at Marcus's heavy handedness but the next second, he was dragging her into the room and closing both the bottom and top half of the door as well as locking it.

Then he pushed her up against the rack of coats.

"I don't appreciate being contradicted in public," he growled, his eyes dark. "By anyone but especially not by my wife."

His wife? Cora couldn't help scoffing. "Let's not pretend I'm anything more than a convenient...what did that despicable woman call me? A fuck toy? And every time you fuck me, you're getting revenge on my father, so I guess I'm a two-for-one special."

If it was possible, Marcus's gaze got even darker. His voice was dangerous when he said, "What woman?"

"I didn't catch her name and she wasn't wearing a collar, but apparently you like to have threesomes with her, so I hope you at least know her name."

"Lucinda."

Stupidly, hearing her name on his lips hurt. Because Cora was a stupid, stupid girl.

But apparently Marcus was moving on without any more comment on his former or perhaps still current fuck toy. "If you think telling that reporter that I'm keeping you against your will will help you—"

Cora laughed bitterly. "If you have the New Olympian Police Department under your thumb, I'm pretty sure you'd handle the third most popular newspaper in the city without much effort." She leveled her gaze with his, which unfortunately meant she was still looking up to him, a disadvantage not even her three-inch heels could help.

"I want to see my friend, Maeve. She's got to be worried about me since I haven't even spoken to her since the wedding."

Even talking about the wedding hurt, remembering how hopeful and excited she'd been on that day.

Cora lifted her chin defiantly. "Besides, surely a mobster like you will take any good press he could get because that's how it works, right? The hypocrisy of this city? Everyone knows what's actually going on but you all come to parties like this and rub elbows and smile at each other and pretend you care about charities when it's all a smokescreen for the terrible reality?"

"Careful," Marcus barked and his hand came to her throat.

Cora kept glaring at him. "Lock me back up. Starve me. Hit me if you want to. It's nothing I haven't had before. I told you, I survived before and I'll survive you."

Something flickered in his eyes but before she could try to figure out what, Marcus grabbed her by her waist and twirled her so she was facing away from him. He dragged up the skirt of her dress and the next second, had her panties down.

There was the noise of a zipper and he pulled her back against himself. She felt the heat of his long shaft against her buttocks and her sex clenched in anticipation.

Such a stupid girl.

He bent his head over her shoulder so that his five o'clock shadow bristled against her ear.

"You will never disrespect me in public like that again. You'll do as I say. When I say."

He thrust inside her drenched sex. Her eyes all but rolled back in her head at the fullness of him. His fingers had felt good but this, oh, *this*—

"Sorry if I'm not your usual mindless bimbo fuck."

His arm circled around her chest and curved up until his hand was at her throat again. "Language," he growled.

And as if for good measure, he gave her ass a sound *smack*.

Cora let out a hiss of outrage even as her sex clenched around him. His other arm that was a bar around her waist dropped until his fingers were strumming her clit and immediately the pleasure started to rise again. It was always like this, she'd noticed. After having one orgasm, the second was easier and quicker to rise, as well as often being harder and more fulfilling.

"This doesn't change anything," she panted even as her hips bucked back against him in pleasure. "I still," gasp, "hate," gasp, "you."

"It's time to shut that pretty mouth of yours," he barked.

When he'd taken her virginity, he'd been gentle and patient.

It appeared that patience was at an end. He clutched her to him with both arms and he thrust deep and wild and violently.

Cora stopped thinking. She only felt with all her senses.

The wet sound and feel of his thick cock sawing in and out of her. The harsh noise of his breath in her ear. The smell of his sweat mixed with cologne. Looking down and seeing his strong, manly hands clutching and working her.

He was usually so in control. So studied and cold. But his thrusts were wild and his noises animal as he took her. He couldn't hold himself back any more than she could. This thing was bigger than the both of them.

Cora couldn't help the cry of pleasure that escaped her mouth when the climax hit this time and Marcus's hand moved from her throat to her mouth to muffle her noises. Somehow that made it even sexier, him fucking her so hard in this coat closet, hand over her mouth to keep her quiet. She clenched on him as the spasms rolled through her, involuntarily at first and then voluntarily as he swore in her ear and pumped even harder still.

He crushed his face into the hollow of her neck and thrust the deepest he ever had yet as she felt him, the heat of him as he spilled inside her and she felt a high beyond that of climax, of womanly triumph.

He pulled out and thrust in again, and again and he stilled, like he was unwilling to let go of the moment. He stayed there a long time, his breathing ragged and Cora clutched around him with every ounce of strength she had.

She didn't let the thoughts back in yet. Not yet. Not yet.

There was only Marcus and her in this moment, so perfectly connected.

She didn't know how long they stayed like that. A full minute? Two?

Before he finally pulled out and she felt his seed begin to slide out and down her inner thighs. Her sex clenched again, involuntarily, as if to keep him inside her.

She was glad she was faced away from him because she didn't know what he would have seen on her face in that moment.

She was only sure of one thing as she stared forward at the rack of coats, exhilarated and horrified by all that had just happened.

That had *so* not been part of the plan.

TWENTY

Three days later, Cora entered the dog shelter. A pause and she ran, flinging herself into Maeve's arms.

Maeve squeezed her close but only for a little bit before pulling back and holding Cora's shoulders. "Let me get a look at you." She'd been grinning, but her smile dimmed at looking Cora up and down. "Sweetie, are you all right?"

Cora's bottom lip trembled and she fought back tears as she nodded. She hugged Maeve again, hard.

"Oh, sweetie," Maeve said, rubbing Cora's back soothingly.

Cora closed her eyes and sank into her friend. She hadn't realized how much she'd needed a friendly face. Tears crested and fell down her cheeks but she didn't make a noise. She clung to Maeve. For a long time.

When she finally let go, she swiped at her eyes and gave a short somewhat false laugh. "I don't know what's come over me. So much has happened since I've seen you." She reached out and grabbed Maeve's hands, giving them a squeeze. "I'm sorry I didn't reach out sooner."

Maeve squeezed her hands back. "It's okay, I understand. I remember what it was like being a newlywed." Then her eyebrows furrowed. "But honey, seriously, are you okay?"

Cora swallowed hard and nodded.

Marcus had made it more than clear at breakfast that she wasn't to disclose any of the truth of their situation to her friend. He hadn't gone so far as to threaten Maeve's safety should she not comply but Cora wasn't about to put her in that position. Maybe it was selfish to even come back here. Marcus was dangerous. Putting Maeve anywhere on his or his Shades' radar wasn't doing her any favors.

But things between her and Marcus had continued to thaw even more since the gala. He was still letting her move freely throughout the apartment and they discussed letting her volunteer again at the shelter on a temporary basis, once a week. Today was the trial run.

Well, by *discussed*, she meant Marcus had decreed it, with a long list of conditions, including having his Shades guarding the front and back of the building and Sharo escorting her at all times.

Marcus worked all day and sometimes nights but they had meals together at least once a day, though they never did much in the way of talking. Sometimes he read to her, though. First from the newspaper. And without discussion, he'd plucked a book from the bookshelf and started reading it aloud. It was a Thomas Hardy novel and it was very beautiful and very sad.

And every night, without fail, he came to her room. He took his time with her. Sometimes it got a little rough, but it was never quick and, as much as she hated to admit it, it was never unwanted.

She'd begun to look forward to him coming home with an excitement that disturbed her.

He was the enemy. Wasn't he?

She. Was. So. Confused.

All that to say, Cora could use a friend now more than ever.

"I'm all right," Cora said and her smile was a little less tremulous this time. "I mean it."

The bell over the door jingled and the man from the gala walked in, the reporter, this time not in a tux but in jeans and an attractive gray Henley. He smiled as soon as he saw Cora and she waved.

"Maeve, this is the reporter I called you about, who wants to do a story on the shelter."

Maeve looked briefly at the man but her eyes came back to Cora. "We'll talk more later, okay?" Her eyes searched Cora's and Cora nodded.

"Definitely," Cora said.

Cora showed the reporter, Joe Garcia, around the shelter and explained how things worked as she went from cage to cage, feeding the dogs.

"We accept any and all strays and drop-offs, no matter what. Maeve has committed to this being a no kill shelter, which means that other than for dogs that are simply too old or too ill for us to care for, no animals are euthanized here. But that puts a huge burden on us to get these animals adopted and to continue caring and housing the ones that remain. We depend on donations and volunteers to stay afloat."

Joe nodded and made a couple of notes on the small pad he had with him. "And how long have you been volunteering here?"

"For about two and a half months, ever since I came to the city."

"Where did you live before that?"

Cora stopped in front of Puggles' cage as she opened his door and scooped in his food. "Out West," Cora said noncommittally. "We work hard to walk the dogs at least once a day, depending on how many volunteers come in. And when we can, we advertise our adoptive services. The more we're able to get the word out about this place, the more dogs we can save."

"Have you always had a love for animals?"

Cora saw what he was doing. He obviously wanted this to be an article more about her than the shelter, and no doubt any reporter worth his salt would try to dig to get what scoop he could.

Cora smiled sweetly at him. "This is Boris," she introduced him to a large German Shepherd. She opened the cage and poured in his dog food, giving him a belly scratch before closing it again. "Now I have a soft spot for him. He's big and intimidating looking, but once you get to know him, he's really a sweetheart." She leaned in. "A little like my husband."

Joe's eyebrows went up at that. "Oh really? Are you saying that Marcus Ubeli has a soft underbelly?"

Cora laughed. "Oh I wouldn't go that far. Marcus is many, many things but I wouldn't call him soft. Let's say he can be a perfect gentleman when he's of a mind to be."

Joe scribbled furiously at his pad, no doubt trying to record the quote.

Cora moved on. "A lot of people think adopting a dog from an animal shelter means getting an older animal, but that's a misconception. We have a lot of puppies, as you can see. It's unfortunate, but too many people take on animals they simply aren't ready for."

"But we work hard here to match potential owners to pets that are compatible with exactly what they're looking for. We don't want to see a dog back here in several weeks any more than an owner wants to bring them back. So we talk to people and have them fill out questionnaires. We spent time with the dogs to learn their quirks and habits, all so that we can make the best and most long-lasting matches."

Joe nodded and made a few notes, but not nearly with as much enthusiasm. "So how did you and Mr. Ubeli meet? Obviously you had a short engagement if you only came to the city two and a half months ago."

Cora gave a slight, enigmatic smile. "Something like that."

"Oh come on," Joe said. "Give me something for my readers. Marcus Ubeli, consummate bachelor, suddenly ties the knot after knowing you only a few months? The news set New Olympus buzzing. Surely you can give our readers some insight into your whirlwind romance. Did your families know one another?"

Cora stopped at that and turned her back to him. Did he know something? Did he know she was a Titan?

She worked to suck in an even breath as she took another scoop of dog food from the plate and poured it into the bowl of a stray border collie Jack Russell mix. No, there was no way he could know about who her parents were, otherwise the news would've been splashed all over the headlines long before now. She'd seen unpleasant headlines about Marcus before, and news *that* big… Even Marcus with all his power and influence might not be able to suppress it.

But most likely, Joe Garcia was shooting into the dark, hoping something would land.

Cora dragged the bucket over to the next cage and felt Joe follow behind.

Still not looking at him, she said, "I don't really know how to explain Marcus and me." Ha. That was the understatement of the century. "It was raining one night and I ran into his club to get out of the storm."

She finally looked back at Joe. "He dazzled me." More truth, even though the pang in her chest was more like an ax blade.

"And I guess I made an impression on him too. Have you ever experienced a moment and known, with everything inside you, that it was going to change the rest of your life? That's what meeting Marcus was like. There was my life before meeting him and my life after. And that's the way it'll be defined until the day I die. Before and after."

Joe had stopped scribbling. He stared at Cora, absorbed, as she told him the simple truth.

"I'm starting to see why Mr. Ubeli might have been dazzled in return," he said.

Cora tilted her head and smiled at him. "Flattery will get you everywhere, Mr. Garcia. Now come this way, I want to show you the puppies."

"THAT WENT WELL, I THINK," Maeve said, looking at Cora over her steaming cup of tea. Maeve always said there was nothing that couldn't be solved over a good cup of tea. But Maeve had only met Marcus once, and briefly, at the wedding.

"Hopefully the publicity will bring in more people to the shelter looking to adopt," Cora said.

"I was eavesdropping," Maeve admitted, making Cora smile.

"I would expect nothing less."

Maeve's face went serious. "But how are you really?"

She reached out and squeezed Cora's knee. They were sitting in the back of the shelter in Maeve's cramped office on stools beside the tiny rest area where a microwave, coffee, and tea station had been set up in a corner.

Cora tipped her head back and let out a heavy sigh.

"That bad?"

Cora looked back at her friend. "Not bad, necessarily," Cora said. She wondered how much she could say without revealing the true extent of it.

"Marriage is... Well, marriage to a man like Marcus is... more complex and intense than I was maybe prepared for."

"Honey, you're only what, nineteen? I'd be shocked if it wasn't, though I wish the honeymoon phase would've lasted a little longer."

Cora smiled. "Marcus works long hours and he's not always the best communicator." That was putting it mildly. "And I guess I worry that..." How to put this? "I came to the city to try to find myself. To be free of my controlling mother and now..."

"Now you're married to a controlling man?"

Cora nodded. Again, an understatement.

"It's not that surprising, honey," Maeve said gently. "It was what you were used to all your life. And it's true what they say, unfortunately. We are attracted to partners like our parents because it's all we know."

Cora dropped her face into her hand and groaned "Don't say that," she said. "The last person I want to be married to is someone like my mother."

Maeve laughed. But then she got serious again. "Is he good to you? Is he kind?"

Cora stared at the floor for a long moment before finally admitting, "Yes."

She looked up at Maeve. "He's not like my mom. He's not petty or mean for meanness sake." Then she wondered if that was true. "I don't know, it's still early. What if he really *is* like my mom?"

"Honey, you listen to me. You ever want to get away from that man, if he ever lifts a hand to you or starts being abusive with his words, you tell me. I don't care who he is, we'll get you away from here."

There it was. Everything she'd wanted to hear ever since Marcus had flipped the script on their wedding night. Someone willing to help her escape him.

But Cora shook her head and reached out to give Maeve's hand a squeeze. She told herself it was because she didn't want to bring down the world of trouble Maeve's words might incite from Marcus.

But she was afraid she believed her next words more. "I think I could be happy with him. It's been an adjustment and we're still learning to communicate but… I think I could be happy…"

She looked around her at the dogs in cages. Were the dogs happy there? They were well fed, taken out for walks once a day, and some of them in far better situations here than the abusive homes they'd been in before.

The dogs were grateful every time she poured food in their bowls or gave them a belly rub or took them outdoors for a walk.

But always they came back to the cage.

"Do you think they're happy?" Cora asked suddenly. "Spending their whole life waiting in these cages until someone thinks they're worthy enough to adopt them?"

"It seems to me," Maeve said quietly after a moment, "happiness starts in here." She leaned forward on her stool and pressed her fist to Cora's chest, right over her heart.

Cora looked up at her and her eyes stung again like when she'd first gotten to the shelter. She swallowed hard. "It's not that simple. All I ever wanted was freedom."

Maeve gave the slightest shake of her head. "You already are free, baby. You always were. Where it counted."

She lifted her fist and pressed it to Cora's chest again. "I want the best for you, girl, whether you want to leave or stay, and I'll help you whatever you choose. But till you demand your freedom here," she opened her palm over Cora's heart, "it won't matter who you're with or what rules they or their lifestyle puts on you."

"I don't understand," Cora said.

Maeve smiled. "You will."

TWENTY-ONE

Marcus sat at a table in the back of Paulie's with Sharo and several of his lieutenants. They did not have good news for him.

Angelo, a junior lieutenant, was animated as he spoke. "They hit us in the Westside, all at different parts of our business. One dealer was hit, two men approached him to take over his corner. He got away. A truck was targeted; we found it empty and abandoned on the Ape."

The Ape, or Appian Way, was the main highway that linked New Olympus to Metropolis.

"Obviously it was the Titans," Marcus said. "But you got anything more specific for me?"

"We're looking for the driver now. Could be that fucker defected. But the worst hit was Santonio's girls' incall house."

Shit. The incall house—as opposed to when the girls met clients at a hotel or on an *out*call—was usually filled with muscle to protect them. "What happened?"

"Two guys came in separately and booked overnights.

Drugged the girls and then snuck out of the rooms and set the house on fire."

Marcus got very still. "Casualties?"

Angelo shook his head. "Guys downstairs smelled the smoke and got everybody out in time, but the two girls are in the hospital for smoke inhalation. And one of the guys did some things to the girl while she was out. We're still waiting for her to wake up."

Prostitutes worked illegally but they lived in the Underworld and were therefore under Marcus's protection.

"Santonio's putting double protection on his stable."

"They weren't after the girls," Sharo spoke up, moving forward from the side of the room. His gaze met Marcus's across the table.

Marcus nodded. Sharo slept at the incall house a few times a week. Always with different girls. If he wasn't there, he was at a different incall house, but this one was his favorite.

He didn't even have a place of his own. If the man like sleeping next to a warm body at night, who was Marcus to judge? But the fact that the Titans were targeting Marcus's right hand man?

"They're getting bolder," Marcus said.

Angelo nodded, eyes locked with Marcus. "They hit us, we gotta hit back ten times as hard." He smacked his fist into his hand.

"How we gonna strike, boss?" asked Carlo.

Marcus could feel the energy from his lieutenants all around the room. This was a war they'd all been waiting for.

Marcus most of all.

But now that it was here?

Marcus felt uneasy. Those girls who'd ended up in the hospital tonight? They were just the beginning.

And while they might not be innocents in the eyes of the public, they were to him.

How much collateral damage would an all-out street war cause? How many innocents would have to die?

And for what?

All because he'd had to have his revenge and capture Cora. They'd been at an uneasy détente with the Titans for almost a decade now. He'd been the one to turn a Cold War hot again.

He hadn't even considered any other options at the time. He got report that Demi Titan was back in the city and he had to see for himself.

But of course it wasn't her. It was her daughter. And as soon as Marcus had seen her, he'd had to have her.

Chiara would finally be avenged.

It was all he could see. Only now, months later after having gotten to know Cora, had he started for the first time in years to remember Chiara's life and not just her death.

He thought he'd been honoring her memory by avenging her death, but all of this... More war? More death? It was the last thing she would've wanted.

"It's time to make our play," Angelo said when Marcus stayed quiet. "We send them the video Marcus took on his wedding night. We put the bitch up for ransom to draw the leadership out. Ambush those motherfuckers and kill every last one of them."

Only years of discipline stopped Marcus from throwing himself on Angelo and beating his face in for calling his wife a bitch.

Noises of assent came from all around the circle at Angelo's words. Clearly it was a popular idea.

It had been Marcus's idea in the first place and he'd

shared it with his lieutenants when he first began courting her.

"Can't," Marcus said sharply. "I fucked it up when I tried to transfer the video to my computer. The file got corrupted."

Angelo stared at him, obviously confused. "So make another one."

But the place he and Cora were at now, Marcus couldn't imagine doing anything that would make her cry like she had after he'd said that stupid shit.

And he'd lied to his lieutenants just now. The file hadn't gotten corrupted. He'd deleted it.

He'd been watching it, about to email it, and it made him sick to his stomach. For the first time in years, he heard Chiara's voice in his head. *Marcus, what are you doing? Do you think this is what I want?*

Before he could think better of it, he'd trashed it and emptied the trash.

"Marcus?"

Marcus glared at Angelo. This little shit was getting too big for his britches. He was only a junior lieutenant and he had a lot of nerve, questioning Marcus and throwing his balls around like he had any say.

"I'll think on it and get back to you."

Angela looked at him like he'd grown a third head.

"But boss—"

Marcus had had enough. He jerked Angelo up from his seat and shoved him back until he was flat against the wall, his hand against Angelo's throat. "It would behoove you to respect your elders. You've been in the organization what? Eight years? Everyone else at the table has fifteen years on you. So don't speak unless you're spoken to. And Cora might be a Titan but she's also my wife and as such she deserves respect. Do you hear me?"

Marcus pulled out his weapon and put it to Angelo's forehead. "Tell me you hear me."

Angelo's body started to tremble underneath Marcus's hand at his throat. "I hear you," he whispered shakily.

"Good," Marcus said with one last shove.

He turned back to the table and holstered his side arm. "The Titans will be dealt with. Their violence will not go unanswered. But we do it smart. Tiny, Fats, find out who their major supplier in Metropolis is. Double up the Shades' presence on the Westside. No more Titans get in our city that we don't know about. No more surprises. And find that damn driver, see what he knows. Meeting adjourned."

There were nods all around and the guys stood up and hurried off. Smart. Most people knew not to mess with him when he was in a mood. Angelo skittered off with his tail between his legs. Marcus would have to watch that. Angelo had a big ego and he was ambitious. That could be a dangerous combination.

Marco glanced at his watch. He knew he was old school, not staring at his phone every damn second, but people were on those things too much.

He looked to Sharo. "Everything considered, it might make sense for you to lay low for the time being."

Sharo nodded and left without another word.

Probably why the big man was his closest friend, if the term applied to anyone. He knew when it was best to keep his mouth shut.

TWENTY-TWO

It was a different driver than Sharo who picked Cora up at the shelter. She'd changed into a dress and heels as per Marcus's request and she fiddled with her purse strap. It felt strange to be driving in the car without Marcus. Strange to be anywhere without Marcus. And yet, Cora found herself doing the exact same thing she'd be doing if Marcus was in the car anyway.

She stared out the window, silent, hand on the glass as she watched the beautiful glittering lights of the city.

"Um, sir, can you put on some classical music? I think it's preset one?"

The strains of Rachmaninoff filling the Bentley made Cora relaxed back against the chair. Between the gentle lull of the music and the soft leather seats, Cora felt her eyes drifting closed.

She'd watched a TV show while Marcus was gone at work yesterday about these beekeepers who used smoke to daze the bees, lulling them into a false sense of security while the beekeepers emptied their hives of honey.

Was that what was happening to her? Being lulled into

a false sense of security by routines and little gifts after periods of hardship her husband himself had inflicted?

Was she being manipulated by a master?

She rolled her eyes at herself. What was with all the animal metaphors today? But maybe it was natural that she couldn't help thinking about traps and cages on the one day she was free.

The driver pulled in front of Paulie's, where apparently Marcus was already waiting. Several Shades shadowed Cora as she stepped out of the backseat and, looking both ways, they ushered her out of the car and hurried her into the restaurant.

She'd been here a couple of times, before they were married when Marcus had stopped in briefly for business and she'd drunk coffee in a front booth while he was in the back. Today though, Marcus was in the booth in a little room separated off from the rest of the restaurant. He was alone, not meeting anyone, as if he was waiting for her.

The waitress took Cora directly back to him and Marcus waved for her to take the opposite booth seat.

Cora nervously fingered her purse and sat down, scooting over until she was in front of him, the narrow table between them.

"How was your time with your friend?"

"It was good. Thank you for letting me go." The words were a little hard to get out. She shouldn't have to ask *permission* to go see her own friend. But she kept her temper in check because she really wanted him to award her more and more freedoms like this afternoon.

Marcus tilted his head at her and she wondered what he was thinking. Seemed like she was always wondering what he was thinking lately. His face was so unreadable and his actions often inexplicable. He'd eased up so much from the wedding night but she didn't know why or what was coming next. She was back to constantly waiting for the next shoe to drop.

"I don't suppose we could talk like real people?" she asked with a sigh.

Marcus's eyebrows went up in surprise. "By all means."

But that was all he said. She sighed again. He'd never make anything easy, would he?

"How was your day?" she asked.

He continued studying her, and shrugged. "I dealt with business."

Cora rolled her eyes. "Fine, don't tell me about your day. I'll tell you about mine. It was great to see Maeve again. And the dogs. The reporter was nosy but I kind of expected that." Her eyes had been wandering the restaurant but they came back to Marcus. "Don't worry, I didn't tell him anything."

"I wasn't worried that you would."

This time it was her looking at him in surprise.

"I give you more credit than that. You're smart. It's one of the things I like about you."

It was one of the things he liked about her?

"Though I might have let it slip how grumpy you are in the morning before you get your first cup of coffee." The teasing comment slipped out but she couldn't deny the way her chest warmed when she saw his lips twitch.

No. Stop it. No smiling at the sadistic captor. Getting on better terms with Marcus so he gave her more freedoms was one thing, but...liking it?

So she just started babbling so she wouldn't have to think about it anymore. "One of the golden retrievers was a little too eager to meet Joe when we took him out for his walk and started humping his leg. Maeve got him under control, though. She's trying to train him in some of the basics because she thinks he'll make a great family dog. We were hoping Joe would feature him in the article but *that* plan went a bit awry, what with the whole humping incident."

"Joe?" Was Cora crazy or was there an edge to Marcus's voice?

"You know, the reporter from the other night. Joe Garcia," she said, dismissing the thought. "Anyway, I think the whole thing went off pretty well. Hopefully it will bring some recognition and publicity to the shelter and will get more people in, wanting to adopt."

Her eyes lifted over Marcus's shoulder. "And it was good to see the dogs again..." Wait, she'd already said that. She bit her lip as she watched the waitress, Maria, approach with their food. Cora hadn't ordered anything or even seen menus.

"I took the liberty of ordering for us when the driver messaged that you were on your way."

"Oh," she said. She didn't like his high handedness, but it was Marcus. And when she leaned over her plate of pasta and took a deep inhale, she smiled. "Thanks. I'm famished."

"Enjoy," Marcus said, eyes still on her, not his food.

Feeling a little self-conscious, she dug in anyway. The meatballs and marinara were delicious. Simple fare but excellently executed. "Oh my gosh, this is amazing," Cora said as she finished chewing a large bite.

Marcus watched her with what looked like amusement as he ate his meal. She was embarrassed when she looked down and realized she'd polished off almost her whole plate and he was only halfway done.

"I'll give your compliments to the cook."

Cora felt her cheeks heat but decided, screw it. Good

food was good food and she wouldn't be embarrassed about enjoying it.

Hadn't Maeve impressed on her the point that happiness and freedom started with her? She wasn't sure she fully understood what Maeve had meant but she could guess that it had something to do with attitude and outlook. She could sit here and sulk about her situation and pick at her food.

Or, she could enjoy the fuck out of this amazing pasta, be satisfied that she'd had a great day at the shelter with her good friend, and tonight, if the pattern of the last week was anything to go by, she'd probably end the day with at least one earth-shattering orgasm.

Was it really that easy?

Be happy in her cage and move on with life?

"What are you thinking about so solemnly over there?"

Her eyes jerked back to Marcus. She didn't know how long she'd zoned out for, but he looked almost done with his pasta now. He gazed at her over his glass of red wine.

"Nothing," was her knee-jerk response, but then she took a deep breath. She was the one who said she wanted to talk about real things, right?

"I guess I was wondering...well I'm always wondering... what it is you want."

Marcus looked surprised again. "What do you mean?"

Was she really doing this? Maybe it was the afternoon with Maeve, maybe it was the fact that Marcus had been relatively nice to her lately, but she decided to take the plunge.

"Well," she started slowly, "I can't help but notice that things have been...different lately."

He didn't say anything so she went on.

"...And I guess I was wondering if you are still determined, um, for me to be...well, miserable."

Her eyes dropped to her plate but she glanced up briefly at him. Pointlessly, because his features gave no indication of what he was thinking.

So determinedly, she went on. "Because I was thinking, um, if you're out for revenge on my dad, us being together whether I'm happy or miserable still does that job. Because I'm guessing you're the last person on earth he would want me with."

Time to get the rest of it out quick. "I've never known the guy so I don't necessarily feel any loyalty to him and things were never that great with my mom. Anyway, what I'm trying to say is that may be a life here in New Olympus, a life with *you*, could be good. I mean, I could be contented if you were okay with me doing things like I did today, going out and not being locked in the apartment all day."

"And I could make it a good home for you," she hurried on to say. "I could cook and clean—"

"That's what the maid is for," Marcus said sharply.

Cora jumped at his voice, but hurried on. "Well I could do other things. Um, wifely things." Cora couldn't help but looked down at her plate again. "The gods know we're compatible in that department."

She took a quick breath in and forced herself to look back up at him. "I guess what I'm proposing is a cease-fire between you and me."

"A cease-fire," he repeated.

She nodded, forcing herself to keep his gaze even though like always, the intensity of his gaze made doing so a difficult feat.

He was quiet a moment but then he moved swiftly, standing and moving around the booth until he stood at her side, hand held down to her. "I accept."

Cora felt her mouth drop open. He accepted? Just like that?

"Okey-dokey," she whispered. She reached up her hand and he clasped it firmly.

"Tomorrow I'll have another stylist come in," he said as he swiftly walked to the front door, dragging her along with him.

Well he was full of surprises today. "Where are we going?"

"To the theater. But right now we're going home."

TWENTY-THREE

The driver turned off the boulevard of respectable brownstones into a private drive and radioed ahead for the caretaker to open the iron gates. A twenty-foot-tall railing ran all around the property perimeter, along with a thick evergreen hedge. It hid the grounds from the view of the street, and in the forested areas, delineated the property woods from the rest of the park.

Maybe Marcus hadn't liked her cease-fire idea after all and he'd brought her out here to kill her and bury her in the woods.

But no, the step forward they'd seem to take back at Paulie's had felt real enough.

Even now, while Marcus wasn't talking, just listening to music like normal, his hand was still outstretched towards hers, their fingers interlocking.

So she dared to ask, "Where exactly are we going? I thought you said we were going home."

"We are. To the Estate."

When he didn't say anything else, Cora pressed. "The Estate?"

Marcus let out a sigh, but it wasn't like she'd ever seen this place before and curiosity was natural. "The Estate is the last layover from the old Ubeli family wealth. Twenty acres of prime real estate, still within city limits. It backs up to the larger Park, which spans many more blocks."

"An oasis in the center of the city."

Marcus nodded.

"But hardly a welcoming place, as you can see." He gestured a hand towards the window.

And Cora got what he meant. As the car crept down the winding drive, she tried to picture a young Marcus running around the manicured lawns of the Estate. Even during the day, the shadows lay long under the ancient trees.

No wonder Marcus now preferred a modern penthouse to the dark Estate.

The Estate house itself loomed three stories over a paved forecourt. Built of stone, she'd bet the house could host twenty guests at a time overnight, and entertain a few hundred in the long ballroom. Tonight someone left the light on in one room upstairs. The rest of the windows were cold and grey, staring at the surrounding forest.

It all had a very Gothic feel. And taking a second glance at the Estate architecture itself, she finally saw it for what it was: a fortress, built by the elder Ubeli to protect his family during a war.

Two more cars pulled into the drive. Cora glanced out the cold windows nervously as Sharo and a few other men she recognized as Shades exited the black sedans in the drive.

"Why did we come here?" Cora asked as Sharo approached the house and opened the lock. Several Shades from the car behind him went inside first, no doubt to doublecheck the house for security purposes. Marcus had seemed particularly on edge lately and Cora had noticed more Shades around than usual.

"You said you wanted a cease-fire. And as my wife, you should be familiar with my family Estate. This is where I usually stay, especially on the weekends when I need a break from city life."

He was bringing her in. Letting her see all of him.

"My childhood was a very happy one here. Until it wasn't."

"Your sister," Cora whispered. "How old were you when she died?"

"Sixteen."

Cora watched the way the vein in his throat flexed as he swallowed and she'd bet anything in the world he blamed himself for his sister's death. But still, *sixteen*? He'd been a boy who'd already lost his parents, all alone in the world.

"I bet she was wonderful."

Marcus jerked his head once up and down and then turned away. "Come on, I'm tired. It's been a long day."

It was only about nine o'clock and while yes, the day had come with a certain amount of exhaustion, being in Marcus's most intimate space had adrenaline shooting like crazy through Cora.

Did he bring his girls here often? To impress them with his family's wealth? Somehow she doubted that.

Why hadn't he ever brought her here before?

No doubt tying up a captive and tossing her in the basement here would incur less risk than doing it at the top of one of the most in demand downtown hotels.

What if everything he said in the restaurant was just a lie to get her out here for exactly that purpose?

Cora's hands trembled as she reached for the seat

handle but the driver was already there, opening it from the other side. Marcus came around as well, offering a hand down to her. There was nothing else to do other than take it. The sharp points of her heels dug into the grass as she stood.

"Maybe I should have changed back into my sneakers I wore at the shelter," she murmured quietly.

"Don't worry. There's a stone path right up here."

"Oh. Okay," Cora said.

Marcus held her arm as they walked the narrow flagstone path from the drive to the door where Sharo was already waiting for them. Apparently the Shades' security check of the house had shown nothing awry and Sharo gestured them inside.

"We'd like the residence to ourselves for the evening," Marcus said and Sharo nodded.

"I'll let the Shades know. Only perimeter patrol."

Marcus raised his chin and then he and Cora were over the threshold and inside.

Marcus didn't seem to be in the mood to show her around, either.

No, he carried her straight up the central staircase, in spite of her repeated squeals that she could walk, she could walk! all the way down a short hall to the master bedroom, where he deposited her in the center of the bed.

He followed her down, sliding his knee between her thighs.

Oh, so they were going to start this portion of the evening early tonight, was that it?

He rarely came to her bed before midnight. Sometimes hearing him open the door woke her up, other times she managed to stay awake in anticipation. But it was barely nine o'clock, twilight still hung outside, and when Marcus leaned over he hit a button that turned on two table lamps to a soft muted glow. So apparently they wouldn't be doing this in the darkness, either, as was per their usual.

Cora trembled underneath him.

He planted his elbows beside her head on the bed and dipped his hips, dragging his erection against her most sensitive place. His greedy hands were on her thighs, reaching underneath the skirt of her dress.

His hands on her body felt so familiar.

Too familiar.

She'd gotten used to fucking this way.

But after all they'd said, if he really meant for it to be a cease-fire...

His lips kissed down her collarbone and the next thing she knew he had latched onto a nipple.

It wasn't that things had become routine in bed. Far from it. Marcus was always showing her new positions and ways to feel him inside her and to get her off.

But apart from the first time, he rarely sought eye contact. His kisses weren't often on the lips, and he took his pleasure and left to return to his own bedroom.

And Cora didn't think she could keep giving herself to him if that was the way it was going to continue.

She wasn't sure if Marcus felt her tense up beneath him, but his head came up and, as if he could sense the very thing she was thinking, his gaze caught hers.

If true inner freedom came with taking action and claiming it, well, here went nothing.

Cora grabbed Marcus's face with both hands and drew him down to her face. To her mouth.

She didn't know what she was doing. So she smashed her lips against his. It was awkward. She never initiated kisses and she was terrible at it—

But then his lips gentled on hers and his clever tongue began to tease at her lips until she couldn't help but relax in response. And when his hands on her sex over her dress did something that felt especially good, she gasped.

Marcus used the opportunity to slip his tongue in her mouth and oh—*oh*—

Her tongue moved tentatively to meet his and holy *shit*! The second the tips of their tongues touched, it was like connecting a live wire straight to her clit.

She moaned shamelessly and lifted her pelvis up against his hand.

"That's right," he growled. "That's how it should be. Give it to me."

At this point, Cora couldn't *not* give it to him.

He shoved her skirt up and her panties down, not even bothering to get them all the way off, just to her ankles.

She kicked at them but only halfheartedly because Marcus had shifted his weight above her. She hadn't even heard him undo his zipper, but the heat and length of him was undeniably at her center, the fat head of his cock pressing and teasing for entrance.

Cora let out the highest pitched cry yet. She wanted him. She wanted him more than anything she'd ever wanted in her entire life.

Now she knew her answer. She didn't care if she was caged or free. As long as she came home to this man every night, she would be happy. Deliriously so.

She loved him.

She grinned at the revelation, wanting to tell him so that he could feel her joy.

But the next second it dimmed. Because there was no way he felt the same. And what the hell was she doing, loving him? She was still the naïve girl imagining she was a princess and he was the prince and that there was still a way this could end in anything other than tragedy.

"What?" Marcus wrapped his arms around her and pulled her close. So close their chests were cemented together like...like he couldn't bear to lose her. "What has you looking so sad?"

She forced a smile. Dammit, she wouldn't ruin this. Caged or not, tonight she wanted to fly completely free. She wanted to let it all go. To surrender absolutely to the bliss of being in his arms.

She tried to kiss him and distract him but he shook his head.

"Cora," he demanded, balls deep inside her, invading her everywhere.

There was no getting away from Marcus Ubeli. There never had been.

"You were here, with me. But then you went away."

He was supposed to be some dangerous crime Lord. He wasn't supposed to see shit like that. But maybe reading people had made him so good at what he did.

Cora wanted to hide her face against his cheek. But she doubted he'd let her get away with that either.

So she looked up at him, and meeting his eyes this time was one of the bravest things she'd ever done in her life.

"Marcus," she whispered. "I still feel it. It never went away. Not fully. I still feel it, Marcus. And more."

Marcus's eyes got dark at that but he didn't make her explain further.

This time it was his lips crashing on hers and the way he kissed her, it was like he was devouring her. Did that mean that he, too—? Had he finally developed feelings—?

But there was no time to analyze things because it was moving quickly now.

Marcus fiddled with the zip at the back of her dress, managed to get it halfway down, whereupon it got stuck. And Marcus ripped the rest of the dress in half to get it off of her.

Cora screeched in protest but Marcus only grinned. It wasn't a twitch of his mouth, either. It was a full, all out Marcus grin accompanied by the dimple and it took Cora's breath away.

Which was unfair because then, when Marcus rolled them and flipped them, Cora was unprepared. Especially when she ended up on top.

"Wanna see you ride me, gorgeous."

Cora's mouth dropped open but the way his gaze glittered, Cora wasn't in a mood to deny him. So she undid the clasp of her bra and took it off, shaking her hair out of its pins while straddling him. It had the intended effect of making her tits jiggle back and forth.

Marcus groaned, "Stop with the torture. Get that hot little cunt on my cock again."

"So crude," Cora pretended to chastise, leaning over and wagging a finger in his face. This had the bonus benefit of allowing her nipples to brush the hair on his chest and pebble up.

A sight which was not lost on Marcus. "Fuck," he whispered harshly before reaching for her breasts.

He caught the entire weight of them in his large hands and he immediately began to roll them and gently pinch at her nipples.

She couldn't help the immediate whimpered gasps that came from his actions. "Yes, yes. Like that. Just like that."

She didn't want him to stop for even a second, so it was her who reached down to align his member with her entrance again.

And with him torturing her nipples and filling her again with his thick, long, shaft, she was right on the edge and yet it felt like they'd only barely begun.

She rolled her hips and ground down against him. She didn't care that they'd only begun. She needed it. She fucking needed it. *Now*.

So she rolled and ground down hard and dirty. She grasped Marcus's hair and crashed their mouths together as the orgasm hit her. She screamed it into his mouth and clenched around him as tight as she could. His thrusts started getting more frantic and she hoped he finished soon because she didn't think the orgasm would last for much longer.

Ohhhhhhhhhhhh. Oh! One last little aftershock and it was done.

Marcus had slowed down his thrusts and she frowned. Did he—?

A gentle chuckle from Marcus rumbling beneath her was her answer.

"No, honey, I didn't come yet. That was the first of many for you and when I come, you'll know it."

He rolled her yet again, this time so that she was on her stomach and he was coming at her from behind. He lifted her hips up and sank into her.

SMACK, he spanked her ass.

"Hey!"

Marcus chuckled deeper. "I may have let you be on top for a minute, but don't forget who's in charge."

Chill bumps raced up and down Cora's body. And not out of fear.

So Cora curved her head over her shoulder to look at him and she blinked her pretty lashes and she said, "Yes, Sir."

If she thought his eyes had been bright before, they were nothing to the way his entire face came alive at her words.

He landed another smack to her opposite ass cheek.

And afterwards he soothed the skin he just smacked, sliding a finger down and around his shaft to gather some of her cream and rub it all around her ass, including her asshole.

Where, as he began to fuck her again, she felt one of his fingers start to probe.

That sent her into a full-bodied shudder. What was he — That was so *dirty*—

So why did it feel so damn *good*?

He stroked forcefully in and out of her sex, one hand at her clit, the other at her ass. And it was so much stimulation, all Marcus, everywhere Marcus—

Cora unabashedly howled her second release, squeezing on Marcus as he hit that glorious spot inside her with his every thrust, clenching and releasing around him, and clenching and releasing and *clenching*—

Marcus was right behind her, leaning over her shoulder to kiss her as he stilled, violently jerked back once and shoved back home.

Cora clenched and squeezed around him, wanting to hold onto him forever.

But as the moments always did, this one too came to an end.

Cora felt tears immediately flood her eyes. What was she thinking? How would amazing, soul shattering sex help anything when it came to her confusion over Marcus?

Marcus climbed off her and Cora immediately rolled to the edge of the bed, reaching for tissues from the nightstand to clean herself up.

"Where's my bedroom?" she asked, proud of herself that she managed an even somewhat steady tone of voice.

Marcus didn't say anything but right as she'd tossed the tissues in the trashcan, an arm hooked around her waist from behind.

"Marcus, what—?"

But she was already being dragged back down into bed. Marcus climbed beside her, or rather behind her, spooning her. He threw the sheet and comforter over them.

He turned off the lamps on the side table with his other hand and settled into bed as if nothing was wrong or out of the ordinary.

Marcus had never *once* cuddled after sex.

Usually the man treated the bed like it was a hot potato he couldn't wait to get away from fast enough after they were finished. So what gave?

Marcus slid his hand around her waist. It crept upwards until he was cupping one of her boobs. He slung a leg over hers, all but pinning her to the bed.

Did he think she'd go wandering off throughout his grand Estate and find some family secret?

But as his breathing quickly eased behind her and he began to gently snore she was hit by an even more stunning thought: he'd really meant the cease-fire. The truce.

This was what life could be like with Marcus, as his wife.

Everything she'd said this evening to him over dinner... A big part of her never thought anything like that was possible with Marcus Ubeli. She thought she'd make her big speech and he'd keep on being his normal asshole self and at least she wouldn't feel as bad about running when the time came.

But now?

She sank her head into the pillow beside Marcus, while his arms wrapped around her, making her feel more safe, beloved, and cherished than she ever had in her life.

And what, exactly, was she supposed to do with *that*?

TWENTY-FOUR

Cora was exquisite in the red velvet dress that hugged her curves in all the right places. Marcus stopped in her doorway and watched as she put on her earrings. She was so beautiful, it almost hurt to look at her. She smoothed down the skirt of the dress, eyeing herself in the mirror and touching her earrings, double checking they were fastened correctly.

From the slight crinkle in her brow, Marcus could tell that she wasn't seeing what he was seeing. At first he thought it was an affectation—her pretending not to know the effect of her beauty. But he'd slowly realized she genuinely didn't see it. She considered herself plain. Ordinary. Her mom had really done a number on her. She didn't know how special she truly was.

Marcus wasn't sure if he looked forward to the day she finally realized it or not. With enough time, would she be spoiled and corrupted like everything else in this city?

No, the answer came to him almost as swiftly as the question had.

Cora wasn't like anyone else he'd ever known. She

wasn't afraid of him and she didn't want anything from him, apart from the obvious, to be rid of him. He couldn't help the smile quirking his lips at the thought.

And now?

Now that he'd felt her soften and go pliant underneath his touch, even knowing all she did about him? Could he ever let her go?

Again the answer came swiftly.

Never.

He cleared his throat and Cora jolted, spinning around to look his way.

"The driver is waiting with the car."

Cora nodded. "Of course. Let me get my shawl."

Marcus had it over his forearm and he held it out to her. It was a luxurious mink shawl and he draped it around her shoulders.

He wrapped it around her and captured her arms with it, pulling her back against his chest and dropping his nose to the back of her neck. Her hair was done up, exposing the area.

He inhaled deeply and dropped a kiss right behind her ear. "You look exquisite tonight," he breathed.

"T-thank you," she stuttered.

Marcus smiled against the back of her neck, held her captive another moment, and finally let her go.

"Come," he said, finally pulling back. "We don't want to miss the opening act."

She nodded but Marcus didn't miss the way her breath hitched.

She turned and he took her arm, guiding her out of the penthouse and to where the driver was waiting outside the lobby with the Bentley.

Neither of them said a word until Marcus had her tucked safely in the back of the car.

When Marcus spoke, Cora looked over at him in surprise. "Cora, I want you to know..." He was usually quiet in the car. It was one of the few places where all the noise and people wanting his time and attention stopped.

But right now, he was more interested in Cora. He wanted to make her understand.

"I wasn't always like this."

Cora's eyebrows knit together and she didn't say anything but he definitely had her attention.

"Growing up, my father always wanted the best for his family. He would've done anything for my mother and us kids. But he was an immigrant and powerless to stand up to the Titan family. They used to run the streets."

Now he definitely had Cora's attention.

"The so-called 'protection tax' the Titans asked for ate up almost all my father's income. Everyone else's too. So my father decided to do something. He hadn't come to this land only to be poor and starving like in the old country."

Cora hadn't taken her eyes off him.

"And Gino Ubeli was a natural leader. He built the outfit up from nothing and within five years, he was challenging the Titans for territory. It was all out war. The Titans had held a monopoly over New Olympus for decades by that point, but their supremacy had made them lax in enforcement."

"It was Karl, Ivan, and Alexander's father who had created the Titan Empire, they were just the heirs. They'd never fought for territory before and they were laughably bad at holding onto it."

Cora swallowed hard but she didn't avert her gaze, not even when he said her father's name. *Karl.*

"They thought to crack down by becoming more vicious in their collection endeavors. They went after not only the men who owed them but their families. It had the opposite effect they intended. Because my father promised people that he lived by a Code. No one would suffer but the sinners themselves. The innocent would be left out of it."

Marcus's eyes drifted to the window as he thought of Chiara. "My father held fast to his Code until the day he died."

Marcus shifted his gaze back to Cora. "The Titans, however, lived by no such Code."

"Chiara," Cora said.

Marcus nodded but he couldn't say more about his sister. Not tonight. Maybe not ever. "Anyway, that's how it began. I took over for my father and I tried to enforce his Code. It might not be anything you could ever believe, but I do what I do to keep those like Chiara safe." Even as he said it, though, he felt his own hypocrisy. Because no one was more like Chiara than the woman sitting on the seat beside him.

Cora's small hand found his.

He pulled away. What was wrong with her? How could she look at him like that, with eyes brimming full of sympathy? Her family and his were natural enemies from the day both of them had been born.

She had no business looking at him with understanding. Especially after what he'd done to her.

He didn't even know why he was saying all this. Why was he trying to pretend that he was anything other than what he was?

"Forget about it."

"No. No, Marcus, no."

She grabbed his hand again. "You look at me this time."

He looked at her if only because nobody else had the balls to try to order him around like that.

"I'm so sorry for what happened to your sister, Marcus. I'm so sorry that any of this happened. We should have met in a different world where you were just a man and I was just a woman."

He shook his head but he couldn't help reaching out and caressing a thumb down her face and over the apple of her cheek. So much of his life dedicated to protecting it and he'd almost forgotten what it looked like—true innocence.

"You're a marvel," he murmured.

He continued tracing with his thumb, over to her mouth and across her plump bottom lip. She sucked in a sharp gasp at his touch.

He smiled. She was so affected by him. Even when she'd professed to hate him, she'd always been so affected.

The devil in him drove him to thrust his thumb between those sweet lips. This was *her* effect on him. It was impossible to see her innocence without wanting to have it all to himself.

Her tongue darted forward to lick the pad of his thumb in her mouth and immediately his dress slacks became uncomfortably tight.

He only pulled back with reluctance. As much as he'd like to shove that fancy dress up and pull her into his lap, he didn't trust that he wouldn't rip the damn thing off considering the things he felt like doing to her. And he wanted to give her this night.

She loved the theater. She lit up reading the stupid brochure the night of the auction. The desire to put her needs first was a strange impulse he felt himself giving into more and more.

He was glad when they arrived on Theater Row and the

driver pulled to a stop. Sometimes the train of his own thoughts around Cora unsettled him.

Several of his Shades approached the car as he helped Cora out. He raised his chin to each of them, all men he trusted. They would be on guard at all times tonight both in and outside the theater. Sharo was still lying low.

Marcus took Cora's arm as they headed into the theater. It was the largest and grandest theater on the Row, with a huge marquee all lit up with flashing bulbs. Marcus wanted to hustle Cora inside but she'd stopped, staring up at it all, her eyes wide, perfect lips parted, glowing like a goddess.

Marcus stood there drinking her in for a moment. Too long a moment. It wasn't safe here out on the street. Marcus frowned and grabbed her arm more firmly.

"Let's go," he ordered gruffly.

Cora huffed, obviously annoyed at him but he ignored her. She never understood even the basics of what it took to stay safe in a city like this. Obviously. She'd walked right into his waiting clutches when he was so obviously a lion and she a lamb.

Well she might not have any instinct for self-preservation but he did, and he'd keep her safe no matter what. Safe from everyone but him.

He led her up the grand, red carpeted staircase and down the secluded hallway to the balcony of the box seats. Ushers looked at them as if to ask about their tickets but as soon as they got close enough and recognized Marcus's face, they simply dropped their heads and scurried away again.

Box seats weren't always the best seats in the house but they were in this theater. Marcus helped Cora settle into the front row of the box seat that provided a perfect, unimpeded view of the entire stage and orchestra.

Even though nothing was happening yet, Cora seemed

mesmerized, using the tiny binoculars to look at all the people who were arriving.

"Everyone looks so fancy," she whispered, breathless.

Marcus smiled at her. Her neck was long and elegant with her hair done up like that. He followed the lines down to her creamy chest and the smallest peek of cleavage afforded by the elegant gown. He could barely wait until later tonight. He could imagine it, what the buttery soft velvet would feel like under his skin as he grabbed her around the waist and slowly, slowly slid down the zipper at the back, unwrapping his prize.

"Oh, sorry," Cora said, dropping the little bronze binoculars and holding them out to him. "Did you want to look?"

"Everything I want to look at I see just fine," he murmured, taking another slow perusal of her body up and down.

Her cheeks flushed such a pretty pink in contrast to the pale of the rest of her face. She was so young and fresh, like an unplucked petal.

"What am I going to do with you?"

Her eyebrows wrinkled the tiniest bit and Marcus could have sworn he saw a quiver to her lip. Her features were full of unchecked emotion and vulnerability. As if a word from him could make or break her.

Foolish girl. Foolish, foolish girl.

But how could he berate her for it when it was what he lo—

He shook his head—when it was what he *appreciated* about her most?

But he was disturbed enough by his almost mental slip up to turn away from her. Luckily the lights around the theater began to dim at the same time.

"The show is about to start," he said unnecessarily, lifting a hand and running it through the back of his hair.

He was glad when darkness settled completely over the box and lights focused down on the stage.

The play was a modern retelling of *Romeo and Juliet*. Marcus had sat through it before but not paid much attention to the narrative. The theater was a nice, respectable place to meet up with contacts who didn't feel comfortable coming to visit the Underworld.

He couldn't say he was getting much more out of the show this time around, either. It was much more fascinating to watch the play of emotions on Cora's face instead.

Her hands clutched the wooden railing of the box seat as she bent over, mesmerized for the entire production. At the end, copious tears poured down her cheeks and she jumped to her feet, clapping furiously.

She wasn't shy about sharing her thoughts, either. As soon as the lights came back up, she was talking a mile a minute.

"If she'd just woken up a minute sooner," she gushed, tears still wet on her cheeks. "Or if he hadn't been so stupid and rash in killing himself like that. And nobody should rely on a stupid bike messenger when it's about life and death! What were they thinking?!"

Marcus nodded to his Shades as they exited the theater, putting his hand to the small of Cora's back and leading her to the car that was waiting at the curb.

"How did you not even tear up?" Cora exclaimed, pausing on the sidewalk. "Did you not just watch the same play that I did?"

Did she know how kissable she looked when she was in a pique?

Marcus smiled down at her. "In the car," was all he said.

Cora shook her head at him but scooted into the car after he held open the door for her.

He got in and instructed the driver, "Take us back to the Estate." The driver's head dipped, formal as always with his round chauffeur's cap firmly in place.

"I mean Juliet was so sweet and smart, Romeo should've known she would've found another way to be with him. If only he would've trusted her—"

Marcus silenced her with a kiss. He'd wanted to do it since midway through the first act when she'd begun biting that luscious bottom lip in anxiety over the lovers on stage.

He sucked her bottom lip into his mouth and nipped at it with his teeth until a petite little groan escaped her throat. Fuck, yes. It was so easy to lose himself in her. In the feel of her soft body molded to his as he laid her down across the backseat. In the taste of her on his lips.

She was so innocent. Good. Pure...

Except for the ways he alone could defile her. No other man would ever hear those little breathy aroused noises she made. No one else would ever revel in her delighted giggle as they ran their stubbled cheek along her neck.

He would never let her go. She was his, for always.

She'd come into his life like the sun bursting through the clouds after a long, frozen winter. He'd tried to deny it. He hadn't wanted to admit how precious she was to him. He'd been so blinded by his agenda and his thirst for revenge but now...

He looked down at the face that brought him so much... He shook his head as he pulled back and brushed a wisp of hair behind her ear.

"Cora, these last couple of months with you... I never thought that I..."

Her eyes searched back and forth between his. "You never thought that you...?"

She looked like her life depended on what he was about to say next.

But something had caught his eye out the window—First Athens Bank? Why were they on Athena Boulevard? They were supposed to be heading east out of the city to get back to the Estate.

Marcus frowned and looked in the rearview to try to catch the driver's eye. As if feeling his gaze, the driver glanced back at him.

The eyes were feminine and he didn't have any female Shades.

Shi—

It all happened so fast. The driver stomped on the brakes and the car wheels screeched, Marcus barely had time to wrap his arms around Cora, and they were both thrown forward against the seat in front of them. At least Cora always put her seatbelt on and the driver's seat stopped Marcus from flying too far forward, although it hurt like a son of a bitch when he rammed into it. Cora's terrified scream filled the car.

Marcus didn't bother shouting. There was no time. He had to focus. He had to get Cora out of there. As soon as the car stopped—

The car finally came to a stop and Marcus struggled with Cora's seatbelt to get it undone.

"Take your hands off her. Hands up."

"*Mom?* What are you doing?!"

Marcus turned and there she was. Demi Titan, pulling off the chauffeur's hat that had hidden all her dark brown hair and tossing it to the side.

She held a sizable pistol, the barrel pointed straight at Marcus's chest.

"Cora, get out of the car," Demi ordered.

"Mom, put the gun down!"

Demi never took her eyes off of Marcus even as her voice got sharper with her daughter. "Get out of the car now or so help me, Cora, you won't like the consequences."

Marcus already had reason to hate this woman but her treatment of Cora only cemented it. If he moved quick enough, he could jam the gun upwards and even if she got a round off, it would land harmlessly in the—

"Tell your sister I send my fondest regards," Demi said. "Poetic justice, if you think about it. Mine was the last face she ever saw, too."

Wait, what? *She'd* killed Chiara—

"Mama! No! I love—"

Two things happened at once, simultaneously really. It was a moment Marcus would live and relive over and over again in his memory. Why hadn't he seen what Cora had? Why hadn't he realized that Demi was done eulogizing?

Because there was the explosion of a gun firing right at the same time as Cora's body slammed into Marcus's.

Demi's agonized scream only reinforced what his brain refused to process.

No.

Cora hadn't really just jumped in front of a bullet for him.

She wasn't *that* foolish.

But when he pushed her back onto the seat, her face was ghostly pale and, though not immediately visible against the red velvet of her dress, his hand came away slick with her blood when he touched the left side of her chest.

Demi had thrown away the gun and was screaming and

reaching back to try to get to her daughter, but Marcus shoved her away.

"Drive! She's going into shock, get us to New Olympian General. We're five minutes out."

Blood streamed down Cora's bare arm now and pooled on the leather seat underneath her.

Marcus put pressure on the wound. "Stay with me. Cora, do you hear me?" he barked. "Stay with me, dammit!"

Cora's dazed eyes drifted towards him but he wasn't sure she heard him at all. Fuck!

"Drive faster," he shouted to the front.

Demi didn't say anything but she did run the next red light, barely skirting past an oncoming car. Marcus didn't care. Cora's breath was labored and her eyes were erratic.

"Stay with me. Stay with me, Cora." It was all he could say. He kept chanting it until it was a prayer.

She couldn't leave him. She couldn't fucking leave him now that he'd found her. He couldn't go back to—to— There was no life for him without her in it.

"We're here," Demi called and Marcus looked up to see that they were indeed at the hospital, at the emergency room entrance. Demi pulled the car all the way up to the entrance and several emergency room techs ran out.

Marcus shoved open the back door. "Bullet wound, upper left chest. She's losing a lot of blood."

Several more techs had brought a gurney and together they expertly lifted Cora out of the car and up onto the gurney.

Marcus followed behind as they wheeled her into the hospital. He only spared one glance back for Demi, standing beside the driver side door, watching her daughter be wheeled away.

He should have texted his lieutenants right then and

there to grab the woman before she could sneak out of the city.

Instead, he kept running beside the gurney. Blood, there was so much blood. It was even more apparent against the white of the gurney sheets. So much blood. Just like Chiara. It was just like Chiara, and what if he lost Cora, too?

More people joined the procession running beside Cora as they flew down the hall with her. Nurses, doctors, all of them calling out questions and medical jargon that Marcus could only half follow.

He clasped Cora's hand and kept up his mantra, interspersing, "Stay with me," with, "I won't ever let you go."

But as they finally wheeled Cora into a room for surgery, an orderly pushed Marcus back. "You can't come in here, sir."

Marcus glowered at the man and got right in his face. "She's my wife," he growled. "And she just got shot. You do not want to try to get between me and her right now."

The orderly looked like he was about to shit himself but with a wobbling chin, he repeated, "No loved ones allowed in during surgery, sir."

"Do we have a problem here?" asked a second man, a nurse who had moved from Cora's side to join the orderly, blocking the door.

"Get back to my wife's side," Marcus all but shouted. "What the fuck are you doing over here? She needs you over there." He pointed back to where four people hovered around his wife, all of them working on her. He wanted to be beside her as well, holding her hand, promising her he'd make everything okay again.

But that was a crock of shit.

There was every chance that nothing would be okay. That she would *die*.

The orderly put his hand on Marcus's arm to try to guide him out of the room and Marcus shoved him off. But he turned of his own accord, not wanting to distract them all from the far more important work of focusing on Cora. He stormed down the hallway several paces as they shut the door to Cora's room.

For a second, he was completely at a loss.

What was he supposed to—

How could he—

He turned to the hallway wall and banged both fists against it, letting out an enraged roar.

What the *fuck* had she been thinking?

Throwing her body in front of a *bullet* for him?

Why would she do that?

Why the fuck would she do something so fucking idiotic?

He'd effectively kidnapped her for gods' sake. He'd seduced and married her under false pretenses. Put a collar around her neck and chained her to the bed. Who in their right mind would take a bullet for someone like that?

If she wasn't dying in the other room, he would go and fucking strangle her for her stupidity.

He wanted to strangle someone, that was for damn sure. Someone needed to pay. Blood for blood.

He whipped his phone out of his pocket finally and dialed Angelo before even calling Sharo.

"Yeah boss?"

"You've got your war. Hit the vulnerable targets you've talked about in Metropolis. I want blood. I want the streets to rain with fucking blood."

TWENTY-FIVE

The war with the Titans was begun. And Cora was in a coma.

It was a medically-induced coma, the doctors kept reminding Marcus, as if that was supposed to make him feel better.

They said she would wake up any time now. But they'd been saying that for days. And she still hadn't woken up.

The bullet had entered her chest and gone down into her gut, which was better than if it had traveled toward her heart or lungs, but still—fucking *coma.*

Marcus sat by her hospital bed, her cold little hand lifeless in his. When he wasn't conferring with his lieutenants, he was here. Sitting on this hard, plastic chair, holding her hand.

Oh what the great Marcus Ubeli had been reduced to. He squeezed his stinging eyes with his thumb and forefinger.

"The doctor said it's good to talk to you. That hearing familiar voices might help you, I don't know." He shook his head, looking out the window at the cold, dreary rainy day.

"Might make you wake up faster. Or that you might still be able to hear my voice or some bullsh—"

"Anyway," he leaned forward, giving her hand a squeeze. "I'm not sure if my voice is one you'd be excited to wake up for, all things considered... But I'm all you've got."

None of his Shades had been able to get a beat on Demi before she slipped out of the city. Which was probably a good thing. Marcus didn't trust himself with her if he ever got his hands on the woman. She put Cora in this bed. But not only that.

Tell your sister I send my fondest regards. Mine was the last face she ever saw, too.

If Demi was telling the truth, it hadn't been Cora's father after all who'd killed his sister. And why would she lie? She'd thought it was Marcus's last moment on earth. No, she was telling the truth.

And the more Marcus thought about it, the more it made sense.

The Titans had been a smart outfit back in the day. They hadn't just been brawn, there'd been brains behind the operation as well.

Except that, after they got kicked out of New Olympus and retreated to Metropolis, they devolved to being just brawn.

Because Demi had taken off with her small daughter. And she'd been the brains all along. It was only because she was back that the Titans were able to do the scheming and machinations it took to even attempt to retake their territory in New Olympus.

It had been right under Marcus's nose the entire time and he hadn't seen it. Demi was a woman in a traditionally man's game and she'd used that fact to make everyone underestimate her. Including Marcus.

It wasn't a mistake he'd be making again.

So many mistakes.

"This wasn't supposed to happen." Marcus let go of Cora's hand and shoved his chair back, standing up. "None of this was supposed to happen." He kicked the chair for good measure.

"I had a plan. I had a plan and you weren't supposed to be— I was never supposed to..."

He shook his head, then he walked back to her bed and put a finger in her face. "I didn't ask for this. I'm a simple man. I want simple things. To keep a lid on this city when every damned day some new idiot thinks they are gonna try being a big shot and steal somebody else's territory. I keep the drug running to a minimum, I see that it stays out of the schools, I make sure Santino treats his girls okay, and the gods know no gun goes in or out of the city without my say-so."

He got further in Cora's face. "And do I do it for the money?" He laughed, pulling back. "What the hell would I do with more money? You see how I live. Money is only good because it gets you power. That's the only currency I ever cared about. Without me calling the shots, this whole place would go to shit. I know because I tried once, letting someone else take the lead. But I already told you that."

Marcus collapsed on the side of Cora's bed. Her slim body was so small, there was plenty of room. "What I didn't tell you was that it was *me* that got my sister killed. I should've claimed my birthright the day my mother and father were gunned down. But I didn't." His voice almost broke on the last word. His deepest fucking shame.

"I let them down and I let Chiara down." He bent over Cora's body and whispered his confession with his forehead to hers. "It's my fault she died. We hid. For an entire year, we hid away at the Estate. I *didn't* continue the work my father had started. I let the Titans run rampant in the city, naïvely thinking they'd leave us alone."

He shook his head, his voice a bleak whisper. "We were both kids. Teenagers. I thought they'd leave us alone."

But it hadn't mattered to Cora's mother. Marcus should have known any Ubeli would be considered a threat as long as they drew breath.

Marcus hadn't even considered it, though. Because his father lived by a Code. Women and children were left out of it, kept separate from the business. It was Gino Ubeli's most sacred law.

But he should have known that the Titans had no such scruples. He should have known and, even though he was young, he should have taken up the mantle his father had left behind. He knew the business. His father had begun schooling him from the time he was eleven. All the players knew him well.

They certainly hadn't minded taking orders from him a year later when he was sixteen. Then again, he hadn't been a normal sixteen-year-old. After Chiara's death...

Mom had always said he was a sensitive child. But he'd numbed any sensitive parts he had left and made himself a robot.

He executed men without even the blink of an eye. He felt nothing. And he'd gone on feeling nothing. For so long that it became normal. It was good for business. He could make the ruthless calls without emotion.

"Until you, Cora," he whispered, lifting his head and looking up at her. "Please come back to me. Come back to me, Cora." He cupped her face roughly. "You have to come back to me. You've made me feel again and it scares the shit out of me. I was never supposed to feel this deep ever again. I was never supposed to love anyone—"

He pressed his lips to hers but they were cold and unmoving underneath his.

"Wake up," he commanded. "Wake up!" She was always so good at obeying before. Why the fuck not now?

He shook her shoulders in frustration. With great effort, he stopped. What the hell was he doing? He let her go and stood up again, taking a step back. Jesus Christ. He turned his back on her and scraped his hands through his hair.

What the hell was he doing? He was acting crazy.

And he didn't love her.

He couldn't.

What was he doing here day after day, hovering over her bed like a lovesick schoolboy? It was because of her that he hadn't taken action sooner against the Titans.

Again. He'd been lulled into thinking that there was a path forward that could actually lead to peace, when long experience had taught him that brute force and violence was the only language the world understood.

He turned for the door. No, softness had no place in his life.

He opened the door only to find Sharo on the other side, his fist raised like he was about to knock.

"What is it?" Marcus barked.

Sharo looked him up and down. "Brother, are you all right?"

Marcus glared at the bigger man even though Sharo towered over him. Things had really gone to shit if his second in command thought to question him so intimately. That was not how their relationship worked. Marcus gave commands and Sharo enacted them. Sharo offered wise counsel at times and could play devil's advocate with the best of them. But never did they ask one another about their personal lives or their fucking feelings.

"Report," Marcus demanded.

Apparently Sharo wasn't giving in that easily, though. "It's okay to take a minute," Sharo rumbled. "You care for the girl. I see how you are around her and I like what I see."

Well now Sharo was really starting to piss him off.

"You saw me playing a part," Marcus snapped. "Cora was always a chess piece for me to play against the Titans. And she served her purpose. She drew Demi out and now we know who's the real brains behind the operation. And as an added bonus, wifey dearest made herself a shield and took a bullet for me. I'd say that's mission accomplished as far as she's concerned, better than I ever could've hoped for. Plus, she's a great lay, so—"

"That's enough," Sharo cut him off, stepping up and getting right in his face. "I know you're hurting and that's the only reason I'm not—"

But then Sharo's head jerked up as something behind Marcus's shoulder caught his eye and he pushed Marcus to the side.

"Bella, you're awake!"

TWENTY-SIX

Ten Minutes Earlier

EVERYTHING WAS DARK. So dark and cold.

Cora had never felt colder in her entire life, or more alone. It was like being locked in the cellar but a million times worse. In the cellar, at least she'd been able to feel the floor beneath her feet. She could count the steps up to the door, nine steps up and nine steps back down. There were the brick walls. How many hours had she spent feeling along the contours of each one, memorizing them?

But here in the void, there was nothing. She tried to scream but no noise came out. She tried to flail her arms but they wouldn't move. She couldn't even feel them. She heard voices, muted, coming from very far away through the dark fog.

I'm here! I'm right here. Come and find me!

But no one ever heard her. No one lifted a hand down into the darkness.

The voices moved away.

But they'd come back. Closer. She concentrated so hard. *Please,* she begged.

And she heard it. Clear as a ringing bell.

His voice. Calling her name.

"Cora."

Everything within her, all of her soul, recognized him.

Yes, I'm here!

"Come back to me, Cora."

I'm here. I'm here, can't you see me?

He was commanding her to wake up and for the first time after wandering for so long in the darkness, in that terrible, terrible void, she felt something. Actually *felt* it.

His hands on her face.

She was back in her body. She could feel her limbs, her arms and legs and face and fingers and her nose.

Her lips. Her lips that he was kissing.

But he was gone, pulling away right as sensation came back to her body in lapping waves, a little more each second.

And with it came a terrible heaviness. She was back in her body again, but it felt like she'd gained five hundred pounds. She tried to lift her hand to signal Marcus but it was a lead weight. It wouldn't budge.

Her eyelids felt the same but she cracked them determinedly open.

Blinding light split the darkness and everything tumbled together, the void and the light and Marcus. Cora wanted to cry and she wanted Marcus to hold her again. She wanted his hand in hers. She remembered that, how he would hold her hand sometimes.

Was he even still here?

She dropped her eyes closed again and listened. *Yes.* There was his voice. And Sharo. They were both here.

She had to let them know she was awake. What if they left her because they didn't know she was here? She couldn't let them leave, she couldn't let them—

So, even though it took everything she had, she forced her eyelids open again, but she wasn't any better prepared for the blinding light.

She focused on the voices to help steady her and forced her eyes open even wider.

And that's when she heard his voice again. His precious voice.

But... The things he was saying...

Cora was a chess piece... served her purpose... mission accomplished... a great lay.

Cora blinked. Once and then again. No. Someone was playing a trick on her. Or her mind was. She wasn't awake yet after all. This was a horrible dream because her Marcus would never say things so cold and callous. She meant something to Marcus. Didn't she?

Liar. How many lies had she told herself to make her situation more palatable? She'd done it back when she lived with her mother and all over again with Marcus. Telling herself they loved her. A thousand times even when all the evidence was to the contrary.

Pathetic.

"Bella, you're awake." Sharo at least sounded genuine in his excitement at seeing her awake.

The light was still painful but Cora dragged tired eyes over toward the large man as he hurried to her bedside. Her vision was a bit blurry but she didn't miss Marcus in the background keeping his distance.

Sharo took her hand and, focusing, she managed to give a wan squeeze.

She let her eyes close again.

Now she knew the truth. She and Marcus weren't star-crossed lovers or any of the rest of the romantic bullshit she'd made up in her head.

She was still the puppet and everyone else still thought they were pulling the strings.

"I'm gonna take you home," Marcus told her as he walked over, and she bowed her head in agreement.

One thing was sure, though.

She'd never let herself be taken in by Marcus Ubeli again. She'd escape New Olympus and his clutches as well as her mother's. She'd find someplace she could truly be free.

And in the meantime, she imagined lifting her leaden fist to her chest, she'd be free where it mattered most—the part of her that none of them could ever touch.

MARCUS & CORA'S STORY CONTINUES...

Keep reading for a sneak peek of Awakening.

AWAKENING
A DARK MAFIA ROMANCE
BESTSELLING AUTHORS
LEE SAVINO &
STASIA BLACK

PREVIEW OF AWAKENING

CHAPTER ONE

Cora leaned against the giant window in the expansive living room of the most expensive penthouse in the most expensive hotel in New Olympus.

Far, far below, people scurried like ants down the narrow sidewalks. Cars crawled through rush hour traffic.

If Cora waited long enough with her face pressed against the glass, would she see a woman, young and beautiful with stars in her eyes, step off the bus and spin in a slow circle, mouth parted in awe at the magnificent cityscape? Maybe the young woman would look up and imagine someone like Cora, diamonds in her ears and hair sleekly coiffed away from her made-up face.

Would the young woman be wistful, wondering what it'd be like to live in the penthouse and float in the beautiful world above the streets? If she could hear Cora whisper, *Get back on the bus, run away,* would the young woman escape before the darkness swallowed her whole?

Cora backed away from the window, chest heaving.

Only months ago, she'd been that young woman. The city had been beautiful, overwhelming and alien, a far cry from the blue skies and waving wheat of the farm she'd grown up on back in Kansas.

She been full of so much hope. She'd ascended the heights and now she lived in her husband's penthouse, with everything she could desire. Diamonds and dresses, fine art decorating the elegant apartment.

Every morning someone delivered fresh flowers to a giant vase on a pedestal by the door. The blooms filled the open space with their delicate floral scent. The lilies of the field, plucked and cut and perfectly arranged to live one day at the height of their beauty. And tomorrow? Tomorrow they'd be gone. Thrown away.

Cora crossed to the front door and ran a finger over the silky petals. Here was a rosebud, tightly furled. She could pull it out and place it in a cup of water. It wouldn't look as grand, but it would still be here tomorrow. She could save one flower. It might be enough...

Crossing the room, she caught a glimpse of herself in a giant gilt mirror. A young face stared back at her, pale and lovely under layers of artful makeup. She'd spent all day at Armand's spa and every inch of her skin was plucked, smoothed, and polished. Her hair had been cut and styled as well.

When she'd lived on her mother's farm, she'd wear old overalls, t-shirts, a farmer's tan and freckles her only adornment, and go months without examining herself closely in a mirror.

These days, every inch of her was scrutinized, first by her stylists, then by society when she went out on Marcus's arm. The wife of a wealthy businessman must look the part.

Especially if that man's business had deep ties to the city's criminal underworld.

Marcus Ubeli, the ruler of New Olympus' underworld. Her husband.

When *he* stood by the window, he only saw his kingdom. His abject subjects scurrying far below. They saw only what he wanted them to see, an elegant businessman, handsome and shrewd, with a new and pretty wife.

They applauded his philanthropy and patronized his legit businesses—and only half listened to the whispers about his dark dealings. Only the rich and ultra-powerful knew the truth about Marcus Ubeli. He had a representative on every shadowy street corner. Cops, judges and juries were in his pocket. Even the mayor owed him favors.

By the time you learned the truth about Marcus Ubeli, it was too late. He owned you, too.

And Cora was his most prized possession.

Yes, she lived a grand life, far above the masses. Weekly spa visits, shopping sprees, meals in the finest restaurants, entry into the glittering nightlife of New Olympus high society. Beautiful clothes, a magnificent penthouse with its amazing view.

She preferred volunteering at the animal shelter downtown and curling up on a couch with a book, but it didn't matter. She was a cut flower in a gorgeous vase, beautiful and elegant and dying a little more each day.

Oh yes, she played her part perfectly in exchange for this new life her husband had given her. Because that's all it was: an even exchange.

Four months ago, she'd thrown herself in front of a bullet for him and saved his life. So now he'd given her all the freedoms she desired, even those that he himself had once denied her... She thought back to those days, miserable but also sort of wonderful through the haze of recollection. Because back then she'd been naïve enough to believe her husband could one day love her.

He'd disabused her of those notions while she lay on her hospital bed after being shot, just coming out of a coma. He didn't know she'd overheard him, which made it all the worse because it meant he'd been telling the truth.

Cora was always a chess piece for me to play against the Titans. And she served her purpose... As an added bonus, wifey dearest made herself a shield and took a bullet for me. I'd say that's mission accomplished as far as she's concerned, better than I ever could've hoped for. Plus, she's a great lay, so...

She was just a possession. That was all she'd ever be to him. He'd never loved her. He'd seen her as a commodity and a tool to use against his enemies. And as someone convenient to warm his bed at night. It was all she would ever be to him. He simply wasn't capable of feeling anything more. At least not for her, a Titan.

Not after finding out that her mom, Demi, had murdered his sister in cold blood. And come back fifteen years later to finish the job on Marcus himself, no matter the fact that Cora had begged her not to do it, to put the gun down, to *stop*.

Cora had chosen Marcus.

And taken the bullet meant for him.

She still had the four-inch scar on her stomach from where they'd had to operate to take the bullet out.

But after her recovery, what had there been to come back to? This life, stuck in the no man's land between two rival gangs, shunned by one because of who she loved but never fully embraced by the other.

"Cora." Marcus's deep voice rolled across the room.

She jerked her head up in surprise.

Her husband stood next to the floral bouquet. When had he come in? She hadn't even heard the front door open, she'd been so deep in her own head.

Marcus was as handsome as ever, the most gorgeous man she'd ever seen, if she was being honest. His hands were in his pockets and his face was tilted into the shadows enough that she couldn't read his expression. Not that she'd be able to read him even if the room were lit with a hundred blinding light bulbs. She didn't even try anymore.

She knew who he was and what was in his heart. She'd heard him loud and clear. In the days and weeks following the coma, his coldness toward her only reconfirmed everything he'd said that day.

He was solicitous towards her. He provided the best medical care money could buy. He continued giving her countless gifts but he never delivered them himself. His driver, Sharo, drove her to rehab every day for two months as she regained her strength.

But Marcus worked dawn till dusk and she could go entire days, once an entire week, without seeing him. He was awake before dawn and back long after she fell asleep. Often he'd sleep in the guest bedroom, saying he didn't want to wake her with his erratic hours.

He never came to any doctor's appointments yet still seemed to know every last detail of her care regimen. When he did talk to her it was to remind her to take her supplements or to ask if she'd eaten enough. And the day the doctor pronounced her well enough to resume physical activity, he came to their bed at night and made love to her in the dark.

The sex was as intense as ever. Their chemistry in bed was undeniable. Some nights his kisses felt frantic as he wrapped his arms around her and pulled her against him so tightly it was like he was afraid she'd disappear.

Sometimes it was fast, his mouth or hands on her working to bring her to a desperate, wild release and then he'd bury himself inside her and spill within minutes. Only to wake her up hours later in the middle of the night with his need pressing against her backside, and then he'd take her slowly, so achingly slowly that she thought she might die.

But always in the dark. And when morning came, he was gone as if the night had never been.

Tonight he wore his signature suit, and he looked just as fresh and unwrinkled as he had when he first put it on the day before. His effortless, controlled perfection was as much a mystery to her as on their first day of marriage. He tucked his hands into his pockets and, black hair falling across his brow, looked her up and down.

She stared back out the window, unmoving. "You're home early."

"We're going out tonight—remember? I thought you'd be ready."

She had on makeup, high heels, and a coiffed updo fresh from the spa, but the rest of her was still wrapped in a robe.

She hadn't forgotten but still she said, "We're going out?"

"The concert at Elysium. New act. A big one."

She looked Marcus's way again as he shrugged and she watched his face carefully. She found herself doing this more and more lately—poking the bear to see if she could get some reaction out of him, some proof that he was really human and could show genuine human emotion. As usual, though, his poker face gave nothing away.

"I always give a photo op on opening night," he continued.

"I didn't forget," she said, turning fully towards him and letting the light christen her hair. He had to squint to try to see her. "In fact, I went shopping for just the right outfit."

"Did you now?" He rubbed the dark shadow around his jaw, the only evidence of his long work day.

She undid her robe and let it fall in a rustle of silk. As she moved closer, she watched her husband's eyes grow hot as they took in her body. A black lace camisole with built in bra cupped her breasts. A sexy garter belt was slung low around her waist, holding her sheer black stockings up.

Cora felt satisfaction at the intense look on his face. "What do you think?"

This was all they had between them.

Sex. Fucking. That was how Cora thought of it now—as fucking. Or at least how she tried to think of it.

Marcus liked fucking her.

She was a good lay, after all, right?

Her teeth ground together at the memory. It was just another reason she'd chosen her outfit so carefully. Sex was a weapon that plenty of women used to control the men in their lives, right? No one would ever control Marcus but if she could even get the slightest edge up on him, it would be something. She was determined that the next time they had sex, it would be on her terms. In the light where he'd be forced to see her face.

Marcus studied her carefully, letting the silence lengthen between them. He smirked, the barest upward quirk of his lips.

"I think the paparazzi will eat it up."

He prowled forward, put a commanding hand to the back of her neck, and drew her head to his.

She told herself not to open to him, to play hard to get—after all, what would entice the man who had everything more than being denied the one thing he seemed to crave?—but the second his lips touched hers, her body went liquid. Such was his power over her. Damn it all to hell.

How did he always manage to do that? To get the upper hand? She'd been so determined to master *him* for once.

But when Marcus pulled back for a moment, his dark eyes catching hers, a jolt of pleasure shot through her.

"I like finding you like this," he whispered. "Waiting so eagerly. Wanting."

He lifted her up and settled her on the small makeup bureau. Kneeling, he parted her legs and leaned forward to inhale deeply, his teeth catching at the top of her lace panties. "I like smelling how much you want me."

Cora felt her face flame. For as calm, cold, and professional as Marcus was on the outside to everyone else she'd ever seen him interact with, it was still shocking how crass and brutish he could sometimes be in bed. Or on the makeup bureau, as it were.

She rubbed her legs together but he wasn't having it. He shoved her thighs open wide and stepped between them as he rose back up, the front of his fancy suit pants jutting obscenely. He made quick work of unbuckling and unzipping them. And all her plans went out the window. She just wanted him inside her now, whatever way she could have him.

She thought he might shove into her quick and harsh, like he often did in the dark. No matter how many times she told herself, *not again,* she always ended up welcoming him into her arms, clinging to him, and spending all day living for the half hour at night when his hands would reach for her in the darkness.

In those moments, it was so easy to let herself forget the truth of their situation. That to him, she was only a trophy of his latest victory. Because he *had* been victorious in quelling the brief insurgency the Titans had attempted on New Olympus. It had been months and there was no word from the gang her mother now apparently ran.

Marcus had triumphed, as he always did. There was no point resisting him. He had a will unlike anyone she had ever met and that was saying something, considering that she'd been raised by Demi Titan.

And yet still Cora had to cling to her sense of self. She couldn't let herself be obliterated by Marcus completely. It was why she continued her futile campaign to gain the upper hand in this marriage. She might never escape him but it didn't mean she had to be tormented forever by her unrequited love for him.

But wait, no, she *didn't* love him. It had merely been infatuation.

And it was an infatuation she would cure herself of, one way or another... But she'd been trying for months with no success.

In the meantime, she meant to gain more of an even footing with him. It was why she'd thrown herself so violently into society life. She was determined to have a life apart from him. And maybe, if she asserted herself more in their bed play, then she wouldn't feel so completely overwhelmed by him each time and so shattered in the aftermath.

She could only piece herself back together so many times.

Because while she knew in her head that to Marcus it was only fucking, to her stupid heart it often felt like making love.

Which was why she'd put on her armor today and surprised him in a full-frontal assault.

But five minutes later, he had her on her back and one hand splayed ever so gently across her throat.

His dark eyes searched hers for a quick moment and her breath caught. He was so gorgeous, his face sculpted with sharp lines and commanding angles. Even through the tux she could feel the power of his large body, muscles bulging against the expensive tailored fabric.

She lifted a hand, reaching toward his cheek. How long since she'd seen him like this in the light of day?

But he grabbed her wrist before she could make contact and slammed her wrist to the bed above her head, pinning it there. She couldn't help the whimper that escaped her at the commanding move. Everything he did turned her on. Everything he was.

She thought he would pull himself out and take her right there. She was only a few seconds away from begging for it.

Instead, though, he pulled back and flipped her over so that she was on her hands and knees. He didn't make her wait long, though. He dragged her lace underwear down and immediately stroked inside her. She was drenched and his passage was smooth.

Apparently he wasn't looking for smooth.

He pulled out and rammed into her roughly and gods, it felt so good. Like he was claiming her. Like she'd actually managed to rile him up for once.

She shifted her backside needily against him and he swore, clutching her hips in a punishing grip as he continued to pound into her.

She tried to look over her shoulder at him but he wasn't

having it. He put a hand on her neck urging her down to the bed, ass up.

He followed, his body dominating hers as his relentless thrusting continued. "Next time you think to tempt me with such slinky little underthings, goddess," he hissed in her ear, "remember to be careful what you wish for. You only make me want to remind you who you belong to."

She'd been on the edge since he first thrust into her but his words sent her over. He was hitting that perfect spot deep inside. Yes, oh gods, *yes*.

In order to stop herself from howling Marcus's name as she came, she thrust her face into the pillow.

But he knew her too well. He pulled back and stopped thrusting right as the first astounding bloom of her orgasm hit.

She cried out with the loss of it and he wrapped his arms around her, holding her still. "Say my name," he commanded in a low, guttural voice. "Say who you belong to."

She shook her head in an attempted denial but he just gripped her tighter and gave her a slight shake. "Say who you belong to."

His cock teased at the edge of her entrance, tormenting her, her pleasure was so close and yet so far away.

"Marcus," she finally wailed and he slammed back into her, immediately lighting her back up. She screamed his name again as her pleasure ramped higher and higher and then exploded like a night full of firecrackers.

Marcus thrust himself to the root right as she clenched and spasmed around him, his grip on her body never lessening an iota.

Together, they came, as the light of sunset streamed through the window.

As the pop and sparkle of her orgasm finally dissipated, she panted, short of breath, her entire body alive but languid with satisfied pleasure. And Marcus still held her from behind, though he rolled them so that they lay on their side. Him spooning her, his cock still hard inside her and every few moments he'd thrust again, like he wasn't ready to let go no matter the fact that he'd already spent.

His fingers trailed the back of her neck. "I missed this."

Her heart was heavy, full to bursting with the things she wished she could say. "You can have it anytime you want." *You can have me.*

"Oh, I know." She could hear his arrogant smile in his words.

She was glad she was faced away from him. It made her braver somehow, so she continued. "You've been so busy lately."

"Miss me?" She thought he sounded pleased.

"As much as you missed me." She rocked against his hardness. His cock shifted and swelled. His fingers found the back of her neck, no longer stroking but clamping down on the sensitive points.

"I have a weakness when it comes to you." He pulled out of her and left her side to clean up. When he returned, she was still huddled on the bed, back to him.

He came around the bed and his fingers lifted her chin. "What's wrong?"

She was done bottling her frustration. "Only you would describe it as weakness."

"What would you call it?" No sarcasm, just curiosity.

"I don't know..." His honest expression made her bold. "Affection?"

Her heart pounded through the silent seconds. His hungry gaze dropped to her lips and she felt it like a kiss.

His hands cupped her cheeks, and then he kissed her for real.

"Affection," he agreed. He stroked her hair, petting her like she was an adorable kitten he allowed to sleep on his bed. And her stupid, stupid heart leaped up like he'd declared his love from the rooftops.

"What if we..." Cora's breath hitched but she continued, "what if we just stayed in tonight?" She felt her vulnerability stretched raw, right out there for anyone to see as she asked it. But she didn't take it back. "I— I could make it worth your while." She reached out and placed a hand on the front of his pants, where his cock stirred.

His hand shot down and firmly clasped around her wrist, though, stopping her. She felt her heart sink as he stepped back. He was about to reject her. Again.

"The Orphan is the hottest music act on the East Coast. The press will be there to catch the celebrities attending the concert, and I want them to see you with me. I need you there by my side."

Aha. Of course. He needed Mrs. Ubeli on his arm for a photo op, a distraction to the cameras. Tonight she'd be her husband's arm candy, dressed to dazzle, drawing the camera's eye to the scandalous slit of her dress or her long bare leg exiting the car.

She squeezed her eyes shut to stop a stupid tear from escaping. She legitimized his business, she knew, with her innocent looks and role as the dutiful wife. Like the magician's assistant, she took the focus off him and left him free to whatever quiet business he had in the background.

It was their unspoken arrangement, as contractual as the rest of his business dealings were. She played the role of Mrs. Ubeli and in return he did her the great honor of not killing her and to the best of his ability, pretending she was not a Titan.

But she would never truly be family and she would certainly never be anyone he could ever love. Men like Marcus didn't understand that emotion. They understood power, and in this relationship, he had it and she didn't.

She'd been an idiot yet again, showing even an ounce of weakness by asking him to stay in tonight.

She turned away from him and forced her voice to be steady and cool. "I'll be ready in an hour."

I wasn't capable of love. Not until I met Cora. My angel.
I've claimed every inch of her body and I only want more.
I'm a man who craves control, but her power over me is absolute. She holds my heart in her hands.
She can never find out.

The demons in this city want to destroy her.
It's my job to protect her innocence. Lock her safe in my high tower.
But I'm the danger that she's trying to escape.
The ruthless man in her bed.
A demon worse than all the others.
One who cannot save her from himself.

A NOTE FROM THE AUTHORS

Hey there. It's me, Lee Savino, your fearless author of smexy, smexy romance (smart + sexy). I'm glad you read this book. Marcus & Cora have been in my heart since I wrote their first scene in college. Their story is a rollercoaster, so hang on!

If you want to check out my other books, visit my website...leesavino.com. You can download a few freebies and get on my awesome sauce email list and I send out stuff all the time via email that you can't get anywhere else. ;)

Hi, it's me, too, Stasia! *waves* Lee and I have both loved the myth of Hades and Persephone for FOREVER, and both of our *very* first book attempts were retellings of the myth way before we knew each other. We didn't want to go over the top with the mythological aspect but it's the concept underneath Marcus and Cora's story. Hades = the original Bad Boy. And it's the first beauty and the beast story and just gah, so much romance! Plus evil mothers, this shit is the stuff fairy tales are made of, lmao! Lee and I had so much swoony fun bringing this ancient story to life in a new, fresh setting.

If you love dark romance and want more from me, you can grab a freebie here: bit.ly/indecentstasiablack

ALSO BY STASIA BLACK

Dark Contemporary Romances

Dark Mafia Series

Innocence

Awakening

Queen of the Underworld

Innocence Boxset

Beauty and the Rose Series

Beauty's Beast

Beauty and the Thorns

Beauty and the Rose

Taboo: a Dark Romance Boxset Collection

Love So Dark Duology

Cut So Deep

Break So Soft

Stud Ranch Series

The Virgin and the Beast: a Beauty and the Beast Tale

Hunter: a Snow White Romance

The Virgin Next Door: a Ménage Romance

Freebie

Indecent: A Taboo Proposal

Sci-fi Romances

Marriage Raffle Series

Theirs to Protect

Theirs to Pleasure

Theirs to Wed

Theirs to Defy

Theirs to Ransom

Marriage Raffle Boxset

Draci Alien Series

My Alien's Obsession

My Alien's Baby

Freebie

Their Honeymoon

ALSO BY LEE SAVINO

Contemporary romance:

Beauty and the Lumberjacks: a dark reverse harem romance

Her Marine Daddy

Her Dueling Daddies

Royally Fucked - get free at www.leesavino.com

Paranormal & Sci fi romance:

The Alpha Series

The Draekon Series

The Berserker Series

ABOUT STASIA BLACK

STASIA BLACK grew up in Texas, recently spent a freezing five-year stint in Minnesota, and now is happily planted in sunny California, which she will never, ever leave.

She loves writing, reading, listening to podcasts, and has recently taken up biking after a twenty-year sabbatical (and has the bumps and bruises to prove it). She lives with her own personal cheerleader, aka, her handsome husband, and their teenage son. Wow. Typing that makes her feel old. And writing about herself in the third person makes her feel a little like a nutjob, but ahem! Where were we?

Stasia's drawn to romantic stories that don't take the easy way out. She wants to see beneath people's veneer and poke into their dark places, their twisted motives, and their deepest desires. Basically, she wants to create characters that make readers alternately laugh, cry ugly tears, want to toss their kindles across the room, and then declare they have a new FBB (forever book boyfriend).

Join Stasia's Facebook Group for Readers for access to deleted scenes, to chat with me and other fans and also get access to exclusive giveaways:
www.facebook.com/groups/stasiasbabes

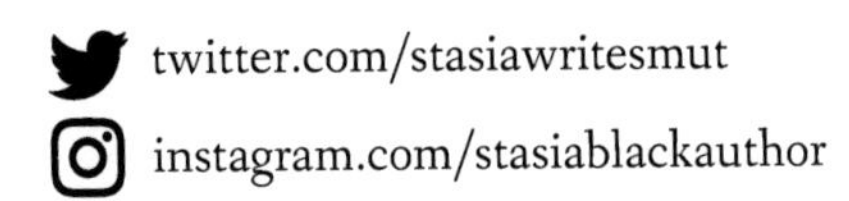
twitter.com/stasiawritesmut
instagram.com/stasiablackauthor

ABOUT LEE SAVINO

Lee Savino has grandiose goals but most days can't find her wallet or her keys so she just stays at home and writes. While she was studying creative writing at Hollins University, her first manuscript won the Hollins Fiction Prize.

She lives in the USA with her awesome family. You can find her on Facebook in the **Goddess Group** at www.-facebook.com/groups/leesavino.

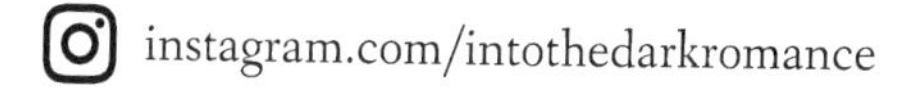

Printed in Great Britain
by Amazon